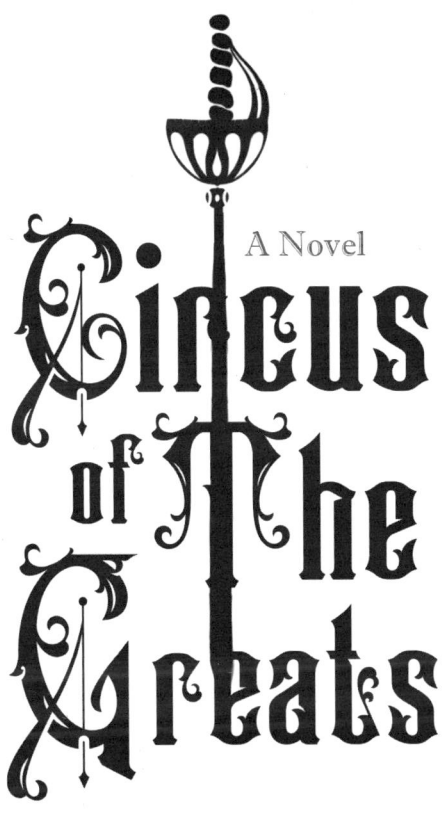

A Novel

Circus of The Greats

ALI AL-NAAMA

دار جامعة حمد بن خليفة للنشر
HAMAD BIN KHALIFA UNIVERSITY PRESS

Hamad Bin Khalifa University Press
P O Box 5825
Doha, Qatar

www.hbkupress.com

All rights reserved.

No part of this publication may be reproduced or transmitted in any form or by any means, electronic or mechanical, including photocopying, recording, or any information storage or retrieval system, without prior permission in writing from the publishers.

No responsibility for loss caused to any individual or organization acting on or refraining from action as a result of the material in this publication can be accepted by HBKU Press or the author.

First English edition in 2022

ISBN: 9789927161292

Printed in Beirut-Lebanon

Qatar National Library Cataloging-in-Publication (CIP)

Al-Naama, Ali, author.

 Circus of the greats / Ali Al-Naama. First English edition. – Doha, Qatar : Hamad Bin Khalifa University Press, 2022.

 263 pages ; 20 cm

ISBN 978-992-716-129-2

1. Circus in literature. 2. Magic. 3. Short stories, English. I. Title.

PZ.1. N33 2022
823.01 – dc 23   202228544900

*To my parents,
who showed me what being great
is all about.*

Acknowledgments

As I create the universe of Circus of the Greats, the enthusiasm and support I have received have been overwhelming. I am genuinely and beyond thankful to every soul who showed interest and encouragement to make this story a publishing reality. Writing this book has been a turbulent journey; at times, it has gotten dark, lonely, and very emotional living with the characters for so long, but it has also been a bliss realizing what the power of writing can do.

I am tremendously thankful to Hala Al Labban, whose intelligent, insightful, and valuable feedback made this book even more prosperous. Thank you so much for your constant support and having faith in the story; this means the world to me. Your passion and interest in the characters are the light that guided me.

Mohammed Al-Jarman, you were the very first that stood by me and saw my potential in writing. I would not have figured out life without you, we have gone through so much, and no matter what, I know you'll always be there for me, and I can always turn to you.

Omar Al-Ansari, you came into my life and immediately believed in me and in what I can do personally and professionally. You have influenced me in ways that only made me the confident man I am today, and I genuinely thank you for being in my life and helping me navigate it. You're such an inspiration.

Dr. Khalid Al-Jufairi, words cannot express how thankful I am for your constant support and always being there for me. You are a gem!

I also want to thank Mohammed Darwish Fakhro, your feedback on the first draft was valuable and appreciated. Finally, a special thanks go to my family members, parents, siblings, and sister-in-law; thank you for your love and support.

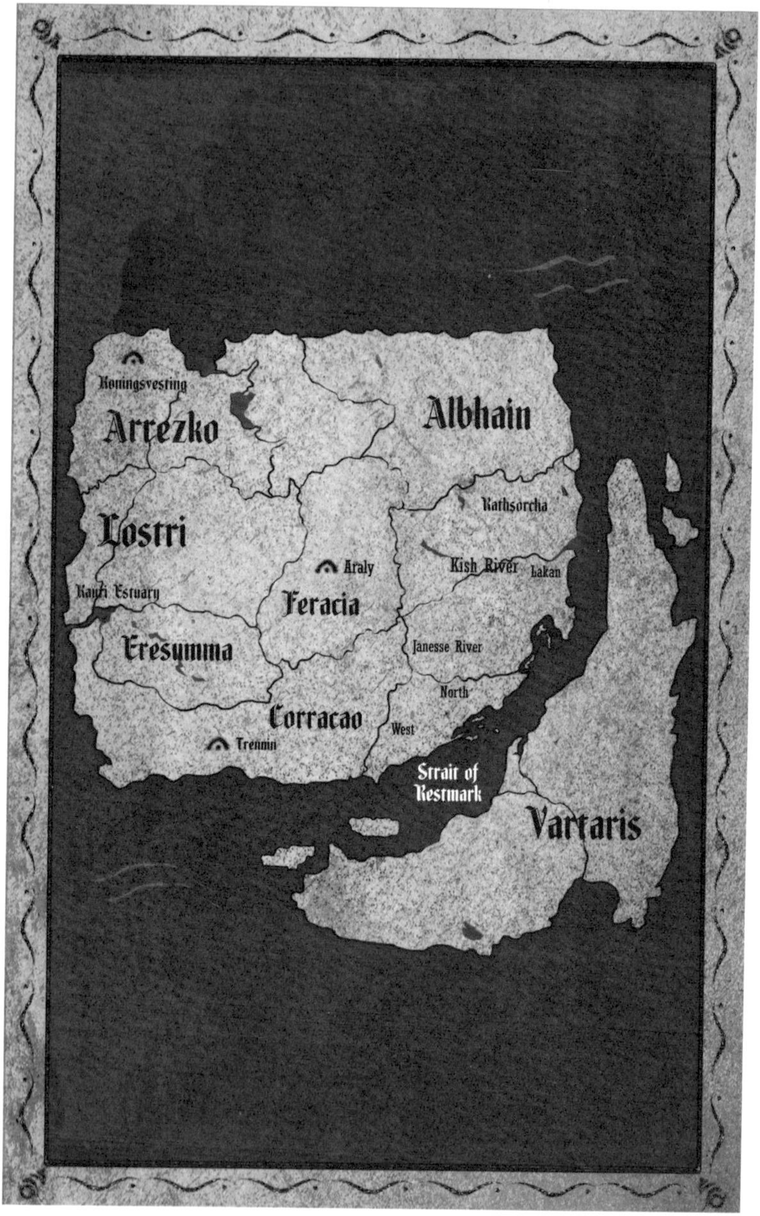

Koningsvesting
Arrezko
Albhain
Lostri
Rathsorcha
Araly
Kish River
Lakan
Kauri Estuary
Feracia
Eresumma
Janesse River
North
Corracao
West
Trennin
Strait of
Restmark
Vartaris

Contents

Acknowledgments *7*

The Dating of Events *11*

Magic in Eiliron *13*

1. Rain Moon, CR 531 .... *15*

2. Harvest Moon CR 531 .... *33*

3. Moon of the First Frost, CR 531 .... *53*

4. Sleep Moon, CR 532 .... *61*

5. Dark Moon, CR 532 .... *73*

6. Freeze Moon, CR 532 .... *81*

7. Snow Moon, CR 532 .... *89*

8. Thaw Moon, CR 532 .... *119*

9. Heat Moon, CR 532 .... *123*

10. Bright Moon, CR 549 .... *131*

11. Thaw Moon, CR 549 .... *147*

12. Rain Moon, CR 549 .... *157*

13. Heat Moon, CR 549 .... *171*

14. Harvest Moon, CR 549 .... *179*

15. Moon of First Frost, CR 550 .... *197*

16. Bright Moon CR 550 .... *241*

17. Rain Moon CR 550 .... *245*

18. Moon of First Leaf CR 550 .... *247*

19. Flower and Berry Moon, CR 550 .... *259*

The Dating of Events

In Eiliron the date is reckoned by the lunar cycle, so there are thirteen months in the year. The year is reckoned from the first moon after the first frost, and continues on through the end of the harvest at the end of the year. While weather and crop cycles vary by year and by location, the following calendar is a rough outline of the different times of the year.

Moon of the First Frost: Ushers in the new year. The harvest is in just ahead of the first frost, and everyone prepares for the winter. It's a busy month for most people.

Sleep Moon: The last of the harvest occurs with the processing of meat for the winter. It's also a labor-intensive time, particularly where the growing season is short, and supplies of grain, legumes, and the like are not as plentiful.

Dark Moon: The days are dark, short, and increasingly cold. There is, in most countries on Eiliron, a Winterfest that celebrates the light in the darkness.

Freeze Moon: Deep, deep cold. In some areas, it is also known as Death Moon because losses to illness are more common in the deep winter, and it's considered an ill-omened time.

Snow Moon: The cold usually abates somewhat by this moon, but there is also more chance of heavy snow, particularly in the mountains. Travel is not undertaken lightly. Communities are cut off from each other in some regions.

Bright Moon: The first signs of spring, particularly in the plains and on the coast. Though the weather remains cold and wet, it's clear that winter is coming to an end.

Thaw Moon: Winter's back is well and truly broken. Even in the mountains, the snows have stopped, and the melt waters swell the rivers that flow into the sea. In warmer parts of Eiliron, new growth is beginning.

Rain Moon: Cool and wet. Trees are budding, herds are increasing, and winter stores of food are nearly spent. Travel can be difficult because the roads are often messy.

Moon of First Leaf: A time of celebration, when new life is bursting out everywhere. Farmers are planting their fields. The days grow ever longer and brighter.

Flower and Berry Moon: Spring gives way to summer with long, warm, sunny days and starry nights.

Heat Moon: The hottest part of the year. Sunshine is abundant, and if the rains come regularly, the crops ripen and grow heavy.

Harvest Moon: The harvest begins as the weather starts to cool again.

Moon of the Ancestors: The harvest concludes as the weather grows colder. It is said that the spirits of the dead are more active, so it becomes a time of deep thought and remembrance.

Magic in Eiliron

Within Eiliron, the use of magic by humans is governed by two sets of laws. The first are the natural laws, which cannot be broken because they are the very wellspring of all magic. These are:

- ◆ The energy has to come from somewhere. If you cast a spell, you're drawing on natural energies. This is the cost of magic. Responsible magickers draw energies from earth, flowing water, even hewn stone, which holds not only earth energy but the energy of its making. These energies are renewable with time. Some magic users can even draw on their own energies, but that means that their ability to work magic is limited by what they're able to endure. Irresponsible magic users drain other people.
- ◆ Magic must be used within the bounds of the natural order. What this means is that the laws of nature cannot be broken, though there has always been debate about this among some of the more adept practitioners. If there is a level of magic that breaks this rule, it has not been documented in Eiliron.
- ◆ Magic can force behavior to some degree, but cannot change a being's essential nature. People prone to doing wrong cannot be made good. Decent people cannot be turned evil.

The second set of laws is man-made, and while they vary from region to region, some laws are common to most of the societies in Eiliron.

- Magic may not be used on people without the person's express permission.
- Magic must never be used to bend another to your will.
- Magic may not be used to harm living things.
- Magic users must be registered and trained.

Some parts of Eiliron still class magic as a capital crime. As might be imagined, these laws are difficult to enforce, and often they're used as political ploys.

Magical practice varies widely, even within Eiliron. The majority of magic is illusion, and it has a life span. An illusion will fade in time. Some magic is sympathetic in that it plays on the natural properties of things to produce a desired effect. Some magic is a thing of powders and potions. There are almost certainly as many traditions of magic use as there are peoples of the world. There is much overlap, as might be expected, but each tradition must be learned from its practitioners.

1.

Rain Moon, CR 531

"A year older if not wiser," Hartan observed as he fingered the newly minted coin bearing the likeness of Pelle Pellires, king of Corraçao. "Jumped up, little no one."

His sister, Roxanna, stood by his side in her stiff and sober gown of heavy indigo silk, utterly out of place in the grand ballroom of the palace, among the candy-colored fripperies and boisterous good humor of the Corraçaoans. She did not care for this place or for the flamboyant court and frivolous monarchs, and her expression was all prim disapproval. Hartan's sour mood didn't help her relax either. "You think anyone who isn't a Talian is vulgar," she observed, though in this case she was inclined to agree. The sheer amount of gold and silver leaf decorating the high-ceilinged ballroom could have paid for the Talian family's estate. The hardwood floors gleamed under the gem-encrusted shoes of the courtiers, and countless candles illuminated the room with a warm glow.

"The Talians are an ancient family, and by rights—"

She cut him off with a wave of her hand. "I don't want to hear about your fantasies again, brother. I don't want to be here, and I don't want to listen to your complaints about how the Talian family has been hard done by. We are here to convey the respects of our king, to King Pelle, on his birthday." Under her breath she added, "Why couldn't he have just sent a letter?"

"I wonder if this is worth anything," Hartan asked as he flipped the coin. It was snatched out of the air by the king's first counselor, who had appeared seemingly out of nowhere.

"Commemorative, nothing more," Revin said as he studied the coin. "Though they can be exchanged for a sweet cake at a local bakery. His majesty's gift to his people." He handed the coin back to Hartan. "He has tasked me to invite you to a private supper this evening, after the festivities." Revin's smile was thin and professional, and never reached his dark eyes.

"We would be honored," Roxanna told him. Revin made a slight bow and moved off into the crowd of guests.

"I don't like that man."

Roxanna didn't care for Revin either; he seemed too shifty by half. But she was tired of her brother's foul mood. "I doubt he likes you either." Hartan was particularly unlikable, in her opinion.

"Roxanna, about our reasons for being here—" The sound of a fanfare cut off Hartan's thought, and the throng of gaily clad courtiers parted to allow Pelle and his queen, Caelea, to enter the hall.

In spite of her bad humor, the sight of them left her breathless, and Roxanna had to admit that the stories were true. The king and queen of Corraçao were a stunningly handsome couple. Pelle, with his broad shoulders and thick mane of shining golden hair, stood several inches above most of the court. That night he was clad in a deep ruby frock coat, stitched at collar and cuffs with gold and silver thread. His golden damask waistcoat covered a shirt of white silk that lay soft against his skin, trimmed in white lace that made him look younger than his forty years. He wore, as he always did on formal occasions, knee breeches with white silk stockings and soft, low-heeled red leather shoes sewn with seed pearls for dancing the night away.

"Peacock," Hartan muttered, but Roxanna looked past the decoration and saw a lion, golden-eyed and powerful.

Queen Caelea was dressed in crimson satin, her enormous skirts ruched at the hips and gathered up with golden bows. Beneath, she wore a white taffeta underskirt and a stiff crinoline. Her gown, like her husband's coat, was tricked out in golden embroidery. Her long, dark hair was dressed with pearls and diamonds, and twisted into an intricate maze of curls and plaits. She was the most beautiful woman Roxanna had ever seen.

"Pity she's barren," Hartan whispered.

Roxanna narrowed her eyes at her brother but said nothing.

In a kingdom full of joy and frivolity, Pelle and Caelea were King and Queen of Hearts, a pair who seemed still to love one another even after twenty years of marriage and a long string of unrealized pregnancies that had taken its toll on both the marriage and the kingdom. They loved each other and loved their people. That night his attention was all on Caelea, sweeping her, laughing gaily, into the first dance, then inviting his court to join them.

Baron Arkeimo approached Roxanna, inviting her into the dance, but she shook her head and looked away from him.

"A little more natural," Hartan hissed at her. "You want to be noticed."

"I do not."

"You do."

She sighed and saw the baron moving away through the crowd. "He won't be back."

"He's not the only man in the room looking for a partner." And sure enough, within a minute Roxanna saw another man approaching again, this time one in even finer garb, though he wore it poorly, as if it had been made for someone else.

"Who is he?" she whispered to Hartan.

"Duke Lakketta."

"My lord, Lakketta," she said, extending her hand and offering a smile which, if a bit frosty, was more than the baron had gotten.

"Your Highness," he said, bowing low over her hand. He turned to her brother. "Prince Hartan, a pleasure."

"It's always good to see you, my lord. And how is the dowager duchess? I've not seen her tonight."

"My mother has little use for such events."

Nor have I, but I'm here, Roxanna thought, and the temperature of her smile dropped by a few degrees.

"May I have the honor?" Lakketta extended a hand to Roxanna.

She looked to Hartan, who raised one eyebrow. "But of course, my lord," she replied.

The duke made small talk as he guided her onto the crowded dance floor and into a slow *pas de vanne*. She could barely hear him, so she kept her smile pleasantly neutral and nodded occasionally. When the dance was over, he escorted her back to her place beside her brother and thanked her for the dance.

"I don't think he'll be asking you for my hand in marriage," she said as she smoothed her pale hair. "How hot it is in here!"

"You can do better."

Roxanna laughed. "We are minor Feracian royalty, brother. A Corraçaoan duke would probably be better than I could hope for, given the state of my dowry."

It was the sort of remark—a reminder that it had been Hartan's mismanagement of their inheritance that had robbed her of a decent dowry—that made Hartan furious. But as he turned, face twisted in anger, the noise in the hall faded. Brother and sister looked to the dance floor, then followed the gazes of the throng to the doors where a small, fair figure stood.

In a froth of pink and white, skirts cropped short to display her slender ankles, Paradis, a newly famous dancer with the Royal Ballet, stepped into the hall, head held high. "Husband, will you dance with me?" she asked in a clear, high voice.

Her entrance made the crowd draw back from the dance floor, looking from dancer to king with horrified fascination. *Husband?* What had Pelle done?

The king came down off the dais, stiff with anger. But then Roxanna saw his anger fade as the girl spoke softly to him and touched her belly lightly. Hartan saw too and cursed softly as a ripple of shock and excitement ran through the crowd.

So that's how it is, Roxanna thought. *He's taken a second wife to secure the succession.*

Pelle gestured to Revin just as Caelea stood and cleared her throat.

"Lords and ladies, it's time for my birthday gift to my dear husband."

The girl gave the king a pleading look, but Pelle turned away from her and walked back toward the dais where his queen waited for him, while Revin led the girl out of the hall.

"My dear husband," Caelea repeated, and touched her own belly with a lovely, beringed hand. "By your next birthday you will have an heir."

Pelle's expression changed and changed again, from shock, to concern, to... what? Roxanna couldn't read it. But the smoothly political announcement had done its job. The dancer and her child were forgotten as the king returned to his queen, put his arms around her, and pressed his face to her hair. There was a ripple of applause.

What of the girl? Roxanna wondered. But Paradis was already being escorted from the hall.

***

Revin steered the girl out of the hall. "What were you thinking?" he hissed at her.

She regarded him coldly, her little cat-like face haughty and unafraid. No wonder the king had been drawn to her. "And who are you to question me?" she demanded, as imperious as the queen she imagined herself to be.

"The man who holds your fate in his hands, child."

"That would be the king," she insisted, and laid her hand on her belly. "And as his wife, I-"

"Second wife. Provisional Wife, taken to ensure the succession to the throne, nothing more," he told her, his voice cool. "You will never be welcome at court, and I can tell you that your game did nothing to endear you to His Majesty. You embarrassed him and the queen. He does not forgive such things."

"Even for an heir?" the minx asked.

Vikar laughed. "Pelle will be appropriately grateful when he takes your child from you to raise at court. And you will be adequately compensated." That sank in, he could see it on her face.

"I don't want money."

"You won't become queen," he warned her, and noted the flush that crept into her round cheeks. "Your child won't even be a royal unless the queen fails to produce an heir, and either way you'll have no part in your child's life. Is that really what you want?" Vikar asked mildly. He gestured to a guard. "You'll have the protection of the crown on your way back to your lodgings," he told her. "If you need help, send word, but don't come back to the palace."

Her fists clenched as if she wanted to strike him. "No one will take my child from me," she insisted.

Vikar shrugged and turned away. She was so young, and didn't understand how these things worked.

"I hate you!" He heard tears in her voice.

For a moment he hated himself. "Yes, well, that's an occupational hazard. Take her home," he told the guard.

The hall was still a scene of confusion when he returned. The orchestra was making a half-hearted attempt at dance music, but all the courtiers were huddled in groups, whispering. The king and queen sat on their polished rosewood thrones, speaking quietly to one another, ignoring the courtiers. Vikar knew someone had to do something, so he ordered the servants to set up the chairs for a performance.

"My lords and ladies, your attention please?" The chatter began to ebb. "Their Majesties have arranged some entertainments for your pleasure," he announced. "Please take your seats. The Circus of Dreams will begin in a few minutes."

The courtiers began to file into the semicircle of chairs that were being placed, and Vikar could feel the atmosphere lighten. Now if the players could be nudged along as easily. He made his way to where the circus troupe was waiting.

"I'm a step ahead of you." Jeskil Gild, the head man of the Circus of Dreams, was marshaling his troops as Vikar approached. "When I saw the girl, I thought there would be a need for distraction."

"When did you start reading minds?" Vikar asked him, though he knew that Jeskil's instincts were almost always on point.

"I could always read yours."

Vikar smiled. "True."

Jeskil's musicians had already taken their places and begun the comedic tuning up that they used to warm up the audience. The squeaks and squeals of fiddles, unexpected crashes of cymbals, and off-key blats of the horns got the entire court laughing while the rest of the players readied their acts. A few practiced pratfalls and stumbles sent the audience into gales of laughter.

"Acrobats!" Jeskil hissed, and the gaggle of tumblers, jugglers, and dancers flowed out into the hall as the musicians began to play in earnest. Vikar watched for a minute or two, nodding.

"Good troupe."

"We're lucky to have so much talent. I'm sorry we couldn't arrange a wire or trapeze in here." He took a moment to tie back his dark hair so it wouldn't tangle in the marionette strings.

"We'll talk about doing that in the summer. Out of doors. Whenever the circus is in the country."

"Whenever you choose," Jeskil told him. Then, "Do you ever miss it?" he asked.

"What do you think?"

"I think you never stopped being a ringmaster in spite of the somber robes," Jeskil replied, making Vikar laugh. "Come and talk later. We can catch up." Then he moved off to collect the clowns.

The tumblers excited the court, the jugglers amazed them, and the dancers won their hearts. By the time they were withdrawing from the hall, even the queen was smiling again. And when the clowns spilled onto the floor to the weird and raucous music of a ghironda and fiddle duo, Caelea began to clap her hands in time to the music, and everyone, even Pelle, joined in.

Vikar felt as if he could breathe again. He knew he could work things out with the dancer, and the incident would soon be forgotten. He relaxed and watched the clowns, laughing at the pratfalls and the deliberate tweaking of noble noses, applauding as one of them made a bouquet of flowers appear out of nowhere and laid them at Caelea's feet. A bold move in a kingdom where magic, if not absolutely outlawed as it was in Feracia, was frowned upon and subject to fines. But Vikar knew that Jeskil would happily expose the trick as simple sleight of hand if challenged. Jeskil never allowed his troupe to perform magic that couldn't be explained away. What happened behind the scenes was something else entirely.

Then, as the clowns withdrew, the ornate puppet theater was rolled forward. There was a low murmur of pleasure as the courtiers took in the hand-painted panels depicting scenes from favorite folk tales such as "The Rain Girl" and "The Stolen Child."

The red velvet curtain opened on a marionette lying crumpled and sad. One of the queen's ladies-in-waiting gasped, "Poor thing!" and everyone laughed.

At that, Vikar recognized the marionette as Lord Merrypike, a ferociously ugly puppet with a huge, warty nose and an under bite that gave him a pugnacious air. He was a great favorite of audiences throughout the seven kingdoms for his often hilarious observations on his sad life.

"Ah, sweet lady, you understand," Merrypike exclaimed as he rose to his feet. "My heart is broken, for my dearest love loves another." He tapped his chest, and one of the musicians rapped on a hollow tube.

Everyone laughed.

"It's not amusing to me!" Merrypike exclaimed. "See where she comes." He stepped back as Petal Fluffbottom, a minxish little puppet with red curls and a voluptuous figure, sashayed onto the stage, sighing, "Ah me..."

"Good day, my love," Merrypike said to her, and she drew back.

"Good day, sir. Do I know you?" she asked. Her wooden features shifted just enough to make her look disdainful, though not enough for anyone but Vikar, who knew what Jeskil was doing, to note the change. It was a subtle magic, but it was clear that Petal wanted nothing to do with Merrypike.

"My love, it is I, your very own Merrypike!"

"Do not speak to me of love, sir, for I am sick with it," she told him. "For I am in love with a man above all other men, and he has eyes only for another." She turned away from him and affected a pose of sadness and dismay, her features shifting again very slightly.

"Who is he?" Merrypike demanded. "I shall challenge him to a duel! I shall vanquish him! I shall win back your love!" he exclaimed, tripping over his own feet and nearly knocking her down. She glared at him. The audience roared.

Petal turned to the audience and batted her eyelashes. "It is... the King of Hearts."

The entire court laughed and applauded.

"But he is in thrall to the Queen of Hearts, and I am downcast." Then she opened her arms and began to sing in a high, thin, wavering voice:

"Oh who is as fine as the blessed moon?
Who sounds as boldly as a bassoon?
Tis our King of Hearts, whose noble features
Set him above all mortal creatures.
He loves me not, oh woe is me,
And I must..."

Here she stopped and scratched her head. "What rhymes with 'me,' my lord?"

"Flee?" Merrypike offered to a round of guffaws. "Bee? Tree?"

"And I must go sit in a tree?" Petal finished. "Does that seem like a thing to do when your heart is broken?"

"I suppose it's as good as anything else," he said.

"I must go find a tree then," she said and left the stage with an enormous sigh.

Merrypike watched her go, then addressed the audience. "I have lost my true love to a king, but my heart really belongs to my queen," Merrypike said. And then he began to sing in Jeskil's fine, clear tenor,

"Our Queen of Hearts is like unto
Our glorious summer morns.
So fair of face
So filled with grace
This kingdom she adorns"

Merrypike got down on one knee, pressed his wooden hands to his wooden chest, and stared up at Caelea, oddly worshipful for a chunk of wood. "Oh my lady, dare I hope ever to win your heart?" he asked her.

"No, my lord," she told him, and her voice was as gentle as it was amused. "For I love another."

"Oh!" Merrypike said and got to his feet. "Well in that case, I'm going to go find Petal and see if she wants to go dancing." And he did a little jig that took him off the stage to wild applause and laughter.

It had been a surprisingly subtle, even gentle performance by Jeskil, and Vikar knew he owed him a debt of gratitude. The drama of Paradis, though not forgotten, had been turned into a joke and pushed to the back of the courtiers' minds. Everyone was laughing again.

That was one of the circus's secrets, the ability to spread goodwill and happiness.

***

Upon hearing a tapping at the side of the puppet stage, Jeskil popped up from between the curtains to find a jug of hot, brewed mountainberry in front of his face.

"Drink with me?" Vikar asked. He looked tired, Jeskil thought, and perhaps unwell, though it wouldn't do to mention that to him. Vikar could be prickly.

"That smells good," Jeskil observed. It brought back memories of his childhood.

"I remembered your fondness for it," Vikar replied. "And your preference for keeping your wits about you."

"Let me just finish packing up Merrypike and Petal. Have a seat."

"Why aren't you at the supper?" Vikar asked when Jeskil sat down beside him and poured two mugs of the spicy bittersweet brew. "I looked for you there."

"I wanted to finish up here before I ate. I'll join them in a while. By the way, thank you for arranging the meal. We don't often get to enjoy such fine food and drink. But of course, you know that."

Vikar nodded and took a mug from Jeskil. "It's the least I can do. You saved the party." He took a deep, appreciative swallow. "What a day this has been. On top of the girl showing up uninvited, I have Feracians to deal with."

Jeskil shuddered. "I don't envy you. I was wondering what the Talians were doing here. Wismar must want something." He was fishing; it was in his nature. Not that Vikar minded; he felt like talking, and Jeskil had always been his first choice of sounding boards.

"He sent the princess to be lady-in-waiting to Caelea in the interest of fostering closer relations, etcetera. Roxanna had no idea. You can imagine the temperature in the room when she and Caelea found out."

"I shouldn't laugh," Jeskil said, and laughed anyway. "That won't last."

"I worry about the queen. If it were up to me, I'd send the Feracians packing."

"I detest the prince in spite of having worked for him several times. He's mean in all senses of the word. Pretends to be a law-abiding Feracian but uses magickers from all over, even Rogies and Peorans. He's a dangerous man stuffed to bursting with ambition. I don't expect she's much better, though I haven't had much contact with her. Be wary of them."

"I'll keep my eyes open," Vikar said. "Thanks for the warning."

"Speaking of problems, what's going to happen to the girl?"

"What happens to any Provisional Wife? She'll have her child which will be raised at court, and she'll be forgotten. The king may be generous, but after today I wonder. I'll see she doesn't starve, if that's what you're asking."

"I assumed that much. You're a careful man."

"Age has taught me caution," Vikar told him.

"Age," Jeskil said with a snort of laughter. "You like to pretend you're so old and wise; you always did."

"I'm older than you are."

"By fewer than two years, Cousin. And thirty-one is hardly what you'd call a venerable age."

"Point taken," Vikar conceded. Jeskil could always puncture his pretensions and make him smile.

They drank together in silence for a time, then Vikar asked, "Any news of note in the Seven Kingdoms?"

"Nothing beyond the usual marriages, births, and deaths. Arrezko is on its way to being related to every kingdom in the known world. The oldest boy, Menno, has been betrothed to Alasine of Vartaris." That was a surprise to Vikar who had heard that Feracia had been making plans for one of their own princesses and Menno.

"Are you sure? Feracia was after him."

"Completely. I had it from Menno himself, who has a passion for puppets. He's quite good with them too. I told him that if he ever decided to stop being a prince to come see me about apprenticing."

"Wismar won't be happy."

"There are other princes. There are other Arrezkan princes come to that."

Vikar took another sip. "We're falling behind in the marriageable heir sweepstakes," he said sadly.

"What do you think the odds are of a royal heir by Caelea?" It was a blunt question. The succession was a tangle and Pelle had made it worse by taking a Provisional Wife in secret.

Vikar raised his mug. "Let's toast to the heir, my friend. The one the queen has promised us." They tapped their mugs together and drank. "I will do whatever I must to ensure that both children thrive," Vikar said.

"And that means?"

"You know what it means. Can you recommend someone?"

Jeskil nodded. "I'll contact the Archmage of Albhain. He'll know how to help."

"He must be discreet."

"He knows how it stands here. Will Caelea agree?"

Vikar bowed his head. Jeskil thought he'd never seen Vikar look so weighed down by trouble. "I ask you on her behalf."

Later, when the mountainberry brew was gone and Vikar had taken himself off to see to other duties, Jeskil joined the troupe at dinner. Though they had a good hour's start on him and he was certain that they had fallen on the meal like hungry wolves, there was still a prodigious amount of food and drink on the table. Such was the legendary hospitality of Corraçao.

He sat back and enjoyed his meal while the others ate, drank, and entertained each other with songs, jokes, and sleight of hand. They were careful about the magic, Jeskil had made sure they understood that the only place in the seven kingdoms where it could be openly practiced was Albhain, and even then he made sure that every one of his magic users was registered as Albhanian law required.

He turned over Vikar's request in his mind, working out how to phrase it so the Archmage would understand the delicacy of the situation. Caelea had never resorted to magic in all of her failed pregnancies out of respect for the customs of her adopted country and the inherent danger of meddling with the unborn. She must now be feeling desperate. While she was still of childbearing age, each year put her closer to being irretrievably barren. And now, this second wife had inserted herself into the conversation, and made things that much more difficult, though Jeskil did understand the logic behind Pelle's actions.

His attention was drawn to Billam who had jumped up onto the long wooden table. His long, belled sleeves jingled as he juggled half a dozen hawnuts, three forks, and a lemon tart. "Just like the King of Hearts!" he barked as he took a bite out of the tart and the others all laughed and applauded.

Jeskil rapped his fork against his goblet. "Hey, hey!" he shouted over the hoots of laughter. "Respect for our hosts," he reminded the troupe. "Billam, watch yourself."

"Sorry, sorry," Billam muttered as he slumped back into his chair like a naughty schoolboy.

"Respect for our hosts," Jeskil said again. "Always." He leaned down and told Feran to keep an eye on things. "I have a message to send."

"I'll get them all back to the camp safely," Feran promised. "And without offense." He grinned.

"Good man." Jeskil tucked a few dainties in his pocket for later and left the hall, turning up the collar of his coat as he stepped into the cool autumn night air. The Rain Moon was full, an omen of fecundity, he thought. But whose?

Jeskil made his way back to the troupe's camp at the far edge of the palace grounds. His wagon was the only one not gaily painted in bright, primary colors. The matte black exterior made the vardo all but disappear in the night. Only the thin trim of silver edging door and windows reflected the moonlight.

The interior of the Wagon was similarly austere, its wooden walls, floor, and ceiling waxed to a rich, warm glow. It was tidy and smallish by comparison to some of the larger family wagons nearby, but large enough for Jeskil, who didn't need more than a sleeping area, some storage, and a workspace.

He lit a lamp, pulled his deck of cards from under his mattress, and sat down at the table to lay the cards out in a wheel with the Magicker at its head. Then he set the Queen of Cups at the center of the wheel, laid his hands on the table, and concentrated on the images before him. When he saw the figure of the magician rise up from the card, holding his wand above his head, Jeskil laid one hand on his heart and bowed his head. "Magister, thank you for answering my call."

The magician figure lowered his wand and spoke with the voice of the Archmage of Albhain. "I see you are in Corraçao, Jeskil, at the court. Is all well there?"

Jeskil barely knew how to answer that question. "As well as can be expected. The Queen of Hearts is with child again."

"May she be blessed," the Archmage murmured. "Is this why you need to speak with me?"

"Yes, and at the queen's request."

The Archmage knew exactly what Jeskil was saying. "I see. But you both understand that what it is you're asking is proscribed by law. *Magic may not be used without express permission,*" he said, quoting the laws of magic. "An unborn child is not able to give such permission."

"Yes, Magister, but—" Just as he was about to beg for a dispensation, the Queen of Cups card that represented Caelea in this communication began to stir. Though voiceless, for it was not Caelea's person who animated the card but the force of her desire, the queen was eloquent in her gestures, kneeling to the magician card, laying her crown on the ground and cradling the chalice she held. A woman begging for help, not a queen demanding it.

Jeskil heard the Archmage sigh. "I daresay we can find a way," he said. I shall send word to Teamur who is nearby at the court of Lostri in exile. She will be the best person to deal with this. You will wait for her in Trennin and explain the situation. Give her every help and protection."

"Of course, Magister."

"And this goes no further."

"Magister, Vikar Revin already knows. The queen sent the request through him."

The Archmage's annoyance was palpable. "Of course he would be involved," he snapped. "I suppose there's nothing for it, though."

You should be grateful he's involved, Jeskil thought, but what he said was, "He is a loyal servant of the crown."

"Of his own ambition, you mean. I know you and he are close, so we will not argue the point. Let me contact Teamur now." Abruptly the card took its former shape, flat and unmoving, and the conversation was over.

Jeskil hadn't planned to keep the circus in Trennin for long after the party, but he didn't suppose it would matter when they left. The best thing about what he did was that there were so rarely deadlines to be met. And the troupe liked the city and its amusements. There was easy money here as well. Perhaps waiting wasn't a bad thing. They could all do with a bit of a rest.

Jeskil stretched and leaned back in his chair. He ate one of the cakes he'd taken from the banquet, a rougeberry cake crackling with a sugary glaze. There was a lot to like about Corraçao, he thought.

It was late and it had been a wearying day, so he stowed his deck of cards and undressed for bed. He'd earned his rest. Then he noticed that one of the plants in his window was wilted. He took it down and examined it; it looked as if it had been sucked dry. "I'm sorry," he murmured, realizing how tired he must've been to draw the energy out of this plant just to carry on his conversation with the Archmage.

"First rule of magic," he reminded himself. "The energy has to come from somewhere." Normally he had enough of his own to communicate via the cards. This time? Apparently not. He'd have to be more careful in the future. Magic didn't care where the energy came from; it was a greedy power.

2.

Harvest Moon CR 531

For lack of anything more interesting to do, Roxanna watched the maidservant work. The girl slunk around the perimeter of the room, tidying, dusting, shrinking into herself when she had to move past Roxanna's chair. As she fluffed the coverlet on Roxanna's bed, the book the princess had been reading the night before flew into the air and hit the ground with a dull thud, pages splayed and bent.

The girl scurried to retrieve it and set it on the night table. "I'm sorry, milady."

"Your Highness, you stupid child."

The dull, bovine eyes blinked. "What?"

"Get out!" It was intolerable living among people like this. "Don't come back!" she shouted at the girl's retreating figure—the third maidservant driven off in the five months she'd spent on the mind-numbing job of being one of the queen's ladies-in-waiting.

Roxanna had remained in Corraçao by order of King Wismar of Feracia. She was to serve Queen Caelea, though she was, in fact, a spy for Wismar. It was hardly an occupation for a Feracian princess, in Roxanna's estimation, but Wismar disagreed. He wanted her deep inside the court, eyes and ears open, sending him regular reports about the queen's health, her pregnancy, and all the court gossip about it. The tenuous nature of the Corraçaoan succession was of great interest to Wismar, who had designs on a Feracian-controlled route to the sea. He had been denied that single goal in spite of his conquest of all of Eresumma, most of Lostri, and a small portion of Arrezko before the magickers of Albhain had stopped the Feracian armies with their tricks and spells, and who knew what other dark arts. Feracia remained landlocked, cut off from the thriving trade enjoyed by every other country on Eiliron. Now Wismar was reduced by the terms of his surrender, enforced by Albhain, to rely upon diplomacy. And spying, of course. While Feracians weren't very good at diplomacy, they were excellent spies.

Wismar had assembled a herd of young Feracian princesses and duchesses ready in case Caelea proved unable to produce an heir. He'd chosen them for their perceived ability to drop litters of heirs, tying Corraçao to Feracia by blood, and their docility, which would provide Wismar with a strong alliance. In a few generations Corraçao would be just a satellite of Feracia, and Wismar's heirs would control the entire southern coast. There was something to be said, Roxanna supposed, to taking the long view.

No one had expected Pelle to take a Provisional Wife. It was a legal maneuver that had not been practiced in generations. And given that Caelea brought no strong alliances to the kingdom, it was a mystery to many why Pelle was determined to remain wedded to her. But Roxanna knew. She saw it in Pelle's eyes when he looked at his wife. She would have given anything to have someone look at her that way.

She had asked her brother why she was not among Wismar's stable of brood mares.

"You're too old, Roxanna, and too far removed from Wismar's direct line." Too old. At three-and-twenty. How was it possible to be used up so quickly?

"And you've no dowry. You'd bring nothing to Pelle. Wismar is negotiating on your behalf with Grand Duke Coline of Arrezko, who doesn't need a wife with a dowry, or even one who can bear him children."

"Coline? He's ancient!"

"And he has more money than anyone else in Arrezko, the king included, and half a dozen sons. He only needs someone to play hostess. But you'll like him; he's a thinker, like you. He reads. Not like Pelle."

Pelle. Handsome, vain Pelle, who was not unintelligent, but not a thinker. Roxanna supposed that he'd never had to be given his position and power. And yet, for all that she looked down on Corraçaoans, there was something about Pelle that excited her, something that set her heart racing.

Unfortunately, in the months she'd been in residence, he'd had eyes only for Caelea and the much-hoped-for child, and the rest of his attention was taken up not only with matters of the kingdom, but with the Provisional Wife who, it was said, demanded a good bit of attention.

Now Caelea was locked away with that strange old woman called Teamur, who had arrived at court a week after the king's birthday, and there could only be one reason for so much secrecy. Despite treaties with its neighbors and a few old but stringent laws, Corraçao had long been a haven for magic users, registered and otherwise. She suspected that a lot of magic was afoot in aid of providing the long-wished-for heir—perhaps dark and dangerous magicks. Roxanna put nothing past the old woman, Teamur, who had banished all but one of Caelea's ladies. Roxanna was reduced to lurking in dark corners and listening to conversations. The court doctors, though their services were retained on a limited basis, were free with their feelings about the situation. Some were pleased, and some emphatically not so.

Sometimes it seemed impossible to know what to think. These people were shifty, bubbling over with shrewd and slippery plots and cunning magicks. Roxanna hated them, their frivolity and deceit. But she also understood that to get anywhere in this court, to rise above the role she'd been forced into, she would have to become cunning as well. She sat down at her desk and began to compose her weekly letter to King Wismar.

Your Majesty, it is my honor to make my report to you. The queen remains in excellent health, and all the court physicians agree that there is every hope that she will be delivered of a healthy child. I attend her morning and night, and can report that she is in good spirits. Pelle is always at her side, the doting, attentive husband.

She smiled without humor, imagining Wismar's chagrin.

Of course there are no guarantees that things will be different this time, she wrote just to dangle a bit of hope in front of Wismar. *But the doctors all agree that Queen Caelea seems to be weathering this pregnancy far better than any previous one. They report that the child has begun to move and seems strong.*

And of course, the Provisional Wife and child continue to thrive as well, promising a true and secure succession into the next generation.

Your faithful servant, R. T.

The more everyone remained in the dark, the more chance Roxanna had to put her own plans into motion.

***

Vikar noted the tall, slender figure moving like a shade in her dark gray silk, through the gaggle of courtiers, stopping here and there to listen to the gossip. He knew exactly why Roxanna Talian had been sent to his court, and it didn't perturb him. He had agents in courts all over the world. It was how things were done by kings and queens and the people who served them.

But it did strike him as indelicate of Wismar to be spying on the queen's pregnancy. Vikar understood why it was being done, but still, Caelea had been through too much already. So when Teamur barred most of Caelea's ladies from the queen's presence, Vikar had approved. Not that Teamur cared what he thought, irascible crone that she was, but she was so filled with magic he could feel it radiating from her.

It gave him hope.

And then there was Paradis, who was safely tucked into a handsome town house a mile or so from the palace also thriving. She was eighteen and thought kings were very nearly divine, and she sent regular entreaties to Pelle to reassure her of his regard. It did flatter the king's ego, Vikar realized, which was probably why he hadn't sent the girl to some safe place outside of Trennin for the rest of her pregnancy.

He was shaken out of his thoughts when Roxanna approached him. "Good day, Master Revin."

"Your Highness." He made a slight bow. "What brings you to court today?"

"Boredom," she told him, and he had the sense that it was, if not the whole truth, then a goodly part of it. "As I cannot do what I was sent here to do, I must do something. How is the king this day?"

"Well, as always." Pelle was healthy as a horse, as healthy as his wife was not.

"And is he occupied with the arts today?"

Vikar's smile went from professional to brittle. "His Majesty is, as always, a supporter of the arts. However if you are asking if he is concerned with the wellbeing of his second wife…"

"My apologies. It was not my intention to imply anything more than a general interest in the goings on here at court. Though it does seem a shame that the girl remains a distraction at such a delicate time."

"Your highness, I—"

"I understand your position," she said, turning her pale gaze onto the crowd. "I know you would do something about it if you could."

It was a conundrum that had occupied his mind since the king's birthday. His intelligence suggested that there were already factions forming in support of the dancer's child, and other factions which wanted Pelle to take yet another Provisional Wife from among their ranks. It wasn't going to get any easier for anyone, least of all Caelea.

"Forgive me, but I had the impression that you and the queen were not"—he searched for the right word—"sympathetic?"

Then the cool, beautiful gray eyes were turned upon him. "My relationship with the queen has nothing to do with my sense of the rightness or wrongness of her situation. It's difficult for everyone, is it not?"

He knew she was right, and it stung. "He will not be led in this situation. He feels an obligation to the girl."

"Does that obligation extend to keeping her safe? Because you must know that there is idle talk here at court about eliminating her and replacing her with a Provisional Wife drawn from the nobility."

"He knew as much, but said nothing."

"It would be a simple matter of removing her from the city and out of the eyes of the members of court. Keep her safe. And silent," she added.

"And what does Feracia want in exchange?"

"To be quite honest, I don't care what Feracia wants, though if you repeat that I'll deny it."

"Walk with me," he said, and strode off. Once they reached the cloistered rose garden, Vikar said, "Talian Principality borders three states, including Corraçao. It is not only landlocked, but almost entirely mountainous."

"True."

"Talian fortunes have waned."

Her pale cheeks colored, and her lips thinned. "Was that a question or an observation?"

"I'm curious about what benefit you personally will derive from removing the dancer from the court."

To her credit, she didn't try to misunderstand or mislead him. "I'm tired of being Wismar's pawn," she told him with a frankness that surprised Vikar. "But without a dowry, my future is arid. Should my brother marry and have children, I become nothing, a virtual beggar in my own home." That a woman of such beauty and intelligence should be considered unmarriageable seemed to Vikar to be a sin. "I had in mind a chance at an advantageous marriage here in Corraçao. The man doesn't matter; the security of the position does. You are the one who can do this for me, are you not?"

Vikar studied her and decided again that while it might not be the whole truth, it was close. "Let me think on this," he said. "We will speak again soon."

"As you wish." She stepped into the sunlight of the garden, crossing the paths quickly and noiselessly, and Vikar watched her go, wondering what it was she really wanted. Though that was less of a concern to him than that she also saw clearly how difficult the presence of Paradis was. By keeping her so close, Pelle might unwittingly be setting the stage for a future power struggle that could damage the kingdom. Whether Caelea produced an heir or not, Paradis's child would have his or her own supporters in the future. Better to hide the girl away somewhere and then quietly bring her child to court to be raised as a second heir. It removed the girl from all temptations to meddle in the affairs of the kingdom, and it would go a long way to easing Caelea's mind and heart at this difficult time. This was worth some thought.

Later that evening, after a visit to the queen, who looked pale but hopeful, and a conference with Teamur, who remained opaque about the queen's health in spite of Vikar's insistence on being informed, Vikar retreated to his rooms. He had decided on a course of action and wanted to put it into motion before he changed his mind.

He retrieved his deck of cards from behind a row of dull, leather-bound volumes on the economic history of Corraçao, sat down, and unwrapped the silky black scarf that shrouded them. From the deck, which he had drawn himself when he was sixteen, he pulled two cards, Magicker and Counselor, and laid them side-by-side on the table. He placed his hands alongside the two well-worn cards and focused his concentration on them.

When the Magicker ros , it saluted him. "Cousin, is all well?" the figure asked in Jeskil's voice.

"It could be better."

"I'm sure it could be much worse, too." The wry features of the card's figure twisted into a grin. It was no accident that the Magicker figure looked like young Jeskil, just as the Counselor was a self-portrait of Vikar at sixteen. The best, most useful cards resonated emotionally with their owners and contained portraits of family, friends, even enemies, and personal symbolism. "What is it you need?"

"Use of your less entertaining talents."

The figure sobered as Jeskil took his meaning. "I see."

"Can you come to me? Are you far from here?"

"A day's hard travel, no more."

"We will speak when you arrive."

"Very well. Look for me early on the day after tomorrow." The card flattened out and the connection was broken.

In the hours that followed, Vikar argued his case with himself a dozen times, and a dozen times he came to the same conclusion: To allow Paradis to remain in Trennin at this time would risk dividing the kingdom, and he could not allow that.

By the time Jeskil arrived just after daybreak on the morning of the second day, Vikar had made peace with his intentions.

"First," Vikar insisted, "I am not a part of this."

"What?"

"This is a plan that benefits Princess Talian." Jeskil got that exasperated look that Vikar knew all too well. "Not to worry, cousin. It benefits the kingdom as well, but I can't be seen to be part of it at this time because I am the king's representative. What I do will be attributed to him. For now, hear the princess out, and agree to whatever she asks, then return here."

Jeskil shot him the look. "But you're not a part of this."

Vikar smiled. "Not at all," he said mildly.

"What is it she wants?"

"A dowry, a husband. It doesn't matter. What the kingdom gains is more important. Negotiate with the princess as if you're acting independently. Then we'll work out what happens next."

"I'll talk to her about it because you ask so nicely," Jeskil replied with a sardonic smile. "And because there's going to be good money in this."

"Don't price yourself out of the job, Jeskil. But if she balks, I'm sure we'll find a way to make up the difference."

"I'm sure."

***

Roxanna was surprised to find Vikar and Jeskil at her door. "Master Revin, what can I do for you?"

"Your Highness," Vikar said, "I've brought the man who can do whatever it is you wish done."

Slippery devil, Jeskil thought fondly.

She stood in the doorway of her rooms staring at them.

"May I enter?" Jeskil asked.

With a sigh, she stepped aside and let him into her study. Vikar bowed to her and disappeared into the shadows of the hallway.

"Our mutual friend has sent me to do a job for you," Jeskil said as she closed the door. "He told me you would give me the particulars."

She said nothing at first but paced from the door to the window and back. In the softening light of the early autumn sun that turned her skin and hair to gold, she looked younger than he had first thought.

Jeskil sank into a chair to wait, and she glared at him. "I didn't say you could sit in my presence."

"Please don't waste my time with nonsense."

She looked annoyed, but said, "The girl, the dancer…"

"Paradis?" Roxanna winced at the sound of that name.

"Yes. The dancer. She is endangering the queen's health and that of the kingdom."

Jeskil's eyes widened in faux horror. "Is she?" he asked, and Roxanna, sensing she was being mocked, snapped back, "I don't expect you to care, but it's the truth. She needs to be removed from the temptations of court."

"By which you mean—"

"She needs to leave Trennin."

"Are you asking me to kill her?"

She went white. "No! By all the saints, no, not that. She is the king's wife, no matter how tenuously, and bears his child. But here in Trennin, she is a danger. And I believe her to be in danger as well."

"I see. You understand that this thing you ask will not be cheap?"

"I do. Name your price."

He did, and she didn't blink. But when he stood, she took a step back as if she feared what he could do to her. "Then I'll take half my fee now, half when the deed is done."

"I cannot be connected with this in any way," she told him. "Your discretion—"

"Is being paid for, yes, I understand."

"Wait outside."

"As you say." Jeskil didn't mind. Her caution amused him. She thought he'd come back and rob her if he knew where she kept her money.

Within a minute of stepping into the hallway, Jeskil had half his fee in his money pouch and was on his way. He took a roundabout path back to Vikar's apartments, through hallways and waiting rooms where courtiers gathered to gossip, picking up snatches of conversation, most of which he felt amounted to nothing. Still, he did hear a few conversations which suggested that everything Roxanna had said was true. The dancer was a divisive presence in Corraçao.

He walked out into the sunshine of the cloistered garden where blown flowers scattered food for birds and beasts as well as for their own future renewal. At the north end of the garden was the remnants of the old wall of the original building with its intact portcullis now supporting climbing roses instead of stopping invaders. The Pellires family had expanded their home from modest keep to superb castle over the centuries without ever losing sight of what it had been.

Tipping his head up to feel the sun on his face, Jeskil closed his eyes and listened to the sound of the fountain, the breeze ruffling the blossoms, and a discussion of the king's marital situation by a couple strolling along the cloister path.

"Mark my words," the man said, "he is preparing to take a new queen, no matter what the outcome is."

"A common dancer?"

"She would bring vigor to the line. We would do well to cultivate the girl."

The woman sighed. "As you say," she replied, and then their words were swallowed up by the stones.

The girl was a bigger problem than Jeskil had imagined. As usual, his cousin had seen the danger and was already six steps ahead of everyone else.

It was odd how different he and Vikar really were. Jeskil was a man of the road, preferring to explore the world on his own terms. But Vikar was at his best as a fixture in a smaller world, moving behind the scenes, making himself indispensable not only to the king, but to any member of, or visitor to the court who might prove useful in some way. He was a political creature, and the cleverest man Jeskil knew.

They'd grown up together in Albhain, cousins and refugees from Eresumma, their families wiped out in the westward sweep of Feracian troops, opening a path to the sea. They were orphans, and they clung to each other, becoming brothers in all but fact. At twelve, they put together an act in which both performed sleight of hand and acrobatic feats, comedy, and (badly acted) skits based on popular folktales. People tossed money in the hat they'd set on the ground and convinced them that they were entertainers.

But they'd both had wild, untrained magic—it ran in their bloodline—and it attracted the attention of the Archmage Goedred, who was then just an archivist who enjoyed street entertainments. He had warned them that they were courting danger by not presenting themselves for registration and training. He became their teacher and mentor.

***

Vikar met him at the door. "So..."

Jeskil laughed and displayed the full money pouch. "I gather she's worried about the queen's health," he told Vikar. "Is there anything to eat?" he asked, slipping into the office where he spied a bowl of hawnuts on the desk, and helped himself to a handful, cracking open the shells with his fingers.

"I've sent for a meal. It will be here soon. Tell me what happened."

Jeskil gobbled down the nuts as he gave Vikar a full account of his interview with Roxanna. "She is a good deal more intelligent than I imagined."

"Too smart by half. I'd send her back to her crumbling castle in the mountains today if I could," Vikar admitted. "But that's not within my power. Nor would it be good for relations between our countries."

When the food arrived, Jeskil set on it like a starving man.

"When was the last time you ate?"

"About midday yesterday. I was in a hurry to get here." He licked his fingers and sat back. "Where do you suppose she got this money?" he asked, remembering how Vikar had characterized the Talians as existing in a state of denial over their poverty.

"I believe she's formed a connection to Duke Lakketta, who is still looking for a wife his mother will approve of. It's not the first time the duke has made a secret engagement. Smart money is on the dowager sending Roxanna packing before spring, but perhaps she'll recognize a kindred spirit in the princess."

"Kindred?"

"Ruthless and determined."

"You don't find it odd, though? I find it odd. Lakketta is a bore, and I doubt he bathes more than once a season. Roxanna seems fastidious, at least in terms of personal hygiene."

"He's extremely well off, or will be when his mother dies. Roxanna herself has suggested that my support would help her make a good marriage, and I would dearly love to see her safely married off to someone with lands far from Trennin. Lakketta fits both our agendas."

Jeskil shook his head. "Maybe I don't understand women."

"No one ever accused you of that," Vikar said with a chuckle.

When they finished eating and the dishes had been cleared away, Vikar told Jeskil what it was he wanted.

"I can't be seen to help you spirit that girl out of Corraçao, but I can make sure you go unhindered to the border of Albhain," Vikar told him as he produced papers that would clear a path through Corraçao for Jeskil and the girl. "Perhaps I'm over-reacting."

Jeskil shook his head. "No. You're on the mark, as usual." He repeated some of the conversations overheard that day.

"I've expected as much. But as far as I know, the girl has shown no interest in anything but Pelle, so I worry less about her motivations than anyone else's. That's something."

Jeskil nodded. "And I'm to leave her where?"

"Nowhere. You're to stay with her."

"What? Vikar, no!" Jeskil slapped the table with an open palm and made the bowl of hawnuts jump.

"Hear me out. She needs protection from herself. She's a stubborn girl who I believe will try to return to the king. I will see to it that he understands the situation, but she must be protected."

"For the rest of my life?"

Vikar rolled his eyes. "It's hardly likely to take her that long to have the child, cousin."

"And how am I supposed to control her?"

"Keep her close in the circus. Let her think you uncovered a plot by me to have her murdered and make her believe that she and her child are in grave danger."

"Why do you do this to me?"

"Because we're cousins, of course! Seriously, though, the longer you can keep her out of Trennin, the more she'll fade from everyone's thoughts. And who knows? Perhaps she'll meet some member of your troupe, fall in love, and forget all about being a queen. Once the child is born the Provisional Marriage can be dissolved, and we'll quietly bring the babe to court to be fostered."

That made Jeskil laugh. "Whenever I see Magister Goedred, he complains about losing you to politics. He always says you were the more promising of us."

"If our positions were reversed, he'd be telling me that about you. He values only what he doesn't have."

"His loss is Corraçao's significant gain." Vikar and Goedred had always struck sparks, Goedred attempting to enforce discipline on the boys, and Vikar rebelling. The irony was that of the two of them, Vikar was the more disciplined magician. Jeskil simply knew how to seem obedient while doing exactly what he wanted.

"Do you miss those days?" Jeskil asked as he folded the safe conduct papers and slipped them into his jacket.

"I don't think about it."

"I don't believe that. It was a good life."

"If you like starving. You're doing better without me than with me anyway."

The circus had been Vikar's idea, and for two years, as they built the show, collected performers, and began to be known outside of Albhain, Vikar had seemed happy. And then one day, he simply walked away from it all, saying he wanted a more settled life.

"That's your problem," Jeskil told him before he left. "You want guarantees. You're a ringmaster at heart, though, and always will be."

***

The next day, after Jeskil left the palace, Vikar was summoned to the Queen's Garden. He found Caelea there, tended by Lady Rosamunda, one of the few ladies-in-waiting Vikar trusted absolutely.

Caelea was pale in the golden sunlight, but her smile was sweet and welcoming. "Vikar, I'm glad to see you. Come and sit with me."

"Is it not chilly out here for you?"

"A bit, perhaps, but I'm tired of sitting indoors. I love autumn, don't you?"

"Very much."

She took a deep breath. "I love the way it smells. But now I think I would like some tisane. Rosamunda, would you mind fetching me something other than Teamur's horrible brews? Something that tastes of apples and honey?"

Rosamunda's smile was fond. "Happily. Counselor Revin?"

"Nothing for me, thank you."

When Rosamunda was out of earshot, Caelea reached out and grasped Vikar's hand. "I am going to say something to you I have never said, and I beg you to listen and not interrupt me."

He nodded, but an invisible force twisted inside his chest.

"This child will be born no matter what I must do to see to it. I hope to survive to be its mother, but if I do not, I beg you to see that it grows up safe and happy."

"Majesty—"

"Hush. You and I both know the dangers; please don't pretend otherwise. Keep my child safe, whatever you must do, even if that means leaving Corraçao with him, as your mother did when she rescued you from the Feracians."

Vikar's mouth dropped open.

"I've always known who you were, Vikar... Cousin."

He squeezed her hand. "I thought I was so clever."

"My mother kept track of her family as best she could. She said she'd hoped that her brothers could send their families to Lostri, but the Feracians made that impossible. She knew who you were the moment she saw you."

"She kept my secret. Why?"

"Because we all have our secrets. She said you must have had a reason. My point is that I trust you with the life of my child. But listen, should the worst happen, should both the child and I not survive, I beg you to serve Pelle faithfully as you have always done. If the dancer produces an heir, support them. If she does not, see that Pelle remarries and has a family." She released his hand and sat back. "I know I lay a heavy burden on you, my friend. I'm sorry that it's necessary.

"I will do whatever I must to care for you, your child, and your kingdom."

"I know you will. Thank you." Caelea closed her eyes and tipped her face up toward the sun, sighing with pleasure in its warmth. "Will we have many more nice days, do you think?" she asked as Rosamunda returned with a cup that smelled of sweet spices and fruit.

"We will have many more years," Vikar said, even though he feared he was telling a lie. She did not seem strong enough to give birth, and if he could have willed his own strength into her, he would have.

Caelea sipped her tisane and sighed happily. "Oh, that does me good," she said. "Thank you, my rose."

***

The girl wasn't difficult to find. Every few days around noon, a carriage left the palace and took the same route to a small house in the Sibi district, a house with a gardener who rarely did much gardening that Jeskil could see, a gardener who was built like a tree and dressed in surprisingly nice clothes for someone who was supposed to be rooting around in the soil.

On each visit, a big man in a black hooded cape alighted from a carriage and entered the house, followed by servants with baskets of food and wrapped packages. Did Pelle really think he was being circumspect? Was a hood his idea of the perfect disguise? The servants came back out and waited with the carriage until the hooded man left the house and went back to the palace. The visits rarely lasted more than an hour, and often just a few minutes, but they seemed to content the dancer, who was always thrilled to see Pelle, and sad to watch him leave.

On the days when the king was not visiting, Paradis often went out to the local market. There were always a pair of guards close by, but they had little to do beyond carrying her purchases back to the house. She was carefree and carried herself with all the assurance of a woman who has found a comfortable place in life. She dressed to show off her swelling belly and paid no attention to the people around her. She didn't seem to care if a merchant snubbed her because there were plenty who fawned on her, knowing that she had the king's attention.

She would stroll home, enjoying the fine weather, and often stopping to watch children play. Jeskil saw her face soften as she looked on, laughing at their games, her hand curving over the swell of the child she carried.

After observing her for a week, learning her habits, Jeskil was ready to act. He obtained a guard's uniform from the palace and arranged for a coach to be waiting a few streets north of the marketplace.

On the day of the abduction, the market was more crowded than usual, with circus people entertaining and Vikar's agents moving restlessly through the crowds. On Jeskil's signal, a fight started over the price of a mackerel, and the crowd surged forward to watch.

Jeskil, who had been standing a few feet away from Paradis, shouldered his way through the crowd to her guard and hissed, "We have to get her out of this crush! Clear a way back to the west entrance." Then he grabbed Paradis's arm and said, "Come with me, lady. You are in danger."

He led her east, then north, quickly losing sight of the two guards who were being buffeted by the spectators who were applauding the fishmonger for slapping his customer with a trout.

"What's going on?" Paradis asked, but he propelled her forward and said, "We have to flee this place, lady."

He nearly threw her into the carriage, climbed in behind, and rapped on the ceiling. The horses leapt forward, and before the girl recovered her wits, they were nearly to the east gate of the city.

"What's happening? Who are you?"

"The king sent me. A plot has been uncovered."

Her blue eyes widened, and she clutched her swelling belly. "Against me and my child?"

He nodded. "His Majesty told me to get you to safety no matter the cost."

She said nothing more, but a single tear rolled down her flushed cheek, and Jeskil understood how she had caught the eye of a king. She had a soft, yielding, irresistible beauty.

3.

Moon of the First Frost, CR 531

Once he had Jeskil's assurance that the girl was safely away and on the road to Albhain, Vikar went to the king.

"Majesty, the dancer situation has gotten out of hand."

Pelle scowled but said nothing.

"She's become the focus of plots and plans--."

"She plots against us?" the king asked.

"No, no absolutely not. The girl is loyal. Unfortunately her presence in Trennin is a divisive one."

"We've spoken on this subject before," Pelle said as if that was all there was to say about it.

"The situation has intensified, and as long as she remains in the city, it will continue to do so. I have had intelligence that suggests--."

Pelle cut him off with a wave of his hand. "Then remove her from the city."

Vikar was taken aback. This was a response he hadn't expected.

"Counselor, she's a sweet girl, but requires far too much attention. I have my queen to think of. Put the girl someplace safe. We'll deal with her after her child is born."

"Of course. I will ensure she's well cared for."

"I know we can count on you, old friend," Pelle said with a tired smile. "Anything else?"

"Not a thing, Majesty."

On his way back to his office, Vikar wondered why everything to do with the kingdom wasn't that simple. But he was kicking himself for having involved Roxanna at all. Now he owed her a favor. Still, it wasn't a bad thing to have her think she had done the kingdom a good turn. A sense of accomplishment was often an excellent reward.

The queen called him to her chambers the next day. "What happened?" she asked, and Vikar didn't pretend to misunderstand.

"The girl was removed from the city."

"Why?" Caelea asked, her voice unexpectedly sharp.

"It was politic," Vikar told her.

"Was she disloyal?"

"No, not at all. But others may have been tempted to be by her very presence."

The queen sighed and laid a hand on her rounded belly. "Vikar you would tell me if I had reason to fear for the sake of my child, wouldn't you?"

He didn't know how to answer her. Part of his job, as he saw it, was protecting the king and queen from such concerns. "I would never allow anything to happen to any of you."

She nodded. "I trust you," she told him, and he felt unsettled for reasons he didn't understand. "And how do you fare?" he asked, changing the subject.

"The prince is moving a great deal today."

"Prince? It's a boy?" Vikar asked.

Caelea glowed with happiness. "Teamur confirmed it. Also that he's healthy if a bit small, but I know he'll grow and thrive. I just feel it. It's everything I've hoped for, Vikar. A strong, lively heir for Corraçao. One day at a time," she added as if she were repeating a mantra. They both knew how fast things could change with a pregnancy.

"That's wonderful news," he said.

"Let's keep it that way." Teamur entered the room holding a steaming cup. "The queen needs to rest," she said and set the drink on the table at Caelea's elbow.

"I called him to me. I needed to know what happened to the dancer."

Teamur's smile was fond. "I know, but it's time to let this concern go, for your own sake as well as for the prince's." Teamur seemed subdued. There was a tension in her features.

"I agree. You must rest," Vikar said. "I hope I've set your mind at ease, Majesty." Then to Teamur: "Walk with me?"

She nodded. "Drink your broth," she told Caelea and followed Vikar out into the hallway.

"Truth now, how is she? How is the child?"

"I have no intention of making any promises," the older woman snapped.

"I'm not asking for promises, just no surprises. She told me that the boy is healthy if small."

"It's the queen who concerns me; she is fragile. The child is healthy and active. For now. I've studied the history of her pregnancies and know that much can still go wrong. She pours too much of her energy into the boy. Why did you never train her in magic?"

"I never knew she had any," Vikar admitted. Though it ran in the family, Caelea had never shown any sign of having magical power or even an interest in it. In fact, she had always resisted the use of magic for any reason.

"It's wild and unfocused. I'm trying to rein her in, but she has such need." She shook her head.

There wasn't much more to say beyond "thank you," so Vikar took his leave. He had a lot to consider.

***

With winter coming on, the notion of being stuck in Albhain wasn't as huge an imposition on Jeskil as he'd made it out to be. The circus normally wintered in Rathsorcha, where they did regular shows at the winter market and a brisk business in fortune-telling. But he complained whenever he reported to Vikar because he wanted to make his cousin feel guilty for setting him to nurse-maiding this infuriating girl whose moods changed by the day.

With respect to her condition, they made slow progress through the north of Corraçao. Paradis spent a full day weeping and bemoaning her parting from her "great love," as she referred to Pelle. Jeskil escaped the carriage and rode with the coachman when it became too much to bear. "So you have some privacy, lady," he told her. He had the sense that she wasn't entirely grateful. She liked an audience for her drama, he supposed. Tiresome child.

By the time they'd reached Lakan, the tears had stopped, and the questions had begun.

"Who was plotting against me?" she asked. Every conversation began with that question, no matter how many times Jeskil feigned ignorance.

"I don't know, lady," he would say. "I was only told to see you safely to Rathsorcha."

"Why Rathsorcha?"

"I don't know, lady. It's what I was told."

Stalemate.

They finally crossed the Kish river and entered Albhain, triggering a whole new set of questions, some simpler: "This is a kingdom of magic users, isn't it?" Some more difficult: "Why would Pelle send me here?"

Jeskil, his patience growing thin, began to snap at Paradis, but stopped once he realized that she was goading him on purpose.

"I've told you everything I know," he insisted.

"You don't know much, do you?"

He bit his lip.

A storm forced them to seek shelter about fifty miles from the city, at a small inn called "The King's Secret". When Paradis saw the sign and gave Jeskil a hard look, he pretended not to understand, though it was difficult not to laugh. He hadn't planned it, but it was a good joke.

Over a dinner of sausage and potatoes, she watched Jeskil with an intensity that was new, as if she was looking for something below the surface. Finally, tired of being studied, he said, "What?"

"Nothing."

"Then stop staring at me."

She looked down at her plate, but a smile twitched at the corners of her pretty mouth.

He walked her to the door of her room and saw her safely inside. "If you need anything, one of us will be right outside your door," he told her, as he did every time they stopped for the night.

She shut the door in his face, and Jeskil wondered what would happen if he just left her on her own. She'd have to pay for her lodging and food by working in the kitchen, he supposed, and the thought made him chuckle.

He settled on the floor, taking the first watch, and amused himself by dealing out the cards to see what story they could tell him. He didn't need magic for this; it was a game to him, something to keep his mind sharp. Vikar's card turned up, and Jeskil muttered, "I owe you a good, hard punch, Cousin." Then the Queen of Hearts reversed, the King of Hearts also reversed, and a run of cards came up, on which the images seemed foggy and indistinct.

He decided he was too tired to do this and gathered them back up. He'd put no magic into the reading and so could take none out.

He heard a bump from inside the room, and something fell to the floor.

"Lady, is everything all right?" he shouted, knocking at the door.

"Nightmare! Go away!" And then another crash, and the girl gave a strangled, faraway cry. There was a heavy thud and then silence.

Jeskil forced the door open onto an empty bedroom. The window was open, and the bed sheet was hanging out of it. Paradis was sitting on the ground below, looking dazed, but she got up and tottered off toward the woods.

"Damn the girl!" Jeskil shouted and went out the window after her, rappelling down until the sheet ran out, and then falling into a roll that had him back on his feet and trailing Paradis into the trees. She was astoundingly fast for a heavily pregnant woman.

The light from the moon shone off her fair hair as she ran, so he had no problem trailing her. And she slowed after the initial sprint, clutching her belly, and finally sinking down between the roots of an ancient oak. "Oh no," she whispered. "Oh no, please."

"You've hurt yourself." Jeskil squatted beside her. "The child... why would you do that?"

"You were going to kill us anyway," she said through clenched teeth.

He laid a hand on her belly and probed with his magic, trying to see what kind of damage had been done in the fall. "Why would I kill you?"

"Pelle didn't send you." She looked him in the eye. "Did he?"

There was no point in lying now. "No. But I wasn't supposed to kill you. I was supposed to keep you safe."

"Why? And who sent you?" she asked, then groaned and doubled over.

"Well for one thing, I don't kill children, and for another, have I been anything but respectful to you? You're safe with me, I swear on my name. Now hold still." He plunged his left hand into the loamy soil and sought the threads of earth energy that would help him ease her pain. Jeskil feared that there was reason to worry about a miscarriage, so he wrapped threads of light and energy around the child and sent them coursing through her muscles, calming them. He eased them into the nerves that were screaming, giving her relief. He held Paradis and her child—a boy, he could see it—in a cradle of energy and light until the spasms passed. Finally, he felt her relax. The child settled, and Jeskil sat back.

"How do you feel?"

"Fine. What did you do to me?"

"Possibly a temporary measure. We're going back to the inn and staying there until I can have a doctor look at you." Her face was pale in the moonlight; she'd been frightened. "I'm not here to hurt you, Paradis. There really is a plot against you, and I'm the only thing standing between you and disaster."

She studied him, then nodded. "As long as we're clearing the air, my real name is Reyna. Is yours truly Jeskil?"

He nodded and helped her to her feet, but before she could attempt a step, he swept her up into his arms and carried her back toward the inn.

"Will you tell me the whole truth, Jeskil? I'm tired of half-truths."

"Not all at once, but yes, I believe I will tell you... most of the truth."

"We will have a lot of time to talk."

"Will we?"

"I don't like being alone. I think you're going to need to sit with me."

"I so look forward to that," he said. Despite his tone, Reyna laughed.

4.

Sleep Moon, CR 532

A young woman came to Roxanna when news of the dancer's disappearance began to circulate in the court. "Master Jeskil sends his compliments," she told Roxanna, "and asks if all has been done according to your wishes." The sweetness and innocence of her face took Roxanna aback, for it was so at odds with the meaning of the question.

"Is the girl safe?" she asked, but the young woman simply replied, "He bids me collect the rest of his fee." The girl stood quietly, waiting.

"Yes. Of course. I have it ready," Roxanna said unnecessarily. She took the pouch from her desk and handed it to the girl, who opened it and counted the coins, making Roxanna bristle. "It's all there."

"He would not be happy with me if I shorted him," the girl said, leaving Roxanna to wonder what the punishment might be for stealing from Jeskil.

"If I should need his services again?" Roxanna asked. "How would I contact him?"

"How did you contact him last time?"

"That path is not open to me now." Some things she would not want Vikar to know.

"You can reach him through me. I work at the apothecary stall in the Sibi market at the sign of the feather and bone. Ask for Elian."

It was time for Roxanna to begin her campaign for the king's attention. That very day, she made sure Pelle saw her sitting in an alcove in the hall outside the queen's chambers when he came to visit Caelea each morning. She was conspicuous in her inconspicuousness, dressed in sober colors, hands folded over a prayer book, sitting so that the light from the window made her hair a fall of gold.

For several days he ignored her, then he took notice but said nothing. After a week, he stopped in front of her. "It's Princess Roxanna, isn't it?" he asked.

She looked up as if startled. "Oh, Your Majesty, I didn't realize." She started to stand so she could make a curtsy, but he waved her down and sat beside her.

"What are you doing here?"

"I come here hoping for good news, but mostly I pray for the sake of the queen and her child." She clutched the prayer book.

He seemed surprised. "That's kind of you."

"I came here to wait on the queen, but the old woman sent most of us away. I do what I can. I suppose it seems like a small thing," she added, turning her face away. "But I do what I can."

"She is as well as can be hoped," he said. "Thank you for caring. And for your prayers. I believe they must be helping."

Roxanna nodded, then laid a hand on the king's. "And you? I see so much care in your face, as if you carry some terrible burden." Then, as if she remembered herself, she snatched her hand away. "Forgive me; I meant no disrespect," she murmured. "But I pray for you as well."

But the touch seemed to have done the trick. He turned toward her like a flower toward the sun and tipped her head up with one finger on her chin. "You perceive much," he told her. Their gazes locked for a moment, and Roxanna lost herself in the cornflower blue of the king's eyes. "I can't burden anyone else with this concern," he told her, breaking the touch and the gaze. "But I do thank you again for your prayers."

"Majesty, I am superfluous here. If I may help in any way, please believe that I am not just ready to, but willing to. I can be a friendly ear," she said. Then added, "And a confidential one."

Pelle nodded, then rose, and continued down the corridor.

Roxanna clutched the prayer book to her chest and stood up, her vigil done for the day.

Back in her chambers, she wrote to King Wismar:

The queen's confinement continues successfully. Pelle is ever at her side, and they are more in love than ever.

Wismar would be furious when he read this. It was a pleasant thought.

There is, of course, no guarantee that this pregnancy will be more successful than the others, but there does seem to be more reason to hope according to all the gossip. For now, I suggest biding your time. If the child is a healthy boy, I will speak to the queen about securing the future of our kingdoms with a betrothal. As I have the queen's ear, I feel she will be amenable.

Oh yes, she and Caelea were best friends, at least on paper. It was a handy fiction, and it made Roxanna all the more valuable to Wismar.

Unfounded rumors circulate at court about the disappearance of Pelle's Provisional Wife. Some believe she was removed for her own safety, others that she has been murdered at the queen's behest, though I think that is unlikely. It is impossible to know the truth at this time and so I hope you will heed my advice in this matter and not press Pelle about ensuring the succession with a younger wife. He will hear nothing of divorcing his queen and rages at any such suggestion. The situation with the young woman has only made things more difficult.

As always, I am your servant in all things, she added, and signed her name with a bit of a flourish. She sealed the letter and handed it off to a messenger, then carried her book out to the garden to read in the last warmth of the autumn afternoon.

***

The doctor from Rathsorcha confirmed what Jeskil had anticipated. Reyna and the child would be fine so long as she rested. Travel was forbidden.

"You're not going to bounce her around on these roads in winter," he warned. "Unless you want a disaster. How did she manage to fall?"

"Um, nightmare," Jeskil told him. "Hers can be fierce."

"Well, keep her down at night. That's your job. I'll be back here in a week or two to check on her."

"You were right," Jeskil told Reyna after the doctor had left. "We do have a lot of time to talk. No more travel until the child comes."

"I don't mind. I like this inn. The King's Secret; it's aptly named, isn't it?" she said, patting her belly and making Jeskil laugh out loud.

"You are so different from the girl I took from the market." He drew a chair up to the bed and pulled out a deck of playing cards. "Do you know how to play pickpocket?"

She grinned. "Since I was a toddler. Deal," she said and popped a candy into her mouth. She had a prodigious appetite for sweets, and Jeskil was happy to bring her treats if it kept her from becoming restless and unhappy.

It was easier to talk while they played cards. A slight distraction meant that they couldn't probe too deeply. Jeskil confessed that Pelle hadn't hired him, but someone else, someone who had good reason to be aware of the plots swirling around court, knew that there were factions growing up around Reyna and her child.

"Some are threatened; some see you as a way to power."

Reyna chewed her lower lip. "I thought it would be exciting to be the king's wife. I had no idea how horrible those people were." She put a queen down on the coverlet and said, "My queen takes your tens. All of them."

Jeskil groaned and threw his tens down. She scooped them up and laughed. "Who was horrible to you?" he asked.

"I suppose it depends on what you consider horrible. I knew the gifts that were sent to me were for favors, so I returned them, but then the ugly messages started arriving. And someone sent me a dead baby in a basket with a note that said, *The kingdom will be better off once you and your brat are dead.* I didn't tell Pelle, and I buried the child myself, poor mite."

Jeskil didn't comment, but he made a mental note to tell Vikar next time they communicated. "Oh, oh," he said, "three aces. I take all your royals."

"Oh damn! That's the game."

"Another?"

"Not right now. I'm a bit tired. Let's just chat for a while, yes?"

"All right. Can I get you anything?"

She shook her head and her golden curls looked like a halo. "I made a mistake," she said. "Going to court like that. I knew better. Pelle didn't make a secret of what a Provisional Wife's position was, but I chose to ignore the truth in favor of the fantasy. It's amazing how much you can grow up in a few months, isn't it?"

"Is it?"

"I thought he loved me. I thought I loved him!"

Jeskil was surprised. "You don't?"

"No. But I couldn't see for the shine on him. He's beautiful and powerful, and he had a way of making me feel important. But I wasn't important, just convenient."

Why Jeskil felt the urge to reassure her was a mystery. That wasn't part of the job, but it saddened him to hear the resignation in her voice. "When we're young," he began.

"We love love," she finished.

He nodded. "Yes, exactly. That's... perceptive of you."

"That's my mother talking. She told me that all the time, and I said, 'I'm not like that. I'll know when it happens.' But I had to learn the hard way, and not just with Pelle. Being pretty can be a curse," she confessed as she gathered up the cards into a tidy pile. "Will you tell me your story about falling in love with love? So I don't feel like the only fool in the world?"

"One day I will, but please trust that you are far from the only fool in the world. We are everywhere." He smiled at her and meant it. He liked this girl. "You should rest now. I'll bring dinner up later."

"Will you eat with me?"

"I wouldn't have it any other way," he said.

Jeskil never thought he'd come to be so fond of Reyna. The prospect of spending the winter with her in Albhain no longer seemed like an imposition, but he wasn't about to tell Vikar that. No point in wasting Vikar's guilt.

***

The king visited the queen every day. Some days he stopped to talk to Roxanna; some days he simply nodded to her and walked on. But on the days he stopped, she felt a warmth growing between them, an ease of communication. She was careful to mirror his sentiments and concerns and to express her willingness to help in whatever way she could.

She was also careful not to overplay her I-feel-useless card. He didn't need to see her as a nonentity. Rather, she wanted him to see her as anything but useless. She did not touch him again until the day he took her hand in his and confessed that he had come to rely on their conversations, particularly when he was most concerned about Caelea and the prince.

So. It was a boy. And while the throne of Corraçao could pass to a female heir—a civilized arrangement in Roxanna's opinion—there wasn't a king alive who wouldn't prefer to be succeeded by a son. "What little I can do," she assured him every time they spoke, "I will do."

Eventually he spoke about Paradis and how he feared he'd made a terrible mistake. "She's a sweet girl, doesn't ask for much, though she does like a lot of attention," he admitted with a wry smile. "I should have known better."

"Do you care for her?" Roxanna asked, comfortable enough to ask such a personal question. "In your heart, I mean?"

Pelle considered, then shook his head. "No, I don't love her, if that's what you mean. There's only one woman I love."

Well that complicates things, Roxanna thought, even as she smiled with the intent to express her approval. What it meant was that she had to keep him at arm's length. A mistress couldn't take him from Caelea, but a beloved friend might ease his sorrow should the queen die in childbirth. And in the throes of grief, well... anything could happen.

It was not an easy path to walk. She wanted to provoke his interest and suggest her own, but had to stand apart from any physical expression just as she was doing with Lakketta. So long as the duke was willing to loan her money without any collateral, he was useful. And he would be a fallback should Caelea survive. Becoming a duchess was no small thing.

Roxanna would do what she had to do to make her own way. She was not going to be a supplicant in her own home, an inconvenient sister or maiden aunt. Nor would she be married off to the octogenarian Grand Duke Coline of Arrezko. She was young and healthy; she wanted a husband and children. Hartan had stolen what future she might have had when he lost her dowry, so she had to create a new one.

Aim high, she told herself every day as she sat down in her alcove and opened her prayer book. *Aim high and do not waver.*

***

Reyna grew increasingly restless over the next days. She begged the doctor to let her get out of bed, then once he told her she could sit in a chair instead, she begged him to let her go for a walk.

"The weather will be growing too cold soon, and it's so beautiful out. Please don't make me miss the last of autumn. You never know," she said as she touched the swell of her belly. "It could be my last one."

Reyna had a talent for handling people. And inevitably, the doctor gave in and said she could go for a short walk.

"You minx," Jeskil said to her after the doctor left. "That was brilliantly played."

"I feel fine. Why should I sit around like someone's grandmother?" She looked fine, too, the picture of health, in fact—bright of eye and pink of cheek. "Now go away while I dress, and then we can go for our walk."

"We?"

"You have to come with me. I might decide to run away again."

"I could just let you get eaten by bears." She pursed her lips and gave him a look that made him laugh. "All right, all right," he said. "Don't take forever."

She met him at the door to the inn, and he sighed when he saw how she was dressed in the same light frock she'd been wearing when he'd snatched her off the street, though it was now riding high over her belly. "It's not warm enough for that dress," he told her, "fetching though it is."

"It's all I've got," she reminded him. "My kidnapper didn't think to let me pack. You should speak to him about it."

He borrowed a cloak from the innkeeper and wrapped her in it. "How on earth did you get the nickname Paradis?"

"I gave it to myself."

"Why?"

"Because men believed it. They thought it was a promise."

"Was it worth it?"

She shrugged as they stepped out into the chill autumn afternoon. "I had fun while it lasted, I suppose. And a girl has to make her way somehow. Oh how beautiful!" she exclaimed as the sun made the autumn colors blaze. "I love this season."

They walked slowly toward the woods together, her arm hooked through his.

"There was a temple to… oh I don't even recall the saint's name now, but back home, the sun shone through the stained glass the way it's shining through the leaves. I used to hide there and just watch it move across the row of windows."

"Where's home? Trennin?"

"No, I'm from Carcalon; it's on the coast."

"I know the place and the temple, I think. Saint Hysis?"

"That's it, yes!" She seemed pleased. "How do you know it?"

"The circus has played there a number of times."

"Circus? Not the Circus of Dreams?"

"The same."

"I love the Circus of Dreams! I wanted to join it at one time, but my mother told me I was selling myself short. I wonder what she'd think of me now." She sighed. "What do you do there?"

"A bit of everything," he told her. "Do you remember the puppet show?"

"Merrypike and Fluffbottom? Of course, they were hilarious. Was that you?"

He nodded. It was strange how pleased he was to think she remembered his work.

"I'm going to sit down on that log for a bit, and you're going to tell me all about the circus."

"Are you all right?"

"I'm fine, Jeskil. I've been abed for a week and need to build my strength again. Now sit and talk to me. How did you join the circus?"

Jeskil sat beside her on the fallen tree and told her some of the story of how he and Vikar had started the circus as boys, starting out as street acrobats and fortune-tellers. They had drawn together other street performers to create a small troupe with the intent of building a regular audience who would be more generous with their donations.

"And if they weren't?" she asked, rubbing her lower back.

Jeskil shrugged. "We helped them be more generous."

"I imagine you did. Street performers often have clever

fingers. I've known a few in my time, and even danced in public squares." She got a faraway look. "I have to say, now I think about it, those days were a lot of fun. Sorry, I didn't mean to interrupt. How did it grow into a circus?"

"It was Vikar's idea to get to know the regulars and offer them free passes when the troupe grew big enough. My cousin understands people and knew that appreciative regulars would bring friends, and those friends had friends. As we sold more tickets, more performers came to us, asking to be included because it would mean a more regular income. But Vikar had rules. No overt magic ever. All magic tricks and fortune-telling had to be fakery."

"Why?"

"To avoid the notice of the magisters. The rules in Albhain are strict despite the country being a haven for magicians. So every trick had to have an explanation that would satisfy anyone who had suspicions."

"That's smart."

"As I said, my cousin is a smart man."

"And what did you do?"

"Everything else," he said, and she laughed.

"I can quite see that."

"I pulled the troupe together, rehearsed them, and created themed shows to keep things fresh. You don't want to give people the same show every season."

"You do not," she agreed, looking amused. "But the... other things, what you do on the side?"

"That was the two of us. We realized what a good intelligence network we had. A group of people who could go anywhere, perform for the quality as well as the people on the street. We became couriers, gatherers of information. We became useful, as well as entertaining."

"So you were spies?" Reyna asked.

"Of a sort. We were young, we had to learn the craft. And my cousin learned it so well that he left the circus and went to work for Pelle." He glanced at her face. "What? You consider it a low occupation?"

"We all do what we can, yes? To get by?"

"We do. Yes."

"It must have been exciting," she observed, and Jeskil laughed out loud.

"It was. It is still. Sometimes."

They talked until the sun was blazing orange on the horizon, and it began to grow cold as shadows of twilight fell.

"We really will be eaten by bears if we stay out much longer."

"You'll finish telling me everything over dinner, won't you?"

"If you like. But then you'll have to tell me about how you came to Trennin." He stood and gave her a hand up. She tilted her head and smiled at him, and Jeskil's heart gave a lurch.

5.

Dark Moon, CR 532

The winter cold came early that year. Reyna's health seemed good, but Jeskil could see that she tired easily. They did a little exercise together each morning, but mostly they sat together in Reyna's room and played cards or talked. Sometimes Jeskil read to her. She enjoyed romances, but when he teased her about it, she said, "They're fun to listen to, but I'm not soft-headed enough to believe they're real. Not anymore, at least."

"You've become so worldly," he joked.

"You have no idea."

One overcast day he found a volume of satires by Kelonia Giraud tucked under the mattress of his bed. "It could explain the dreams," he told her, and she laughed her lovely, musical laugh.

"Have they been satirical?" she asked.

"More farcical. Shall I read to you?"

"Please. It feels good to laugh on a day so gloomy."

Jeskil was halfway through a story about a knight and a clever donkey, when Reyna suddenly stopped laughing and went pale. "Something is happening," she whispered, clutching her belly.

Jeskil stared at her, mouth open, and she began to laugh again. "Please don't tell me that you didn't expect this to happen. Oh... oh dear." She scrunched up and gave a little moan.

"I'll send someone for the doctor," he said and raced out of the room.

The innkeeper said, "You'd be better off with the midwife. She's only down the road a bit. The doctor could take hours."

Why couldn't he think of what to do? "Yes, of course. Can you send for them both?" he asked, and the innkeeper looked at him with amusement.

"First child, eh?" he asked. "It'll be fine. She's a healthy girl."

"What?" What was the man talking about?

"I remember our first." He waved his wife over. "Solya, it's little Reyna's time. I'll send one of the boys to fetch the midwife if you stay here and reassure our friend. It's their first."

"Is she alone up there?" Solya asked.

"I—yes."

"Let's go keep her company." She followed him up the stairs, chattering the whole time about her own children and how it was the most natural thing in the world. When she saw Reyna, she smiled and said, "Well, isn't this exciting? Your husband tells me this is your first." She bustled around the room, lighting more lamps. "Let's give the child a bright greeting, shall we? Though a Winterfest child will bring light into the world. Are you hoping for a boy or girl?"

Reyna stared at Jeskil in surprise, then, when Solya had turned away, she crossed her eyes and put out her tongue at him. He was too startled to respond, but it took some of the edge off his near panic. He grinned.

"I don't care either way," Reyna said as Solya helped her to her feet. "But I think Jes wants a son. Don't you, my heart?"

"They all do," Solya said, and patted Reyna's shoulder. "Let's walk you around a bit. It helps."

"I'm so thirsty," Reyna told her.

"I'm not surprised. Jeskil, go downstairs and fetch a pitcher of fresh water, will you? And there's a bit of bread and cheese in the larder. She'll be hungry, too."

Jeskil was so relieved to leave the room that he almost flew down the stairs. Why was he acting like this? Why so nervous? Women gave birth every day. But his hands were shaking as he carried the water and food back up the stairs, and he was forced to ask himself why Reyna and the child were so important to him, more important than just a job. They were...

He stopped outside the door of Reyna's room, frozen by the realization that this was love, this madness, this giddy happiness and anxiety all tangled up together. And it was impossible. Reyna was little more than a child herself, just eighteen and still new to the enormous possibilities the world held for her. To say nothing of being wed to a king, if only as a political tool. He was also a dozen years her senior. Even if she cared for him now, would that feeling last?

And why was he fretting so? She might feel nothing for him save gratitude to a protector. She might feel nothing. But Jeskil felt everything.

He took a few deep, calming breaths and stepped back into the room. The two women looked up, Reyna smiled at him, and Jeskil thought that he had never seen anything so beautiful in his life.

Solya had Reyna sit, and she told her to eat and drink all she wanted. She'd need the energy.

"I'm just going to trot downstairs and see to things. I'll be back soon."

"You're leaving?" Jeskil asked.

"You two will be fine. Honestly, new parents." The older woman chuckled to herself as she left the room, leaving the two of them staring at each other.

"How do you feel?"

"Oddly fine. Hungry. Thirsty." She gulped down a glass of water and held it out for a refill. "You look worse than I do. What's wrong?"

"Um." He couldn't think of a thing to say.

Reyna grinned at him. "She told me I was lucky to have such a good man."

"Um," he said again.

"Not many men would keep to a separate room to let me rest more comfortably," she said. "Fortunately, there was a pain so I couldn't laugh."

"People see what they want to see."

"Sometimes they see what's there. For what it's worth, she's right. You are a good man. Please don't say 'um' again, Jeskil. Just finish the story."

He suspected that she said it more to give him something to do than because she wanted to hear how it ended, but he picked up the book and began to read again.

When he looked up, she was staring at him. Something in her expression made his heart swell with happiness.

By the time the midwife arrived, Reyna's good humor had dissolved. Between birth spasms, she glared at Jeskil as if he were responsible for her situation. The midwife got Reyna on her feet and walking, and sent Jeskil away. "She won't want to see your face until the babe comes," she told him. Then she chuckled. "I've had mothers try to kill the men who brought them to this pass, and afterward tell them how loved they are. You'll see. Babies make us all quite mad."

This was a magic Jeskil couldn't comprehend, so he did as he was told and retreated to the room he'd been sharing with the coachman. He laid out the cards, hoping to talk to Vikar.

It took a few minutes to connect, and when Vikar's image appeared, it looked tired. "You look the way I feel," Jeskil told him. "How is the queen?"

"We're still waiting. How's Paradis?"

"Hating the sight of all men today. The midwife is here."

Vikar's response was a sharp intake of breath. "Already?"

"Babies come when they choose, Cousin."

"Will you go on to Rathsorcha when the child comes?"

"No, I'm not moving her in the winter. You know what travel is like after Winterfest. We can wait until spring. It's a good place. Good people. They think I'm the father, and Reyna and I aren't saying otherwise."

"Reyna? She told you her real name?"

"Why does that surprise you?" Jeskil asked him. "You knew she had to have a proper name."

"Because she's been canny about hiding it. She's smart, she understands how powerful the fiction is. It surprised me that she'd open up to you that quickly."

"I don't know why she did, but she asked me to call her that. Sensible girl," Jeskil added, almost absentmindedly. "The king, how did he take her loss?"

"As if it was all his own idea. I doubt he remembers her name now. Almost everything he does is for Caelea." He hesitated then and Jeskil sensed it.

"What?"

"He's become friendly with Roxanna Talian. I suggest no impropriety," he added. "I just find it odd."

"Well, it should surprise neither of us," Jeskil observed. "She's capable of anything, isn't she?"

Vikar's figure nodded. "I should have seen this coming and didn't. I must be getting old. Never mind, I think I can handle one ambitious woman. Take care of Reyna. Is she naming the child for you?" he asked.

"Very funny. If you need me, just let me know."

"Of course."

Jeskil said his farewell and flipped the cards, watching Vikar's image dissolve into the shadows.

As he put the cards away, he heard an infant's cry and his breath caught. It was the sound of life announcing itself.

Solya met him at the door to Reyna's room. "Give us a few minutes to clean up," she said, but then Reyna called out, "Is that Jeskil? I want to see him!"

"I can take it," he said as he edged past Solya.

Reyna was holding the squalling child and laughing. "Look what I made!" she said as he came to her side. "Ignore the blood. Isn't he beautiful?"

"The most beautiful child I've ever seen," Jeskil agreed as he took in the red, angry little features. How could something so ugly be so beautiful?

"What shall we name him?"

"Don't you have any names picked out?"

"No," she said and tucked the blanket around the baby more tightly. "Why so angry, baby? Look at him. He wants a name, Jeskil. He'll cry until he gets one. Look how blue his eyes are!"

"Most babies have blue eyes when they're born."

"His will stay blue. Azur then, because he'll have beautiful blue eyes, and luck with the girls."

"Perfect," Jeskil agreed, and he had no sooner spoken than Azur left off crying and gurgled happily.

"You see?" Reyna said. "Told you. Are you happy?"

He didn't even think to ask her why she would ask him that. He just nodded and said, "I am happy. It's been a long time since

I had a family." He knew then that he could not let go of either Reyna or her child. Not ever.

***

It was a brilliant, sunny afternoon when Roxanna walked in the rose garden, appreciating the last late-blooming flowers that scented the cool air. She did not expect to see Pelle again that day, particularly as he had barely nodded to her in the hallway that morning. She thought then that he looked fretful and distracted and hoped that it meant her time was coming.

But as she stopped to smell a particularly beautiful, blood-red blossom, she saw Pelle in the shadows of the cloister. He was watching her so intently that she found herself trembling. She pretended she hadn't noticed him and sat down on a bench, breathing deeply to calm herself.

She heard the scuff of his boots on the pebbled walk.

"Your Highness... Roxanna." His deep voice was husky. She looked up and offered him her most guileless expression.

"Majesty, you surprised me. Is everything all right?" she asked, trying to move the conversation to safe topics. "Has something happened?" She could see all the emotions warring inside him. "Sit with me and talk, if it helps," she told him, holding out her hand. "You know I'm a good listener, and I know you are burdened."

He sat, and she could feel how unsettled he was. "What troubles you?" she asked him.

"I've had word of a sad event," he said. "The girl, the dancer... her child was stillborn."

The news surprised her. "Majesty, I am so very sorry."

"By the terms of the provisional agreement, the marriage is dissolved, which is just as well. She was a mistake. I should have known better."

Silence fell between them, broken by a faraway bird's cry. Finally Pelle said, "But we have everything to hope for still. The queen thrives." He stood and shook his big, golden head as if trying to rid himself of bad thoughts. "I just thought you should know. You're a good friend," he told her, then he nodded and walked back into the shadows of the cloister.

Roxanna was left alone to consider what it all meant. Why had he sought her out to tell her this news? She shivered as a chill breeze swept through the garden.

6.

Freeze Moon, CR 532

The queen's labor began a little before midnight; Vikar received word of it not long after retiring for the night.

"Teamur told me to tell you that you are not needed. She sent me as a courtesy," the page told him. "Any answer?"

Vikar shook his head and closed the door. *Nearly over*, he thought, but he couldn't feel any relief in spite of Teamur's assurances that things were under control. She reported that as far as she could tell, the child was strong. "The mother is less so, but I will do what I can to keep them both safe. If only one may be saved, I will save the child. It is the queen's wish."

Of course it was. He had never seen Caelea so determined to produce an heir for the kingdom. The very fact that she was resorting to magic for the first time told Vikar that the queen would do anything to bring this child into the world, including die to save him. Likely she knew that either way, this would be her last pregnancy.

He looked out the window and saw a sky purple with clouds. The first snow of the season would be on the ground for the prince's birthday. Vikar scrubbed at his face with both hands and sat down to read since there would be no more sleep that night.

And yet, he must have dropped off over his book because the next thing he knew, there was a pounding at his door. It was the page again, and the boy looked unhinged.

"You must come," he said. "You must come, Counselor, please come now."

Half addled by his disturbed sleep, Vikar raced after the boy, across the courtyard dusted with fresh snow, and up into the queen's tower.

The door to the birth chamber stood open, and a brilliant light shone out as if the sun had been trapped inside. Distantly, he heard a child crying as he moved into what felt like a raging storm. The pressure was crushing. Magic was flowing unchecked, tearing open the air so that portals gaped, closed, reopened. Teamur, or what had been Teamur, lay crumpled on the floor. And Caelea was at the center of the storm, shining like a collapsing star.

Vikar slammed the door in the boy's face and fell to his knees. He had to send the energy away, had to dissipate it and channel it deep into the earth. It was already very nearly out of control. He reached for the blaze of power, caught hold of its threads, and pressed them downward into the stone beneath his knees, down through all the levels below, knowing that he would probably lay waste to anything and anyone in the rooms below and kill himself in the process, but that couldn't be helped. He gritted his teeth and drew the magic into himself, channeling it downward, forcing it into the ground beneath the palace. It burned within his bones and blood, and the building shuddered with it. Unchecked, this power would raze the castle and kill everyone in it.

He could feel Caelea's presence in this magic, and Teamur's. He felt them rushing through him like a river of power. Vikar lost himself in them for a time, but eventually their presence faded as the storm ebbed. He sprawled on the floor, barely able to think, to understand why he had survived that much magical energy.

But none of that was important now. He crawled to the queen's bedside where she lay in a pool of blood. She was gone, but there was still a crackle of magic on her skin. Teamur's body lay nearby, an empty, blackened husk. Caelea had drained the magicker of every drop of energy, sucking not only her magic, but the old woman's life.

Then he realized that the child's crying had stopped. In a panic, Vikar stumbled back to the door and opened it. Silence pressed down on him.

"Where is the child?" he asked the page. He barely recognized his own voice. But the boy just stared.

"Counselor?" A voice from inside the room. Vikar looked around and saw Lady Rosamunda huddled under a heavy table. She was clutching a bundle, and Vikar prayed it was the child.

"Come out, Rosamunda, it's safe."

"I have the prince," she told him. It was probably why she was still alive.

He nodded and crumpled to the floor. "Thank God," he murmured. "Is he alive?"

"Yes, but he's stopped crying," she said, and Vikar could tell from the tone of her voice that she wasn't happy about it.

"If he's alive, we'll worry about the crying later." He sprawled on the floor. "Boy, close the door, and don't let anyone in here, not even the king." Not that he expected a page boy to stop Pelle.

As the door closed, Vikar said, "What happened?"

Rosamunda crept out from under the table and sat down on the floor, clutching the child, rocking him. "I don't know. There was so much blood, and Teamur was weaving a spell because the prince came out blue, and then the queen--." She began to cry. "Teamur was consumed," she sobbed.

He knew. Caelea, untrained and desperate, had pulled the magic out of the old woman, had sucked out every ounce of energy, and even consumed her own life force to save her child. Why hadn't he known how powerful she was? He should have sensed it. He felt sick with guilt.

"I took the prince and hid when I saw what was happening," Rosamunda said. "I thought we would die too. The Frozen Moon is an ill-omened time," she added, holding the prince close as if he were some kind of talisman.

"You did well." Vikar could barely think. He was grateful that the child had survived, particularly since the dancer's child had not, but then all he wanted was to sleep and forget everything that had just happened. "You'll need to bathe and swaddle him." Giving her something to do would occupy her mind.

"Yes, of course."

They both jumped as someone pounded on the door. Vikar heard the page protesting, and then the door banged open and a phalanx of guards burst into the room.

"What is happening in here? Where is the queen?" the captain demanded.

Vikar sighed and stood up. His legs were shaking. "The queen is dead."

The soldiers looked around for someone to skewer. "What happened?"

"She did not survive the birth of the heir." He gestured to Rosamunda, who brought the child forward. "Prince Corius Pellires," he said. It was the name Caelea had chosen, after the founder of the Pellires line. "Captain, we will need a little time to make things right in here before the king is informed. He mustn't see his wife like this. Can you send me several of the queen's women? Not the Princess Roxanna," he added.

"Of course. But what happened? I must know. The rooms below—"

"Was anyone hurt?"

The captain shook his head. "They were empty, but everything in them is in shambles. Scorched in some places."

Vikar took a deep, calming breath. "That's a mercy; the magic that saved the prince went wild," he said. It was at least partly true after all.

"I thought that old woman was trouble. That's why magic should be outlawed, as it is in Feracia. With due respect, Counselor Revin."

Vikar didn't feel like arguing. "Let's worry about the prince and his father right now," was all he said in reply. "Oh, and remove the magicker's body."

"It must be burned," the captain insisted, and Vikar shrugged. "It already has been, it seems," he told the captain.

He was so tired, so drained by his effort and by the grief he felt at the loss of the queen. So very tired.

***

There were whispers as Roxanna moved through the courtiers that morning. The halls were filled, and gossip flew about what was being called "The Storm."

"Someone tried to kill the king!" she heard.

"It was in the queen's tower; they were trying to kill the queen."

"It's the Freeze Moon," many whispered. And, "Damned magickers!" That was a common thread. The one certain thing was that nothing was certain.

Roxanna made her way to the tower as she did every morning, noting that it was filled with guards, the halls were heaped with rubble, and windows had been blown out. Something enormous had happened there, but none of the guards looked approachable, though they didn't try to hinder her as she made her way up to the top of the tower.

She had to pass the queen's chambers to reach her alcove, but the door was closed, and a huge, grim-faced guard stood in front of it. Roxanna moved on.

In the shadows of the alcove where they had talked together, prayed for the good health of the queen and her child, and where Roxanna had made herself a part of Pelle's life, she found the king huddled, weeping.

She knew then what had happened; the queen was dead. Roxanna stopped, took a deep breath, and put an expression of concern on her face. "Oh no," she breathed, touching his shoulder lightly. "What has happened?"

"I have lost the thing I loved best in life," Pelle said, his voice thick with tears.

She looked away quickly, her emotions in an uproar. "Your Majesty, I am so very sorry." She sat beside him. "And the child?" she asked.

"He is safe. By the mercy of God," he said, his voice raw and tinged with sarcasm.

"A prayer?" she asked. "Will it help?"

"No. I'm done with prayers," he told her. Death had taken away his faith. Nevertheless she slipped an arm around his shoulder and murmured a prayer she'd memorized for just this occasion. One about the dead not being truly gone from us, and other things that were supposed to make grief more bearable. As if anything could do that. She spoke in a low whisper, not enough really for him to hear what it was she said, only to let him know she was with him, ready to offer her comfort and support.

He seemed about to speak when Roxanna heard steps in the corridor. She stood again and stepped in front of him, shielding him from the gaze of passersby. Two courtiers slowed when they saw her, straining to see who sat behind her.

"Walk on," Roxanna told them, her voice firm and steady. "Now."

When they were alone again, she sank back down onto the bench. "You cannot stay here. There will be too many people here soon. Come with me."

She hurried him to her chambers, which lay in the upper ward between the queen's tower and the chapel. "No one will think to look for you here. I shall leave you to mourn in peace."

Pelle caught hold of her arm and looked up at her, an unnerving blankness in his gaze, as if he were not truly there with her. "What shall I do now?" he whispered to her, taking her hands between his. "I have lost half of myself."

"You will recover," she told him. "You will. And I will stand by you until you can stand on your own."

As she stood, looking down into his eyes, she saw the blankness replaced by relief. "Has heaven sent you to me to share my grief and bring me comfort?"

She cradled him as she would a child. "I will never leave you," she promised.

7.

Snow Moon, CR 532

The queen was laid to rest after twenty-one days of somber ceremony. While not enough time for all the monarchs of the continent of Eiliron to send representatives, the funeral was well attended. Hartan arrived a few days early, representing Wismar of Feracia, and at his side was the Princess Catenia, the eldest daughter of Rugenius of Vartaris, daughter of his first, Peoran, wife. Catenia, dark and vivid like a Vartarian but with Peoran eyes so silvery-pale they seemed sightless, was a striking presence in the court. She was not beautiful, but there was something compelling about her that drew people. She was gracious and reserved, and spoke in a low, throaty voice that reminded Roxanna of smoked honey. Catenia brought her family's condolences on the death of the queen, but Roxanna sensed that there was more to her presence than a state visit.

Later, when she was alone with Hartan, he said, "I expect you're wondering why Catenia and I are here together."

"I hadn't given it much thought," she said. She wasn't about to give him the satisfaction of seeming interested. "Though I do wonder why she needs so many servants. It seems excessive for a short visit."

"We are en route to Feracia. Catenia and I are engaged."

"Ah," she said because she didn't know what else to say. "I am impressed by your good fortune."

"It's Wismar's doing. The Talian fortunes are rising again, sister. Now perhaps I may be able to give you a dowry to suit your position in life, and perhaps an advantageous alliance of your own. Wismar has been negotiating with the government of Lostri in exile, and there may be a match there which would bring you your own kingdom. And then, since many of the kingdoms of Eiliron joined the Great Council of Nations, there are opportunities off-continent—"

"Indeed. I thank you. But I shall remain here until such time as I am dismissed." She knew it sounded cold, but she couldn't help it.

"You don't seem pleased."

"I appreciate being thought of at all." In fact, the timing couldn't have been more awkward. Pelle had been increasingly attentive since the queen's death, and Roxanna felt that there was a declaration coming from that quarter, one which she had every intention of accepting with pleasure.

"What's wrong? You should be overjoyed. Isn't this what you wanted?"

"To be traded like a commodity? Of course. What woman doesn't dream of that?"

Hartan's lips thinned. "Nothing satisfies you, does it? This place is no good for you either. You'll come back to Feracia with me now that the queen is dead."

"No."

"No? You don't have a choice, Roxanna."

"I will stay until the king releases me from my service."

Her brother stared at her, a frown creasing his brow. "You will come home when I tell you to come home, and you will marry who I tell you to marry."

"I will not," she told him. "I have my own plans right here in Corraçao, and you will not ruin them for me, dear brother, or I promise you I will bring such shame down on the house of Talian that your princess will run back to Vartaris."

After a few seconds of obvious confusion, Hartan realized what she meant. He rose from his chair and stood over her, glaring down, his fists clenching and unclenching. "Who is it? That duke... what was his name? Lakketta? By God, he will marry you before the week is out—"

"It's not him."

"How many men have you given yourself to?" he shouted.

She lifted her chin. "None. But if he reaches out to me, I will not hesitate."

"Oh, you've fallen in love," Hartan replied, sarcasm dripping. "And I was certain you had no heart. Who is the lucky fellow? Some comely stable boy?"

"It's not your business."

"If I find the man who took advantage of my sister, I will kill him."

She shook her head. "You have no power over him," she told her brother.

He uttered an oath when he realized who she meant. "Not the king? Are you insane, sister?" He caught hold of her arm. "Do you really think he'll wed you? Do you? He has an heir now."

"The child is sickly," she said and immediately felt ashamed. The child had nothing to do with her feelings for Pelle. "No, it doesn't matter. I love him and I'll stay beside him as long as he needs me." She knew she sounded like some lovesick idiot, but she was angry, and it was the truth. She did love Pelle. It horrified her to realize how much she loved him.

Then, oddly, Hartan deflated. "I wanted better for you," he told her. "I will not see you disgraced. You'll come home to Feracia. No one needs to know. We'll find a home for your child, and a husband for you, I promise."

"Hartan, I am not with child. Please stop assuming I'm lying about that. I am in love with the king and I have reason to believe that he loves me as well. Leave it alone."

He rubbed his forehead as if his head ached. "Will you at least talk to Catenia? I have not known her long, but I've found her counsel to be invaluable. Perhaps between us, we can help you weather this."

Roxanna stared at her brother as if seeing him for the first time. "Do you love her?" she asked.

"I believe I do," he said. "Or something very like it. She has made me a better person, I think." Then he took a deep breath. "I'm sorry for shouting. But you're my sister, and my first thought is to protect you."

It was strange for her to see this new side of Hartan, the side she'd always wished for when she was growing up and wanted a brother who cared what happened to her. She wanted to believe him. "I will speak to her if she is willing," she allowed.

"Thank you."

Catenia came to her that evening, after supper, and the two women spoke together at length. At first it was a strained conversation with Roxanna resisting the woman's overtures of friendship, but it wasn't long before she warmed to the Vartarian princess, her sister-to-be. Catenia seemed warm and caring, not at all the sort of woman she imagined winning Hartan's heart. But perhaps she'd misjudged him all these years. Perhaps he really was kinder than she'd feared. Or perhaps it was just Catenia's grace that had softened him.

"I make no judgment," she told Roxanna, in her soft voice. "In Vartaris we follow our hearts and never regret the choice to love. I myself—" she began, then stopped speaking and glanced away. "I should not speak of my own situation; I'm here to help you." She patted Roxanna's hand, and Roxanna felt a rush of warmth and affection flow through her. She liked this strangely beautiful princess. "But I assure you I have no secrets from Hartan," she said. "Nor he from me. Have no fears on that account."

That didn't sound like her brother, but the last two days had suggested to her that she knew very little about the man he was.

"What do you want?" Catenia asked her. "Never mind what anyone else wants. What do you want?" She tapped her fingers on the arm of the chair in an odd little rhythm that caught in Roxanna's brain and played itself over and over.

It took Roxanna a few moments to collect herself, to sort through all the hopes and desires she'd had since coming to Corraçao. "I want to be with him."

"The king?"

Roxanna nodded.

"And you would prefer not to become his mistress, I presume?"

"Yes, although if that is all he offers…"

"My dear, I know you are from a place where magic is frowned upon, but in the right hands, it can smooth things that seem difficult and tangled. Are you willing to use some"—she made a graceful gesture—"friendly magicks? All in aid of winning the heart of your king? Will you trust me to lead you through some simple steps?"

Trust? No. Roxanna trusted no one easily, but she heard herself saying, "Yes."

"Then we must find an apothecary." *Tap-tap-tappety-tap.*

"I know of one."

"Excellent! Then we will go together tomorrow morning. Fear nothing, Roxanna," Catenia soothed. "I will take good care of you."

When Catenia left her, Roxanna wilted, as if months of tension and anxiety had suddenly drained away. She lay down on her bed to think about what had passed between them, to think about the feeling she had that Catenia understood her so well that they barely needed to talk. She wondered how that could be possible, and yet it felt right, as if she could finally relax.

Without intending to, she dropped off into a deep, dreamless sleep.

When Roxanna woke early the next morning, she felt briefly confused, not quite recalling what had happened the night before. It came back to her in bits and pieces as she readied herself for the day, the talk with Catenia, the promises of aid and friendship, the sense of relief in having someone to support her. Was this foolishness on her part?

All her musings vanished at the knock at her door. It was Catenia. "Are you ready to go?"

Then it came back as a whole, the plan to go to the apothecary together. "I don't know if this is a good idea," she began.

Catenia caught hold of her hand. "You have nothing to fear, dear sister. But if you are not ready, we can go another time."

"No. I'm fine," Roxanna said. Why had she been so silly? "I want to go. It's just that this is so strange to me."

"I will take good care of you," Catenia promised and embraced her as a sister and a friend. Warmth flooded Roxanna, and a sense of well-being. This was the right choice.

It was a chill morning when Roxanna and Catenia sought out the apothecary in the Sibi market. Roxanna had expected the apothecary to be a benign grandfatherly type with a long white beard and some sort of cap—didn't they all wear headgear? But this one was close to her own age and looked like a goose, with a narrow head; bright, angry eyes; and a long nose. He did wear a cap, a dull green one with an odd stain. She approached him with hesitation.

"I am looking for Elian," she announced. The apothecary looked her up and down.

"She's out on a job."

"I need to speak to her."

"What do you need? Y'know this is my booth, not hers."

"It's... a private matter."

"Women's troubles?"

Catenia huffed with impatience and said, "We need a charm."

"A love charm?"

"A charm of compulsion," Catenia told him. "Strong compulsion."

"One of you needs a husband, I'm guessing."

"Keep your guesses to yourself," Roxanna snapped.

"Now, now, don't get upset. I have to know what the charm is for to make sure it's the most effective thing."

"A charm to compel an offer of marriage, yes," Catenia said. She tapped her fingers on the counter in an impatient rhythm.

"Without the commentary," Roxanna added. She was starting to think this was a terrible idea.

"I've got just the thing." He nudged the boy who stood nearby, grinding herbs. "Chest all the way in the back, red pouch with the pink stone clasp." The boy scurried off. "I miss Elian when she's not here. At least she can read. So... in a condition, eh?"

Roxanna's icy silence was all the answer he got.

The boy returned with the pouch, which the apothecary opened and spilled the contents onto the counter. There was a vial filled with some kind of pink liquid, a bone tied with a red ribbon from which dangled a feather, and a small wooden box. "This is a banic bone," he explained, and it's got all the right virtues."

"I understand what that is, and it's nonsense," Catenia said, cutting him off. "What is this?" she asked, holding up the box.

"Em-Ir. It's for--."

Catenia said, "Yes, I know it well. And this?" She pointed to the vial.

"A little potent Rogie magic, from across the sea. Pretty, isn't it? This goes in his drink. Used all together these three things will bring you the man of your dreams!"

Roxanna stared at the vial in his hand and wondered if this could possibly work or if she was being played for a fool.

"Six pieces of silver, and I throw in the pouch," he said. "You can't say fairer than that, madam."

"Four," Catenia replied, tapping the counter sharply. "And that's more than this is worth."

The apothecary stared blankly at her. "Four then," he said, though he didn't sound happy about it.

Roxanna counted out the silver and handed it to him, taking the pouch in return.

"Thank you, madam, and don't forget to stop back for a charm to cut the pain of childbirth," he said as Roxanna tucked the pouch into her cloak. She turned sharply and ran into Elian, who was startled to see her.

"What?" she stammered, glancing at the apothecary who was watching them with interest. "Do you need something from Master Jeskil?" the girl asked, sotto voce.

Roxanna shook her head. "I have what I came for, thank you," she said as she moved away from the stall. Catenia followed more slowly, watching the girl watch them.

"Who is Master Jeskil?" she asked as she caught up to Roxanna.

"It's not important."

"All right, it just seemed—" Catenia caught hold of Roxanna's arm and pulled her close in a sisterly gesture.

"He did a job for me, nothing more."

When they were back at the palace, safely in Roxanna's rooms, Catenia opened the vial and sniffed, shrugged, and closed it. "The Rogies know what they're about, I suppose. The banic bone isn't worth a copper, but the Em-Ir might help. I'll teach you how to use it."

"You seem to know quite a lot about magic."

"It's part of our culture, especially among my mother's people. Peorans revere magic; they're not afraid of it."

"Aren't you worried about living in Feracia where magic is illegal?"

Catenia laughed. "No, not worried. I'm not a fool. Well, the rest is up to you, isn't it? It only remains for me to wish you the best of luck. And if you do need our help, Hartan and I are here for you." She touched Roxanna's shoulder, and once more, Roxanna was filled with a sense of well-being and hope.

"I am so grateful that you're part of our family," she said as Catenia rose to leave.

"As am I, my dear."

***

"I don't know what to do," the king said. "I don't want to be married again, not yet, not when the memories—" He broke off and looked out the window. "It's too soon."

"Of course it feels so, Your Majesty," Vikar replied.

"But she has been my rock, Vikar. She has given me back my will to go on, to be a king. But you see, our closeness in the last weeks has--."

"Provoked comment?"

"I fear it may have compromised her reputation, and I cannot bear the thought of subjecting such a good, decent woman to that sort of gossip. I feel I should do the honorable thing."

"And you feel that would be to marry her?" Vikar asked. Yes, this was Pelle to the teeth, he thought. Soft hearted and soft headed. And yet it wasn't a bad match, and it might secure a back-up heir. Prince Corius, though not exactly a sickly child, was not thriving.

"What should I do?"

Vikar sighed. "The timing is not good, Sire. Your mourning period has only really begun." Even as he said it, it sounded weak to him. "Have you considered a second provisional marriage?"

"I can do that? With the queen gone?"

"Yes." He didn't add that he'd spent hours researching the laws about provisional marriages when Paradis came on the scene, trying to find a way to be rid of her. With the stillbirth it became moot and the marriage was automatically dissolved.

"So, marry her? Provisionally?"

"It is not the worst choice," Vikar told him with complete if uneasy honesty. It was a good middle way if nothing else.

Pelle seemed to consider this for a time. He cracked a pair of hawnuts between his fingers. "Yes, that seems best," he said at last. "I shall speak to her about it tonight and tell you what she says tomorrow."

"No, don't be too hasty. Give it a few days. Think hard about what it would mean."

"She's so giving. I fear I may not be worthy of her."

Vikar nearly choked on the hawnut he was eating.

Pelle grasped Vikar's hand. "You are a good friend to me, Vikar. Thank you."

"That same afternoon", Catenia, cloaked in a glamour that remade her into Roxanna's double, made her way back to the Sibi market and sought out Elian at the apothecary's stall. "I was not able to speak privately before, but now we must talk," she said, casting a sidelong glance at the apothecary who was at the counter, helping a customer.

"Of course. Come with me," the girl said, and led her visitor to the back room, chasing the apprentice out. "What can I do for you?"

"Master Jeskil. I have need of him." She knew of the man's reputation. It was a stroke of luck that there was an easy way to contact him.

"May I tell him what the matter is?" Elian asked.

The princess laid a hand on Elian's arm. "It is a matter of removal."

"I see. I will contact him immediately."

"Tell him that money is not an object, but time is."

"Understood."

***

Jeskil barely had time to settle Reyna and the baby at the troupe's winter quarters before he was contacted by a sending from Elian. "You told me you wanted to know about anything having to do with the Princess Roxanna," the small figure from the card said. "She wants someone removed, is the way she put it. And she's in a hurry."

He scowled and thought seriously about telling Vikar and letting him sort it all out. "Did she say who?"

"No, but that same day she came to the apothecary for a charm to compel love and an offer of marriage. He was bragging about it, says he's wagering that she's pregnant."

Jeskil swore softly. "I'll return as quickly as possible. If you see her again, tell her to do nothing until we speak. And try to find out who it is she wants removed."

"She won't tell me," Elian said. "I'm no one. But if she is pregnant and wants to keep the child, I'd guess the father is the king, and the obstacle is—"

"Best not to speculate," Jeskil said. "I'll see you when I see you," he added, and swept all the cards back into the deck. Something, some sense told him that he needed to see to this himself, and not involve Vikar until he was certain what was going on at the palace.

But first, the hard part. Leaving Reyna.

She was talking to the baby when he found her sitting near the puppet theater. "Mama needs her sleep," she was saying. "Can't we please agree on that?"

"Oh, did he keep you up again?"

She looked up at the sound of Jeskil's voice.

"I don't mind, really. He's a good baby. I just never knew how tiring motherhood can be. You really should try fatherhood," she said, handing Azur to him.

Jeskil rubbed his cheek on the golden down that coated the child's head and wondered how it was possible to love this deeply. "I'd like that," he said. "In fact, there's something I've been wanting to say, but it never seemed like the right time."

"Is now the right time?"

"No, but it's not going to be a better one anytime soon. I want us to be a family. I want to marry you and be Azur's father."

Reyna laughed.

"What?

"I was thinking that I'd have to ask you. Thank goodness you came to your senses. But why isn't it a good time to ask?"

"Because I have to go away for a while. So that's a yes?"

"It's a yes. Where are you going and why?"

"Back to Trennin, and I'm not wholly certain what's likely to happen."

Her expression darkened. "You're not going into danger, are you?"

"No, no, nothing like that. It's just that I'm not certain about whether I'm going to do the job or not."

"Then say no, and don't go."

"I can't do that."

She looked as if she was ready to argue the point, but then she said, "All right then, but the wedding first."

"I wouldn't do it any other way," he told her. And it was true because it was his promise to return to her and their son.

Their son. He held the child close. "And while I'm gone, you look after your mother for me," he whispered.

When Jeskil arrived at the palace several days later, he was shown to a guest apartment where Roxanna was waiting for him. She looked regal in red silks, and Jeskil sensed a touch of magic about her, which was odd, but not impossible. In spite of old laws, it was everywhere in Trennin.

"Thank you for coming, Master Jeskil." She coughed and touched a handkerchief to her mouth. "Forgive me, but I seem to have taken a cold. With my brother in Trennin, I've taken the opportunity of using his apartment for our meeting. As you and he know each other, it will excite no comment. I know you and he have had dealings, as have you and King Wismar."

Jeskil said nothing. Exposing clients' secrets was not done in his line of work.

"Or perhaps I'm wrong, but I thought I'd heard—"

"Whatever your brother has told you of me is precisely what he has said."

She frowned, then said, "He speaks highly of you. And I have need of your talents."

"So I understood." He sprawled in a chair, and she didn't attempt to stop him but sat down opposite him and drummed her fingers on the arm of the chair.

"Before we discuss the matter, I must ask if you have any reservations about your work."

He frowned. "I'm not sure what you mean."

"Is there anyone you would refuse to dispose of?"

He laughed. "I'm not stupid. I won't take a job that might end with me on the scaffold."

"What about children?"

"What about them?"

"Would you..."

"Kill a child? If the money was right," he lied. "What infant has offended you?"

"Prince Corius."

"I shouldn't be surprised, I expect. But I am, a little. It's a bold move."

"What do you mean by that?"

Jeskil's expression was neutral. "Only that you have one last obstacle to overcome, don't you? And it's a newborn, a sickly one. No one would be surprised if he were to follow his mother, would they?"

Roxanna stared at him, her expression cool. He had underestimated her cruelty. "Will you do it?"

"Of course," he said and named a figure.

"That much?" she asked and reached out to touch him, but Jeskil pulled away instinctively as he sensed tendrils of magic swirling around her hand. This was not Roxanna; he was sure of it now. But he had no idea who he was really dealing with.

"Forgive me, but I came here directly and am travel-stained. As to your question, this will require time and effort as well as discretion, so yes. That much."

She nodded. "I can get the money," she assured him. "When will you do it?"

"When will you get the money?"

"I have it now."

"Then within the week."

"That will do." She went to a cabinet and drew out a money pouch. "If you wish to count it…"

"Do I need to?"

"Of course not."

He rose and made an ironic little bow. "A pleasure doing business with you, Your Majesty."

"Your Highness," she corrected.

"Not for long, I'm guessing."

***

After several days' consideration, and armed with a new determination to be a good man and a good king, Pelle went to Roxanna determined to do the right thing. Her solace had meant the world to him, her company gave him comfort. He could contract a provisional marriage with her that he would convert to a full marriage once his mourning was over. It was the perfect solution.

He sent a messenger asking if she would see him that night, and her reply was swift.

I look forward to it, my dearest friend.

But even as he made his way to Roxanna's chambers his heart was heavy with memories of his beloved Caelea and the joy they'd shared through the years. He knew he couldn't expect to find another love like that, but to have found a like-minded woman, a comfort and a helpmeet in such a sad time, it was good fortune and not to be ignored.

Roxanna met him with a smile and a gentle touch on his arm. "You look tired. Come and sit." She led him to the table where a meal waited. "First, a tonic for you, to increase your appetite," she said, handing him a small glass. "You look as if you've lost weight."

As he drank, she filled his plate with the delicacies. She was so graceful, so lovely. How could he not love her? She was everything he wanted.

"Eat," she said, and he did. With each bite he took, he felt stronger, surer. With each word she spoke to him, he found himself more in love with her.

He put down his fork and said, "I have mourned deeply, but now it's time to live again. I want you by my side, Roxanna. I want you to be my wife." No provisional nonsense. He loved this woman and would make her his wife and his queen.

Her mouth curved into a lovely smile. "If that is what you truly wish, then I will gladly be your wife."

"It is. On my name, it is." He wanted to catch her up in his arms and kiss her a thousand times. Had he loved before this?

No, everything else was a pale shade of what he felt for Roxanna. "As soon as we can. Tonight?"

"If you wish," she murmured. So demure. How he loved that about her.

He took her hand and led her to the chamber of the court prelate, who seemed shocked to see them there, hand-in-hand like lovesick youths. In spite of a headache that had sprung up over the meal, Pelle was grinning and laughing.

"You must marry us tonight, immediately," he said, rubbing his forehead.

"Majesty, I—"

"It is my dearest wish, my lord, and that of my lady."

"But, the mourning period." It was a feeble protest. Pelle reminded him that the period was custom, not law.

"Come in then," he said and waved them into his chamber. He did not seem pleased, but he didn't have to be. He only had to do his job.

Without much ceremony they joined hands and spoke the words. Pelle's head was splitting by then, shooting showers of pink and red sparks across his field of vision. His stomach churned, and he swallowed hard, stammering his vows. Roxanna's voice was clear and strong for both of them.

"Then by the power I hold, I declare and proclaim you husband and wife." The prelate slammed his book shut and turned away, and Pelle drew Roxanna into an embrace just as his consciousness splintered into pink and red shards that stabbed and stabbed until he fell to his knees.

The last thing he heard before he lost consciousness was Roxanna crying out for a doctor.

The king was carried to his bed by guards who were charged with absolute silence. They left Vikar alone with Pelle and

Roxanna, who stood close to the king, looking fearful. As Vikar stared down at Pelle, he understood that things had changed and it would be a fight to keep up. "What did you do to him?" he asked, his voice soft.

"What d'you mean? How dare—"

"Spare me the outrage. If he dies, the throne goes to a Pellires cousin in Vartaris. I will see to it," he promised her. "You will have nothing."

"I have everything I want. He is my husband according to all the laws of this land." Roxanna produced the empty vial from the pocket of her gown and handed it to Vikar. "I was told it was a Rogie love potion."

Vikar opened the vial and sniffed, then touched his finger to the edge and lifted a smear of the potion to his tongue. He winced. "Why?"

"I love him. I wanted him for my own."

"He was going to offer you a provisional marriage. You had only to wait."

"I didn't know. He seemed so uncertain." She frowned. "I thought only to nudge him into a declaration, on my honor that is the truth. Will he be all right?"

"I don't know. I hope so. Who gave this to you?" When she hesitated, he made an impatient noise. "This is not a negotiation."

She rallied. "Pelle and I are husband and wife, and I am to be your queen. How dare you demand anything of me?"

"I dare because the law is quite clear about the uses of magic in Corraçao. You will not be queen for long if I speak to the magistrates. And if he dies, you will not be alive for long."

She paled a little but lifted her head. "The apothecary in the Sibi market, at the sign of the feather and bone. Would you have reported Caelea to the magistrates?"

He pocketed the vial and laid a hand on Pelle's forehead. The king felt clammy. "For the desire to bear a living child? What do you think? And who do you think the magistrates would sympathize with, a desperate mother or a woman trapping a king in marriage?"

At the door to the king's chamber, he turned. "If he dies, you will suffer."

"I am not afraid of you, Counselor," she said, though she grew even paler than before.

He shrugged. "Your choice." But he knew that if she was now part of the Pellires dynasty he would preserve her in spite of his threats, because the monarchy was what he served. The monarchy had to be preserved, and Pelle had chosen this woman to be his wife and mother to his children. He had to serve the good of the king and the country; he had sworn as much to Caelea.

***

The apothecary, whose name was Nevin, gave up information faster than Vikar could ask for it. He'd seen the woman twice. The second time she'd dealt with Elian, who had disappeared. "Left me to run the shop on my own, didn't she?" he grumbled. "Stole from me and vanished into the night. Last time I hire an educated helper."

"The woman who came to you for help," Vikar prodded.

"She'd got herself into a situation," he sneered. "You know what I mean. Needed her man to make it right." He shook his head. "Elian was on a job, so I had to help."

"What did you give her?"

"Banic bone charm and some Em-Ir to bathe in. Nothing unusual."

"And a potion?"

The apothecary frowned. "I don't remember—"

"You'd best remember. Something from the Rogie, wasn't it?"

Nevin pursed his lips. "You know all about it, don't you? Why you asking me?"

"What was in the potion?"

"I never asked. I bought it off a Rogie down on his luck. He said it was an old magick. And it wasn't cheap! Don't know why I bought it," he muttered. "I think he set some kind of spell on me."

Vikar thought that the apothecary didn't need to be spelled to be greedy. "And the second time she came?"

"Same day, but this time she was alone. Don't know what they talked about; I was busy."

"You said she came alone the second time. Who was with her the first time?"

"Some high-handed Peoran wench. Knew her magic, though."

"Peoran. You're sure?"

"Part anyway. No one else has eyes like that."

"All right then, this is what's going to happen. You're going to leave Trennin."

"What? You can't do that!"

"I can. You're going to cross the Janesse and never return. If I hear you're doing business anywhere south or west of the river, I will have you killed."

Nevin's face grew darkly angry. He raised his hand, and Vikar caught him by the wrist.

"If you're thinking of trying a spell, I suggest you rethink it. I would cheerfully cut your tongue out and chop off this hand if I smelled a whiff of magic coming off you." And at this the man paled visibly. "Do I need to have you escorted out of Trennin?"

Nevin shook his head.

Vikar released him. "That's wise."

Once the man was gone, Vikar sat down and made a list of all the Rogie magickers he knew of in the capital. They weren't exactly welcomed anywhere, but Corraçao was an easygoing country, more tolerant of magic than anywhere on the continent save for Albhain, despite the laws that supposedly curtailed it.

It was a pointless exercise, but it was something to do while he worked through the problem. He knew that the Rogie diaspora was broad and ever shifting. The Rogie who had sold the potion to Nevin might be long gone, and even if he wasn't, he might not know what was in the mix. Potion-making was like cooking; every potion brewer had their own recipes.

Vikar contemplated contacting Magister Goedred, just to reassure himself about the potion, but the idea rankled. His relationship with Goedred had always been prickly, and had grown more so after Vikar had become first counselor of Corraçao. There was no point in bringing his mistakes to his old teacher; Goedred would just tell him that this was what came of foregoing his studies to seek temporal power.

Still, if anyone could give Vikar insight into how to preserve Pelle's life—

There was a pounding at his door. It was one of the guards. "Counselor, the king is awake and asking for you."

For a moment, Vikar had to steady himself. His relief was so great that he felt weak with it. "I will follow in a few minutes," he told the guard. Then he wrapped his cards and put them away, grateful to not need them that day.

***

The greatest difficulty, Jeskil knew, would be access to the child's chamber. It was heavily guarded, and apart from the women attending the prince, only the king, Vikar, and the boy's doctors were allowed in. Illusion could only go so far, and maintaining a string of them was hard work. Shapeshifting was a more reliable choice because though the initial change required some formidable magicks, once Jeskil had shifted, his new form would remain stable without expending a lot of energy. While he'd still need minor illusions to do what he needed to do, the combination of shifting and illusion seemed like his best plan.

His shaping choices were limited by physical laws, which meant that he could only shift into something roughly his own size. His voice wouldn't change along with his body, so he couldn't hope to impersonate any of the child's attendants since they were all women.

He could easily impersonate Vikar, down to the voice, but didn't want to involve his cousin in this. The king was impossible since he was much bigger than Jeskil, inches taller, and pounds heavier. That left the doctors. Jeskil would need to study them and choose one closest to his own physical image.

He chose his subject, a Lostrian doctor named Tomeran, of about five and fifty years. Jeskil disguised himself as a medical student and attended several of Tomeran's lectures, studying him closely enough to do a fair imitation of his voice, walk, and gestures. The Lostrian accent was a minor problem, but not insurmountable so long as he kept conversation to a minimum.

When Elian brought him the things he required, she asked him, "You're sure this is all you need? I don't mind staying to help out."

"No, I want you out of Trennin now. I'm sorry to have taken you away from your new job."

"Don't be. I'm glad to be away from the city," she admitted as she accepted payment for her services. "Too sad these days."

"All right. I will see you again in Albhain, at the winter site."

It was time, then, and the faster he went in and did what he had to do, the faster he'd be on his way home. The king's recent illness and his sudden marriage had set the court spinning, but the upper corridors were more quiet than usual. The same night that Elian quit the city, Jeskil found his way into the tower where the prince slept. In the hall, out of sight of the bored-looking guards, Jeskil assumed the doctor's form, reshaping himself into a man older than himself, with a trim, gray-flecked beard; short, silvery dark hair; and a pocked face from a childhood bout of fen fever. He wore the voluminous black robes of a royal doctor, in the pockets of which were all the tools he needed to carry out his plans.

The guards, used to seeing the doctors come and go, gave Jeskil a cursory glance and let him pass without challenge. At this hour, there were only two nurses in the chamber, and one was dozing on the couch, her mouth hanging open. The other, Lady Berhari, looked up from her needlework, surprised to see him.

"Doctor Tomeran, is there something wrong?" she asked, looking concerned.

Jeskil made a calming gesture. "Nothing to be concerned about," he assured her. "I mislaid my copy of Lomashis today and wondered if I had left it up here," Jeskil explained as he laid a light spell on her that gave her a burning desire to find it. "Have you seen it?"

"No, but let me look." She rose and began to search the rooms intently.

With one last glance at the sleeper, Jeskil stepped up to the crib where the child lay, silent but unnervingly awake. He took the vial from his robes and poured a few drops of Elian's compound into the child's mouth. After a few moments the sad, dark eyes closed and the child sighed softly and slept.

Then Jeskil did what he had come to do, making the switch between the prince, and a child Elian had brought him, newly dead of a fever, and magicked into a double of the prince. A moment or two later, Lady Berhari returned, holding what she thought was the book he was looking for. "Is this your book?" she asked, holding it out to him.

In fact it was nothing but a glamoured plate that he had brought with him into the chamber. "So it is! Thank you."

She flushed a little and began to fuss with the prince's cradle. "I'm glad to have found it for you. I know how you medical men rely upon your books," she said, straightening the coverlet around the still child. The belief that she had helped Tomeran made it that much easier for Jeskil to convince her that the prince was soundly asleep. All it took was a touch of the illusion of breath.

"He's finally sleeping," Jeskil whispered. "We should let him rest." He moved toward the door.

She followed him, stepping softly. "Oh, of course. He is a treasure," she whispered, her face soft with affection for the prince. "Such a beautiful child. Such a sad beginning."

"Indeed. Well, now I have what I need, and I thank you again, my lady. May you pass a quiet night." He laid a delicate spell on her to fog the recollection of this visit—not enough to leave an obvious hole in her memories, just enough to confuse them.

"Why thank you, Doctor. It was a pleasure to see you again."

"And you, my dear."

In the early morning hours, the court would learn of the death of the heir. It would be seen as a sad inevitability, a child who had never thrived slipping into a quiet rest, and then into death. It happened every day. No blame would be laid at any door.

On his way out of the tower, Jeskil peeked into the hidden pouch in his robes where the true prince lay sleeping. "You're safe now, little one," he murmured.

***

It was not unexpected, and yet...

Vikar stood a little away from the cradle where King Pelle, still weak from his illness, wept for his son. The child, carefully swaddled after the doctors confirmed that he had died of natural causes, lay like a mummy in the softly padded bed. The little face was wizened and drawn, and it all felt wrong somehow, though Vikar couldn't put his finger on why.

He looked at the faces of the people in the room, trying to read them. In most there was genuine sorrow. The nurses comforted each other, and the doctors conferred in hushed tones. But one of them, the Lostrian named Tomeran, looked troubled.

Pelle wiped his eyes, touched the tiny bundle, and walked stiffly toward the door, stopping only to say, "Walk with me," to Vikar. "Will you do what is necessary?"

"Of course."

"Revin, I don't know what to do now."

"Mourn. Nothing else is required of you at this time."

"The kingdom—"

"Will still be here when your mourning period ends, Your Majesty. You must give yourself time."

Pelle laid a hand on Vikar's shoulder. "What would I do without you?" he asked before he walked down the stairs and away from his hopes, his tread labored and his back bowed.

Vikar waited for the doctors to leave the chamber, and he touched Tomeran on the shoulder. "I would like to speak with you, Doctor." He waited until the others had left the hallway, then asked, "You looked troubled. Is there something I should know?"

"No, no, it's nothing. It's just... Lady Berhari said the oddest thing to me when I arrived to examine the child. She said it was so odd that this should happen so soon after I had looked in on him. When I told her it had been nearly a full day since I saw the prince, she looked strangely blank for a moment, then said that's what she meant. But I don't believe it was."

Vikar's skin crawled, but he put a good face on. "I'm sure she's a bit confused. This is terribly upsetting, coming so soon after the queen's death."

"Yes, of course," Tomeran agreed, though he still looked concerned.

"We'll talk again," Vikar promised him with a pat on the back and a small suggestion that he'd dreamed Lady Berhari's words. If there was anything wrong about what had happened in that chamber, Vikar wanted as few people as possible talking about it.

"I think I must've dreamed it," Tomeran said with a laugh as he took his leave of Revin.

Accordingly, Vikar went to Lady Berhari, held her hands in his, and told her that her dream of Dr. Tomeran had been odd but understandable. She looked at him with cloudy eyes for a few moments, then nodded. "It was so real," she said.

"Our minds do try to protect us, don't they?" Vikar said with a smile of just the right degree of sadness.

He went to the cradle as if to pay his respects and touched the child's brow, seeking some insight. But all he found was a dead child and the slightest whisper of magic where there shouldn't have been any at all.

He was not looking forward to his next conversation.

Roxanna was asleep when he knocked on her door. Her ladies—for now she was queen and had ladies-in-waiting—tried to send him away, but in the end, they were the ones who left the queen's chamber.

"What's wrong? Is it Pelle?" she asked, her face gone pale.

"Prince Corius is dead."

Either Roxanna was a superb actress or she was genuinely shocked. "What happened?"

"I thought perhaps you could tell me."

It took her a moment to catch his meaning, and when she did, she sank into a chair and gripped its arms until her fingers went white. "You think I did it?"

He searched her face and wondered if all that cool beauty held a cruel trick of nature. "I believe you had something to do with it."

"A child? You think me capable of murdering a child?" He could see tears starting in her eyes, but she blinked them back and set her jaw. "On my name, on my life and that of my child, it was not my doing."

So she was already with child by the king. Vikar knew it was for the best, but somehow it rankled. "Then why did you go back to the apothecary?"

"For the love charm."

"No, the second time, when you spoke to the girl."

"I went to the apothecary's stall only once."

"Did you take anyone with you?"

Roxanna hesitated. He could see the question troubled her. "I will not tell you that. I cannot."

She didn't have to because the pieces fell in place, and Vikar realized who must have accompanied her that first time. And who it was who went back to the apothecary. "Madam, I regret having had to question you about this. I understand how distressing these days have been for you. I believe what you have told me and will say no more about this matter. I advise you to do the same for your own sake."

A long moment stretched out between them during which nothing was said, but some kind of deep understanding was reached. He felt how vulnerable she was, and though it surprised him, it also reassured him. "I will go to Pelle now," she told him.

"He is nearly broken," Vikar replied.

"I will do what I can."

He nodded. He believed her.

In due course, the king recovered, to the relief of both the new queen and Counselor Revin. But something was different about Pelle. Vikar set it down to all the king had been through in the preceding months, the loss and grief, and then the illness that had left him weak and disoriented for a time. His strength came back and his mind ordered itself, but a spark had gone out of him. There was no joy left in the king who had once been known as a "merry monarch." He attended to the business of Corraçao without enthusiasm, spoke without vigor, and avoided all human contact, even Roxanna's.

In truth, he looked at her as if she were a stranger. Vikar could feel that there was a gulf opening between them, an inexplicable distance that felt unnatural. Pelle was an affectionate man. He would, under normal circumstances, treat the mother of his child with tenderness. But for Roxanna he seemed to feel nothing at all. And if it was so obvious to Vikar, what must it have been like for Roxanna?

To her credit, she did not complain. She held her head up and behaved as a queen ought. The advent of an heir was made public, and Corraçaoans shrugged and went on with their lives. A Feracian queen wasn't a popular choice, but with Caelea and Corius both in the tomb, their concerns were pragmatic; the kingdom needed an heir, and if the Feracian woman provided one, they were willing to accept her.

Vikar made it clear to her that she could look to him for help, and the two settled into a state of truce.

For Roxanna's part, she was a little relieved to be spared Pelle's grief. Her pregnancy was already wearing on her, and much as she loved her husband, she was finding it difficult to be around him when he was in his dark mood.

Hartan wrote to her from home.

It seems your campaign is bearing fruit, if you will excuse the word play. Wismar is furious at the way you ruined his plans but also sees the sense in it, so you can look to him for (grudging) aid, should you need it. I will be sending a gift in a few days. Keep it close, and use it well.

When the gift arrived, it proved to be a Peoran woman with the characteristic dead white skin and silver eyes of her people. Even the sight of her made Roxanna shiver, for the true Peoranu were rumored to be cannibals.

"There are nurses aplenty in Corraçao," Roxanna observed. "Why would my brother send you?"

The woman's smile was oddly both motherly and frightening. "Because he knows the value of a nursemaid whose milk has special virtues, of someone who can give special help where it is needed." She waved her hand, and there was a brief flare of rainbow light in the air.

A magicker? Hadn't she had enough of that already? "I do not want your magic."

"I can ensure a healthy child. Ensure a son," she added more quietly. "It is my special gift to serve mothers and children."

Roxanna's skin crawled at the sight of the woman, but her words struck home. To be sure of producing a healthy male heir would be worth much. "I see."

"My name is Nori-Gant, and I am at your service, my queen. Your brother will provide my payment," she added, as if it was a point in favor of keeping her there at court. "What a kind and thoughtful brother you have."

"Yes. He is a paragon," Roxanna agreed archly.

"And his wife-to-be is a great lady. A cousin of mine as it happens."

So this nurse was a gift Roxanna couldn't easily dismiss. "She and I became close friends." It wasn't exactly the truth. With Catenia gone from Trennin, Roxanna couldn't think of why she'd felt so warmly toward the princess. But it never hurt to take advantage of a connection. "Very well, we shall be pleased to have you serve us."

Nori-Gant's wide, white smile was dazzling.

8.

Thaw Moon, CR 532

Roxanna disliked going to Nori-Gant's rooms. For one thing they were always overheated, even for winter. But worse, the rooms were filled with tools of the woman's trade. The scents of the botanicals drifted and blended, sometimes in pleasant combination, but sometimes in odors that had Roxanna covering her face with her hand.

And the jars? Things floated in them that she didn't want to think about, things that made her shudder if she accidentally caught a glimpse of limbs, or scales, or—worst of all—sightless eyes staring out from the murk inside the glass. Going there for anything, no matter how necessary, was a thing Roxanna hated.

And yet she was there in her fifth month, miserably uncomfortable, with aching legs and back, cramping in all her muscles, and persistent indigestion.

"How do you fare, my queen?"

"Everything hurts. My back, my legs..."

The old woman chuckled. "A woman's burden. Believe me, I know, I've had six myself, two grown now and wed, four in the ground; my youngest taken by fen fever about the time the little prince was laid to rest. Well, that's a mother's lot, I expect." She sighed. "Not to worry though, we'll see you have a healthy son."

Roxanna couldn't imagine the woman having children, much less a husband. She seemed so singular.

"I have something that will help." Nori-Gant held up a blue bottle. "A massage with this will ease the pain in your muscles. Let me apply it and you'll see."

Willing to try anything to ease her discomfort, Roxanna disrobed and lay on her side. She flinched at the first touch of the calloused fingers, but almost immediately a warmth began to spread through her back muscles, and she felt the ache ease.

"Better?" Nori-Gant asked.

"Yes."

"Let me massage your legs."

Roxanna rolled onto her back, relaxing into the massage and the warm, calming scent of the oil.

"Do they cramp?"

"Yes."

"Drink more water." Then the old woman rubbed oil into Roxanna's swelling abdomen. "And this will ease the marks. You'll be perfect in spite of your burden. I have made a bottle for you to take with you."

"Nori-Gant, it has to be a boy. A healthy boy." Nothing else would cement her place in the Corraçaoan court as certainly as a healthy prince.

Nori-Gant checked a battered old pot heating over the fire. Whatever was in it, it smelled strange; not bad, nor good, but like nothing Roxanna had ever smelled before. She prayed she wouldn't have to drink any of it.

When the nurse returned to the queen, she laid her hands on Roxanna's belly. "I know what it is you're asking, and no good can come of it." Then she bent over Roxanna's swelling abdomen and whispered as if talking to the child within.

Then Nori-Gant filled a cup with her brew and handed it to Roxanna. "Drink."

"Will this make it certain?" Roxanna asked and the nurse scowled at her.

"Don't you listen? No good can come of what you're asking. No, this draught is for the health of mother and child, nothing more. Drink."

Somehow Roxanna lacked the will to refuse. She drank, feeling as if the woman had taken control of her. A warmth spread through her, reaching all the way to her womb where the child floated. She relaxed in spite of herself.

As Nori-Gant was helping Roxanna dress, she said "You carry a boy child."

"Truly?"

"He whispered his secrets to me," the nurse said with a chuckle. "It's going to be a son. You will have all you desire." She pressed a bundle of herbs into Roxanna's hands. "Hang this in your chamber to freshen the air. A strong child needs to breathe freely."

9.

Heat Moon, CR 532

The remainder of Roxanna's pregnancy was peaceful. She let go of her concerns, and concentrated on being a good wife and mother. The doctors told her everything seemed normal.

She rubbed the oil into her back and legs, and it eased her discomfort. She exercised, she ate and slept well, and the child exhibited no signs of distress. It would be a fine, strong boy to carry on the Pellires line.

Pelle seemed disinterested, but Roxanna set it down to understandable caution. He had lost much and was afraid to hope, she told herself. When they were together, she gave him good reports of her progress. "I want to make you happy, my love," she told him.

"I know that," he would reply and look away. And the terrible thing was that she did want to make him happy. She had seen him as a prize but had been caught up in his love and tenderness, in the affection he'd shown her before the night when she used that Rogie potion on him. It was as if the charms had worked on her heart more completely than on his, and she'd trapped herself in love with a man who might never truly care for her without the aid of magic.

She was too heavily pregnant to attend Hartan's wedding in Vartaris during the Flower Moon, and she was glad of it. Even the thought of her new sister-in-law made her uneasy. She and Pelle sent a representative and a generous gift, but neither Hartan nor Catenia responded.

The time wore on, and the weather grew warmer. Roxanna's body felt unfamiliar to her, unwieldy, still prone to aches and pains and internal disturbances that were alien and troubling. The massage oils helped with some of the troubles, and she used them liberally, asking for a new bottle every few weeks. But nothing eased her entirely, and she prayed that the time would move more quickly and she would be delivered.

The date set for the birth came and went. Doctors assured her that often the first child was late, and it was nothing to worry about. Nori-Gant said the same, but Roxanna did worry. And she was miserable. She massaged the oils into her aching back and legs and told her son that it was time for him to come out and meet the world.

She ran out of the oil on a day when nothing was going well. She felt ill, the baby was moving and kicking and being difficult, and everything hurt as if her muscles had all caught fire. Roxanna grew angry and stormed down to Nori-Gant's rooms to demand... what, she didn't know. Something. Some help. An end to the endless discomfort. Or just the chance to take her irrational anger out on someone.

The old woman seemed surprised and not particularly pleased to see her. "What can I do for you, my queen?"

"This has to end!" She pushed her way into the room. "I can't bear this a day longer."

"They take their time; you've been told as much." She tried to herd Roxanna out of the room, but the queen sank down into a chair, hoping for a moment's ease.

"I know that," she said. "But surely there's something—" Her vague gaze had taken in the sight of Nori-Gant's meal, passed over it, and then registered what she'd seen.

It was a human hand. A roasted human hand, partly disjointed and devoured.

And for a moment there was neither pain nor illness, just a cold, clutching sense of horror as Roxanna realized that the stories were true, the Peoranu were cannibals.

And she realized then what was in those packages Hartan sent Nori-Gant every month.

"I—I—" She struggled to her feet and doubled over with a wave of pain so intense it brought tears to her eyes. "Oh no," she breathed. "Not here."

Roxanna stumbled to the door as the pain eased. "You will leave Corraçao now, today," she ordered. "I will not have this"—she gestured at the plate with its grisly portion—"this abomination in my kingdom."

But Nori-Gant's face hardened and split itself with a mirthless smile. "I will do as I choose," the witch told her. "Go off and farrow now." She pushed Roxanna out of the room and slammed the door in her face.

Making her way down the empty corridors, Roxanna wondered how her brother could have made such a bargain. Why would he care so very much about the Corraçaoan succession? Because it wasn't brotherly love that drove him to these ends, that much was certain.

Finally she saw a guard and called out to him for help, and he supported her all the way back to her apartments. "Fetch the doctors," she said, feeling another crushing wave beginning. "Hurry now!"

The man ran out.

Why hadn't she thought to tell him to fetch her ladies first? "Rosamunda!" she cried. "Lady Rosamunda!"

There was only silence. "Lady Alyce!" Nothing.

The pain rolled through her like thunder, and she gasped out, "Help me, please!"

Not that she expected help. They hated her. This was a bad moment to have second thoughts about her reputation at court.

"Damn, damn, damn." She clutched at her belly and shuddered as the pain passed. Why did women choose this?

And then finally the doctors were there, preparing her, soothing her with their promises and the medicines that took the edge off the violent pains. She sank into their ministrations, her muscles relaxing, and fears dissolving as they took charge.

Through a haze she saw Counselor Revin looking concerned. He was probably hoping she'd die and leave a healthy heir. That would be like him.

Why did everyone hate her?

And then she stopped thinking and eased into a drugged sleep.

***

The call from Vikar came after Reyna and Jeskil had retired for the night, and Jeskil was inclined to ignore it. He was tired; his cousin could wait.

But the sense that he was wanted persisted, so he stumbled out of bed, found his cards, and crept down to the kitchen to lay them out. "What is it?" he asked as Vikar's card came to life before him.

"Did I wake you?" Vikar asked, though he sounded anything but repentant. "I thought you needed to know that the queen is delivered of a healthy male child who has been named Oreyn. The king is pleased, as is the court. Let this be the end of the uncertainty. I hope watching over the dancer hasn't been too onerous for you, but that's at an end now. You're free of her."

"About that," Jeskil said. "I should tell you that I've married the girl."

There was a long silence from the figure before him. "Married? You?"

"I know I said I would never marry, but people change. Don't make a huge issue of it," he said. He could almost hear Vikar's eyes rolling. "We're fine. Forget all about us, Cousin. We'd prefer it that way."

The small figure nodded. "Yes, of course. It makes sense. Go back to bed. Get some rest."

"You do the same," Jeskil told him and gathered up the cards with a sense of relief as well as some small feeling of guilt for having deceived Vikar not once but twice. He'd be called to accounts for that one day, but for now, they were all safe.

Jeskil crawled back into bed, trying not to wake his wife, but she was always half on the alert because of the two boys tucked into cradles beside the bed: Azur, already large and healthy, and showing signs of being golden-haired like Pelle; and Corius, Caelea's son—who Reyna had renamed "Vari"—who seemed now to be thriving, though he remained small.

"I missed you," she said, her voice warm with sleep.

"I needed to talk to my cousin. He tells me that Queen Roxanna has had a son."

"Really? Well, she must be proud of herself." The comment had a sharp edge. "Actually, that's good news for us, isn't it?" She stretched. He admired the way the soft fabric of her gown lay over her curves. He had become a connoisseur of those curves since Azur was born.

"It is. How are the boys?" he asked.

"Precious," she told him. "Of course. Jeskil..."

"Hmm?" He drew Reyna into his arms, and she rested her head on his shoulder.

"I would never have given either of them up. I hope you know that. Not for any reason, not even for a throne. I may not have given birth to Vari, but he's as much mine now as Azur is."

He kissed her forehead. "I believe you. I'm glad we don't have to fret about that any longer."

"Pelle didn't lose any time, did he?" Reyna observed as she settled into his embrace. From any other woman that might have been a biting comment, but Reyna just sounded amused. She was over Pelle, had probably been before Jeskil had kidnapped her and taken her out of Corraçao. "But Roxanna Talian... wouldn't you think he could have chosen someone better? Someone less—" She searched for a word that fit, then let the thought go. Jeskil knew what she meant and shrugged.

"Someone had to be queen and make little princes and princesses for Corraçao."

Reyna made a disgusted noise. "That's how she is rewarded for planning the death of Vari. And my death!" she added indignantly, raising herself up on one elbow to stare down at Jeskil, a frown creasing her lovely brow.

"About which no one knows," he reminded her. "And I am still far from convinced that it was she who hired me to kill Corius. But we need to let go of it. It's over now. Vari is no longer a little prince, just our child."

"I know. I do know. It just makes me angry when I look at Vari's little face, to think that someone wanted him dead, even if it wasn't her. Who could want to kill children? I don't understand that." She reached over and fussed with the blankets covering both boys. She loved touching them, caring for them. Jeskil could feel the love spilling from her onto her boys.

"They're safe." He drew her back down against himself and kissed her fair curls. "They're our sons now, and they are safe and happy, as we are. Nothing can change that. I won't let it."

"I love you," Reyna told him. "Do I say that often enough?"

"I can always stand to hear it again." With a sigh, Jeskil closed his eyes. The rain poured down outside in the unseasonably cool and raw late summer, but inside their rooms, with Reyna and the children, it was warm and safe with a briskly burning fire, and a deep, warm pile of coverlets. Jeskil had never felt so perfectly happy in his life.

Just as he was dropping off, he heard a fretful cry from one of the cradles, and he winced. "Do they never sleep?" he asked, but he didn't mind getting up to comfort the babies. "You sleep," he told his wife. "I'll take care of them."

"You're a prize, my love," Reyna said and yawned.

Jeskil got up and went around to the cradles. It was Azur who was fretful, so Jeskil picked him up and rocked him. "You're the one who makes noise," he told the baby. "You'll get what you need." With the other hand he rocked Vari's cradle. "And you're the quiet one." He looked down into the sad, dark eyes of the little prince. "You'll need to work harder than your brother to get your due."

He hummed a little tune and Azur quieted. Vari's eyes closed, and the child's little mouth curved up in soft contentment. Instead of putting Azur back in his own cradle, he laid him beside Vari and covered them with the blanket. The boys seemed to melt together, each seeking the other's warmth.

"Your mama and I will watch over you until you're grown, but you're brothers now, and you'll have to look out for each other," he told them. "Family first. Never forget that." He looked up to see Reyna smiling sleepily at them.

"Family first," she whispered.

When the boys were asleep, he crept back into bed beside Reyna and spooned against her, wrapping his arms around her softness.

"Everything is good," she whispered, her words thick with sleep. "Isn't it?"

"Perfect," he told her. "I am the luckiest man in the world."

"That's what I thought," she replied, and they both chuckled.

10.

Bright Moon, CR 549

Albhain, Seventeen Years Later

The pretty red-haired girl dimpled when she smiled up at Azur. He handed her a pass to the puppet theater. "Pretty girl like you needs to have some fun, yes? And you'll love the show," he promised. "And after."

She giggled. Vari decided that one of them needed to get the passes out to the citizens of Rathsorcha, and turned away from where his brother continued to flirt, offering tickets to the puppet theater for that afternoon. "Circus of Dreams!" he called out. "Come see the famous Merrypike and Petal. Free pass for this evening," he cried, handing the chits to the townspeople.

"Free?" the redhead said, and Vari chuckled.

"I'll be there," Azur assured her. "You'll see the show, and then we'll see what happens, yes?"

The dimples showed themselves again.

"Hey!"

Vari looked up to find trouble. The sort Azur was so good at attracting. An angry, thuggish-looking young man pushed his way through the crowd. "What are you doing with my girl?"

Azur's handsome, leonine head turned slightly, and he appraised the man with a careless glance. "Nothing yet, but give me time," he replied.

The boyfriend lunged, Vari's leg shot out and tripped him, and he face-planted at the feet of the redhead who giggled again, probably making the situation worse.

"Here, let me help you," Azur said, lifting the boyfriend up off the damp cobbles. "Oh dear, horse shit," he said, staring at the man's jacket. He handed the man a pass. "Come and see the puppet show; you'll feel better." Then Vari shouted, "Free money!" and threw a handful of passes into the air. In the confusion that followed, Azur and Vari sprinted off together, doubling over in laughter as they rounded a corner out of sight of the girl and her thuggish lover.

"I can't always save you from yourself, you know," Vari pointed out.

"Of course you can! What are brothers for?"

"I never need saving," Vari pointed out.

"I know. You're letting me down, brother, forcing me to make all the mischief in the family. It's a lot of work."

"It's my fault?"

"Entirely. Ooh, hot hawnuts!" Azur strode off, following his nose, and Vari strolled after. By the time he caught up, Azur was already trying to charm the seller into giving him a cone of roasted nuts in exchange for a pass. She wasn't having it, and she held the paper cone just out of reach. "I'm too old for your tricks, young man. Pay up or they go back in the warmer."

"Vari, do you have any money on you?"

He sighed audibly but paid the woman what she asked. "You can still have a pass," he told her. "They're free."

He took another stack from his pocket and gave her one. She shot Azur a look, and he shrugged.

"Oh, Circus of Dreams, I know that name. You're here every winter season, aren't you?"

"That's right. Rathsorcha is our base. You should come."

"I always did like that Merrypike puppet," she admitted. "He's a saucy one."

Vari grinned. "That he is. More mettlesome by the season. One day he'll own the circus and we'll all be working for him."

She laughed a rich, alto laugh and Azur sighed. He loved women, all women. He found them amazing. "How can I make you laugh again, bright spirit?" he wheedled.

"Oh, go on with you," she told him, but she didn't sound annoyed any longer. In fact, she scooped up a second cone of nuts and handed them to Vari. "Can I get a second pass for my man?"

"Of course!" Vari handed her another.

"You're married? My heart is broken."

"My brother is quite mad," Vari told her. "Don't let him scare you."

"He's your brother?"

"That's right, we're twins," Azur said, putting his arm around Vari's shoulder.

She frowned, but said, "I suppose around the eyes."

"And nose," Vari said.

"That is to say the mouth as well," Azur added, and the three of them burst out laughing.

"You're really twins?"

"That's what our parents tell us. But you never know. I think the fair folk left my brother, Vari, on the doorstep one cold night."

"It was the trolls that left Azur," Vari confided. "Because he was too ugly for them. Thank you again. Hope to see you tonight."

They walked off together, shoulder to shoulder in the hazy dusk. Streetlamps were flickering on with mage light cutting through the shadows.

When not indulging their wits, or practicing their patter, the brothers were often silent together in perfect harmony, and it was then that the resemblance between them showed most clearly. They were handsome boys, tall and agile, with cat-like faces and clear blue eyes. But where Azur was muscular and golden like a desert lion, Vari was a sleek, dark mountain cat.

"Thanks for the nuts," Azur said at last. "And the distraction back there."

Vari nodded. "Family first," he said.

"Family first," Azur agreed.

By the time they returned to the arena that housed the winter circus, the boys had finished their snack and were ready for dinner, and they slid into their seats just as the bowls of stew and dumplings were being passed.

"Did you give out all your passes?" their father asked as he put a bread roll on his plate and gave one to his youngest daughter, Mera.

"Almost all," Azur said. "Lots of pretty girls should be here tonight. Make the show extra racy, will you?"

"I think we'll have to tone it down instead," Jeskil told him. "You're going to get yourself into some trouble one of these days."

"Mother, tell him I'm fine," Azur begged.

"You're not fine, and he's right," Reyna said, and Vari leaned over and kissed her cheek.

"I take care of him. Family first," he told her.

"I like pretty girls," Donnr observed as he shoveled the stew into his mouth. The youngest boy of the family was twelve and precocious. His older sister Ibeth replied, "Shame they don't like you," and earned sputtering laughs from Vari and Azur.

"All right, all right, let's calm down and eat. We have a show to do, even if it's just a preview of the winter circus," Reyna reminded them all. "We have to make the effort tonight."

"They'll come. What else is there to do in Rathsorcha in the winter?" Ibeth asked. She loved being on the road and always chafed at being stuck in the winter camp. When Azur wagged his eyebrows at her, she scowled and said, "Oh stop it!"

After their meal, the boys helped Jeskil at the puppet theater while Reyna and Ibeth dressed for their short preview of the wire-dancing act. The musicians were tuning up while the acrobats leaped and tumbled, and the seats began to fill with excited patrons.

Because it was the winter show and they were in a big arena, the puppet theater was much larger than the one they took on the road, and the puppets were nearly full size. Both Azur and Vari helped Jeskil behind the stage, pulling strings and moving the big, ungainly figures so gracefully that their audience often felt as if they were seeing real actors, not wooden ones. Many of the spectators set it down to a glamour because Rathsorcha audiences were sophisticated and used to an atmosphere of magic. But the truth was that there was little magicking involved. The boys and their father simply had a feel for their puppets, an affection for them that conveyed itself to their audiences.

Vari had become the voice of Petal, and he was hilarious, flirting with the men in the audience. Azur remembered one potato-faced merchant whose dour expression hadn't changed a bit during the show. Vari took that as a challenge.

"I like a good, solid man like you," he said in his sweet Petal Fluffbottom voice. "I could take good care of you," the puppet cooed, to the delight of the audience.

The man's face flushed crimson, but he was smiling now, enjoying the attention, not only of Petal but of the audience, which was vocal in its appreciation.

"You look like a man who could take good care of a woman," Petal purred. "Come see me after the show and you may propose marriage to me."

There were hoots and whistles, and though the merchant seemed embarrassed, he also seemed rather pleased.

He was less pleased when he waited until after the show to meet "Miss Petal" and found her to be a good-looking young man.

"All in good fun," Jeskil had told him when the man began to sputter with disbelief. "Your friends will be slapping you on the back and asking you how it went."

"Just tell them Merrypike challenged you to a duel and Miss Petal fainted," Vari suggested, and the man seemed to regain his sense of humor.

"Well, all right then," he said. "That Petal is a lovely little piece of fluff, isn't she?" he asked and took his leave of them.

With the women in the audience, he would often seek advice on Merrypike's philandering, his tightness with a penny, or simply compliment them on their shoes, pointing out that her own feet were so dainty that she couldn't, of course, wear such things. Then he'd do a little dance and chirp, "And my ankles are famous!" Azur often found himself shaking with barely suppressed laughter as Vari delivered Petal's lines, many of them ad-libbed, with such a combination of innocence and guile that he nearly eclipsed Jeskil's Merrypike during some shows.

Acting was not Azur's forte, but he didn't begrudge the talent to his brother; he reveled in it. "Family first" was a motto that he took seriously. He also had no magical talent to speak of, though with his father's help he'd mastered a few tricks. But he was a natural leader, and a natural lover, and he made the most of both gifts.

After the show, he greeted the hawnut seller who had been sitting right at the front of the audience, kissed her cheek, and told her husband what a lucky man he was. "Were I Merrypike, I'd try to steal her away from you," he told the husband. He supposed it would earn him free roasted hawnuts all winter, but he loved how happy he made the two of them with so little effort.

While he was on the floor of the arena, blending with the crowd, thanking people for coming and explaining what the full circus would be like, Azur noted a man standing near the orchestra, watching him. He seemed startled, as if they knew each other. And in truth the man looked vaguely familiar. Azur supposed they'd met on the road. Maybe Azur had stolen a girl from him. He suppressed a grin and moved along, shaking hands, flirting with the women and girls, being a relentlessly charming ambassador for the circus.

The crowd thinned, and Azur joined Vari, who was cleaning up the arena alongside a few of the acrobats. Jeskil always insisted on keeping their sites orderly; it was a point of pride to him that the circus left things neat and clean when they left a site. And often they improved their surroundings. Jeskil had plans to repair some areas of the arena that were run-down.

Azur admired his father; he was a good businessman and a good man, someone to look up to and emulate.

When he and Vari returned to the puppet theater, Jeskil and the stranger who had been watching Azur were in conversation, and Azur bristled with a sense that all was not right. The men looked up. The stranger looked at Azur, then at Vari, and his eyes widened.

"How many other things have you lied about, Cousin?" Azur heard him ask Jeskil.

Cousin?

"It was necessary."

"Really?"

"Really." Jeskil sighed. "Boys, come and meet your uncle Vikar." He motioned them forward and introduced them to Vikar as "my twins, Azur and Vari." Vari, picking up on Azur's unease, perhaps, was more reserved than usual.

Jeskil said, "We usually share a light meal after a performance. Why don't you come and join us?"

"Are you sure I'll be welcome?"

"I believe so. As long as you don't expect her to give up anything."

It felt as if they were speaking in code, and Azur hated it. He decided he disliked this strange man he was supposed to call "Uncle Vikar." He hung back as they made their way from the puppet theater to the space the family shared.

"What's wrong?" Vari whispered.

"I don't trust him."

"Why not?"

It annoyed Azur that he had no reason he could share. "I just don't."

Vari was silent for a moment or two and then nodded and said, "Then I won't either."

The meeting between Reyna and Vikar was strangely tense. She looked him up and down, and observed, "You haven't changed."

"You have. You're more beautiful than ever. I owe you an apology."

After a drawn-out moment, she shook her head. "No. Jes told me everything. I owe you my life and that of my sons.

And you sent me a good man. You and I are even." Then she added, "So long as you're not here to try to take either of them from me."

Vikar shook his head. "That's long over," he assured her.

They all sat down together at a table laid with bread, cheese, fruit, and a pitcher of black plum water, which had a mild relaxant effect and would help them all sleep well when they retired. Jeskil introduced his three youngest children to their uncle, who easily charmed them. Azur could see how Vikar and Jeskil were alike in many ways, and it reassured him a little. He relaxed, and Vari, sensing the change, relaxed as well.

The meal was pleasant enough, though there were currents running through the assembly that made Jeskil uneasy. He had the sense that he and Vikar were going to be having a loud disagreement quite soon.

The boys excused themselves after bolting their food, and Reyna, with her unfailing sense of her family's emotional state, took the other children off with her not long after, leaving the cousins alone together.

Jeskil sipped the plum water. "Why are you here?"

Vikar's reply was a thin smile. "I came because I have been questioning my entire life's work, and I arrive to find that there is much more to question." He tipped his head and stared at Jeskil with an expression that was both quizzical and challenging. "You have no idea what life is like at that court, Cousin. None. Why could you not tell me that there was some hope of restoring a rightful heir to the throne?"

Jeskil set his jaw. He would not be moved. "Because there is no chance. You need to leave my family alone, Vikar. They are nothing at all to you or to Corraçao."

"Jeskil!"

"Vikar, no. Enough. Those boys are my sons now, and I will not allow you to pull them into that mess."

"I never thought you'd lie to me like that," Vikar said. "Family first, cousin."

"It cuts in both directions, cousin. They're my family too. Look," he said as he set his cup down. "Reyna wouldn't have given up Azur for anything. And someone, I'm still not sure who, wanted Vari dead. Wanted it badly. My first duty was to a pair of innocent children."

Vikar sat back and picked at a piece of bread. "Azur is nearly the double of Prince Oreyn. Did you know that?"

"Stop."

"And Vari—"

"Stop!"

"Why didn't you at least tell me you'd stolen him?"

"It was safer for everyone that way. Only Reyna knew. She's his mother now, and nothing will ever make her part with him. They're still children, Vikar. I won't let you take them from us. They know nothing of governance, nothing of your world, and I don't want them ever to have to live in it."

"Not just my world, it's yours as well. Caelea was your cousin too."

"And I owed her son a secure future, not a throne and the constant danger of murder. What kind of a world considers children to be such threats that they need to be eliminated?" He pushed his cup away. "The circus does not go to Corraçao. Ever. Or Feracia. Someone, perhaps the queen, perhaps someone in the guise of the queen, called me to kill Prince Corius. I'm grateful it was me. Anyone else, Vari might... would be dead now. I left a glamoured dead child in his place. Some poor orphan mite got a royal funeral, and a living child grew up into a fine, happy young man. I wouldn't give that up for the world. Don't ask it."

Vikar held up both hands as if in surrender, but Jeskil knew his cousin too well to trust it would be that simple. "You're right, there's a lot more to that story, and when you're ready to hear it, I'll tell it."

Jeskil nodded. "Though perhaps I don't want to know who wanted Vari dead. I'm not above taking revenge, you know." Then he brightened. "Vari wants to study magic," Jeskil said. "I've spoken to Magister Goedred about taking him on as a student when he turns eighteen in the autumn."

Vikar nodded but said nothing.

"Azur loves the circus."

Another nod.

"They will have the lives they choose, Cousin."

"Of course." Vikar sighed. "I came here only to seek some kind of resolution to my own concerns about my life's path, but meeting Vari has given me much to think about."

Jeskil repeated that the boys would have the lives they chose. Then he said, "Stay with us. Stay with the circus. It was our dream, remember?"

Vikar's slow nod told him that his cousin did remember, that it was, perhaps, one of his regrets that he hadn't remained an entertainer. Jeskil pressed a little harder. "It would be like old times. Better."

"I don't know what I want," Vikar admitted. "Nor am I in any condition to decide tonight. My travels have taken their toll, Jeskil. I find I'm longing for a bed, and perhaps several days of uninterrupted sleep." His smile was wry. "I do feel at home here, I won't deny it. But my sense of duty to Corraçao gnaws at me. Give me time to think."

"That's the least I can do," Jeskil said, leading him to his bedchamber. "No one will disturb you. Sleep as long as you need to."

The two men embraced as they used to when they were boys and alone in the world with only each other to rely on.

***

Vari sat with his brother at the side entrance to the circus building. Azur was waiting for a girl, as usual, and Vari waited with him for want of anything better to do that evening.

"You need a girl," Azur observed.

"There's time enough. There's the whole world to see, isn't there?"

"It's better with a girl. Or several." Then Azur laughed. "You're right, of course, but I'm a weak man when it comes to a beautiful woman."

He stood up, did an easy, graceful back flip, and grinned. "That's how being in love makes me feel."

"And are you? In love?"

Azur shrugged. "Why not? Oh, there she is," he murmured as the red-haired girl who had taken his fancy that morning stepped into the pool of light from a nearby lamp. "Isn't she wonderful?"

"Very. Much more so without her young man trying to kill us."

Azur snorted with laughter. "Salt and spice, brother. Salt and spice. Don't you have somewhere else to be?"

"No, I'm not expected anywhere," Vari said, all wide dark eyes and innocence.

"Go on with you!" Azur hissed, but he was laughing.

Vari left his brother, certain that Azur could take care of himself, and wandered back into the near-silent theater. Toward the back of the building where the circus wagons were parked near the sleeping rooms, he saw a small group sitting around a fire that was magicked to be nearly smokeless.

The group was trading magical tips, trying out new spells.

"Ho, Vari!" they said, waving him over. "Watch what Coll can do."

Vari sat down and waited, watching Coll frown and grunt as he pushed at the spell. It made Vari laugh to see how his features twisted like a man whose guts were bound up. "You'll do yourself an injury!" he observed, and then suddenly Coll was gone, and in his place was a sleek, golden oroszlán with a black mane and tail.

"Women like the big cats," the oroszlán observed in Coll's voice, and the others laughed.

"You're getting good at that," Vari told him. "The magisters all say that you have to be born a shifter, but you're proving them wrong. Well done."

In a moment Coll was back, though his hair was still black and shaggy with residual magic. It faded slowly to his usual brown. "It does take a lot out of me," he admitted. "But it's easier each time."

"I think," Davia said, "that the shape of magic is changing. No, listen," she added quickly as the rest of the group hooted at her. "Coll does something he shouldn't be able to do. He wasn't born a shifter, but he can shift. More babes are born to magic every day it seems, and those with magical parents grow stronger than either parent."

"So you've made an exhaustive study of this?" Maygora asked, a bit more archly than was necessary, and Davia frowned and poked at the fire.

But Vari thought that perhaps Davia was right. Coll was shifting more easily every day. And he, Vari, had started to be able to shift as well. He'd told no one, not even Azur, but in private he practiced and had learned how to cover his body with feathers or fur or even scales, how to change his features enough to resemble a cat or a hound, and had nearly taught himself how to grow the great, tearing beak of a mountain eagle. Nearly. The effect was currently more amusing than alarming.

But he was learning. Perhaps soon Magister Goedred would consent to take him on as a student. Though he wanted badly to study magic, he was worried that the magisters would try to hold him to all the old rules of magic when he believed that many of them were outmoded. Not the ethical rules—those Vari agreed with entirely: harm no one with magic, inflict your will on no one with magic; those rules made sense even if Vari guessed that they were not always easy to enforce.

Rather, Vari had the sense that some of the regulations that had been made about magic were, at best, wrong-headed and based on mistaken notions. At worst? Designed to keep magickers in check, to force them into the open and control what sorts of magic they could work.

If Goedred accepted Vari as a student, Vari would have to register as a magic user and give the magisters a list of all the talents he possessed. He was not sure he wanted to do that. Control of one's power should be a personal thing. It occurred to him again to wonder how his father viewed those rules. Jeskil had never spoken out either for or against. He was opaque about his magicks. Vari couldn't recall ever having seen him cast a spell, but all the same he sensed that Jeskil was more skilled than any other magicker Vari had ever met. There was a banked power about his father that Vari found intriguing. He had never encountered anyone else with that sort of aura. Until he met his uncle Vikar, that is.

What sort of lineage did they come from, he wondered? Who were they? He must have inherited his powers from Jeskil because Reyna had no magic at all. Not that she needed any to bewitch people. Jeskil's story about having been a street orphan had never seemed like the whole story to Vari, but his father insisted that was all there was to the story. He wondered if his uncle Vikar could be cajoled into telling him something more.

***

Vikar slept.

For the first time in months, perhaps years, Vikar slept deeply, his mind at rest, his heart lighter. He slept around the clock, got up to share a meal with Jeskil's family, and returned to his bed to sleep away another night.

On the second morning, he knew what he would do. He went to Jeskil. "You've done me a service," he told his cousin. "I've determined to leave Corraçao."

Jeskil gave a whoop of happiness and clapped Vikar on the back. "Good choice. Your place is here. You'll have a rest, and then we'll find you a place in the circus—"

"No. I won't sneak off like this. I have to go back, put everything in order for the next person to hold the title of counselor, and make a formal resignation."

"But why?" Jeskil asked.

"Because that's who I am." It was the best answer he had and the only one his cousin would understand.

Instead, Jeskil said, "They'll drag you back, Vikar. They'll pull you back into their scheming, and drama, and misery, and you won't have the heart to leave."

"I will."

"No you won't."

"I swear I—"

"Don't. Don't swear on this." Jeskil sighed. "At least stay a few more days and refresh yourself. Get to know the children and Reyna. Enjoy the circus. And give me the pleasure of having my boyhood companion back for a time."

Vikar nodded. "Gladly."

11.

Thaw Moon, CR 549

After a few weeks of rest and relaxation, Vikar returned to Corraçao to find the royal family in the usual turmoil. Roxanna summoned him to her sitting room immediately and began the interview with a rebuke over how long he'd been gone. Then she said, "We have a decision to make."

"We?" As far as Vikar was concerned, there was no more "we" or wouldn't be once he found a successor and resigned.

With a heavy sigh that said she hated to include him in the discussion, she admitted that yes, she needed his expertise. "Marriage," she said. "For Oreyn. He is of an age."

Vikar wanted no part of this. "He's only sixteen. It can wait."

"Not if we want a choice alliance."

Realizing that she wouldn't be put off, he asked, "Who are the lucky contenders?"

"The Princess Saskia of Arrezko, and Duchess Wilhelmina Haase fonFulkenheim of Feracia."

"Who?"

"She's no one, but the match is being promoted by Wismar and my brother, so it must be taken seriously. Fulkenheim," she grumbled. "A little backwater only recently elevated to the level of a duchy. I'm sure her family paid a great deal to the crown for that honor."

"I gather that your choice would be Saskia of Arrezko," Vikar said with just a touch of irony.

"Arrezko offers a huge dowry that will replenish our coffers."

"It's a powerful incentive," Vikar admitted. Much more money flowed out of Corraçao than in, and the kingdom was often in peril of not being able to pay its bills. "What does Oreyn say?"

"What do you imagine he says? Today it's no, tomorrow it may be yes, and yesterday he wanted to wed a Peoranu woman like Nori-Gant. He says she's the only one who has ever loved him," Roxanna said with an expression of disgust.

"Sadly, the Peoranu use shells for money, making such an alliance pointless."

She rewarded his flippancy with a thin smile. "You've become sarcastic in your old age, Revin. It certainly makes you seem more human."

Why stay? He wondered. He should resign his position immediately and leave Corraçao to sink into the mire of its own making. But he thought that if he could see Oreyn safely married and under the sway of a real ruler like Wouder of Arrezko, or even Wismar, as loathsome as that thought was, then he could retire with the sense that he had done his duty to his adopted country. "I shall be happy to arrange meetings between the prince and representatives from both countries."

Just then the door banged open and Rhaenne, the elder of Roxanna's daughters, came screaming into the room, followed closely by Oreyn, who brandished a candle. The smell of burnt hair followed her.

"Mother, stop him!"

"Oreyn, enough!" Roxanna shouted, pulling the girl into her arms. "What have you done to your sister?" She fingered the burnt ends of Rhaenne's golden braid. "Why do you do these things? Put that candle down at once."

"Stupid. The candle is out," he said, waving a smoking candle at them. He noticed Vikar and scowled. "I thought you were gone for good."

"Sorry." Vikar got up and snatched the candle from Oreyn. "This is a waste of reading light. Rhaenne, are you unharmed?"

"I don't know."

Vikar closed his eyes.

"She's fine," Roxanna said, stroking her daughter's hair. "Just frightened." To Oreyn, she said, "Don't torment your sisters."

"Why not? They deserve it."

"Prince Oreyn, will you sit with us for a time and hear some news?" Vikar asked.

"About?"

"Your future."

The handsome face twisted into a grimace that could almost have expressed amusement. So like Azur, and so unlike. "How could I refuse?" He slouched into a chair and kicked out at Rhaenne, catching her in the ankle. She yelped, and Roxanna barked, "Stop that right now."

"Make me."

"I'll make you behave, little one." Nori-Gant stood in the doorway. "Haven't I taught you anything about the manners of a king? Did you take no wisdom from my care?"

She never missed an occasion to hold it over Roxanna that she, not the queen, had wet-nursed Prince Oreyn; that she had all the love that should have gone to Roxanna.

Nori-Gant sat down, and Oreyn came and crouched by her side. "You're the only one who loves me," he told her.

"Then don't burden my heart with your mischief, little one, and leave your sisters be." She petted him like a beloved dog, ruffling his fair hair with slender fingers. "What news have you?" she asked Vikar as Oreyn slumped down onto the floor, resting his head in her lap.

Vikar and Roxanna exchanged glances. "Marriage," he said. "The prince is of an age to marry, as you know."

"I won't. I won't!"

"Hush, my boy, hush. This is part of life. Who offers for my little one?"

"Both Arrezko and Feracia," Roxanna told her.

"Which Arrezkan princess?"

"Saskia."

"A third daughter?" The woman spat on the floor. Oreyn giggled, and Roxanna turned away. "Which Feracian?"

"Wilhelmina Haase fonFulkenheim."

"A nobody."

"A duchess," Vikar countered. What he wanted to say was that it was a miracle any noble or royal family would be willing to sacrifice a daughter to the Pellires heir. Oreyn's reputation was already foul. What he'd be like in ten or twenty years almost didn't bear thinking about. What Vikar said was, "A good marriage will bring advantages of alliance and dowry."

Nori-Gant reached out and took a black plum from the plate on the table, bit off a piece, and put it into Oreyn's open mouth. "Why does my sweet boy not want to marry?"

Oreyn chewed, saying nothing.

"It couldn't hurt to talk to the ambassadors from Arrezko and Feracia."

"I want to see them," Oreyn said. "I won't wed a fright."

Vikar went from Roxanna to the king to discuss the proposed marriages. Not that he expected Pelle to care one way or another. The king cared about nothing much these days beyond food and drink. He had changed dramatically in the years of his marriage. There were no more lavish parties, though he often gave expensive gifts to his courtiers. He cut taxes and raised the pay of all servants of the crown, and when he was feeling particularly low and unappreciated, he would ride through the streets distributing alms and food to the people of the city. He was beggaring his kingdom in a vain attempt to be the beloved Pelle Pellires of the past, the King of Hearts.

But the sight of the king nearly broke Vikar's heart. In spite of his prodigious appetite for food, Pelle seemed shrunken in stature, soft and rangy, all his muscle having melted away. His hair and skin were dull, as were his eyes, and they were sunken in dark circles. He looked much older than his not-quite-sixty years, and horribly unwell, but no doctor in Corraçao was able to find anything wrong with him.

"My king," he said, and was taken aback by Pelle's sneer.

"So you came back. Why? I thought you'd shaken off our dust."

"Majesty, I am your servant. This is my place." He felt horrible telling what felt like a lie now, particularly to this wreck of a man.

"Where were you when I needed you, eh?" Pelle demanded. "When that brat worked foul magic on me? Look at me!" He ran a bony hand through his hair and pulled out a clump. "Look at me, Revin. They're trying to kill me, and you left me alone with that pack of vargs."

"Prince Oreyn couldn't work a spell with a talisman and a sheet of directions, Majesty. He has no head for it, no patience, or discipline."

"Then it's that witch."

Vikar wasn't entirely clear which woman Pelle referred to, so he side-stepped the discussion, which would lead nowhere.

"Majesty, I've come to discuss the possibility of Oreyn's marriage."

"Who'd take him?"

"Arrezko, apparently. There's a second offer, but I don't consider it particularly worth your time."

"Arrezko?" Pelle leaned forward. "What sort of dowry are they offering?"

"There is no firm amount mentioned yet, but the suggestion is that it will be substantial, at least according to the queen. It will be up to the ambassadors to make a formal offer, and that's why I've come to you now. I want to tell King Wouder that we are open to a negotiation."

"I don't know." Pelle's fingers scraped the arm of his chair. He had scraped a rut in the wood.

"We can use the money, though I'm not sure it will make the kingdom wholly solvent again. And so I would also like to discuss the possibility of raising taxes very slightly."

"No."

"Majesty—"

"I said no, Revin. The people love me for keeping their taxes low." He sat back and sighed. "Someone has to love me."

"Then at least speak to Wouder's representatives."

There was a long silence while Pelle's dulled eyes stared out the window where a sarcot tree was budding in the warming sunlight. "If he marries and gets a son from his wife, Pelle is no more," he said. "Perhaps that's for the best, eh Revin?"

Vikar didn't know what to say. He had never seen Pelle in such a state of mind.

"Tell Wouder we will entertain his suit. Tell all the petitioners that we will consider their offers. I might as well sell the brat to the highest bidder."

"Should we make inquiries off-continent, Majesty?" Vikar asked.

"No, not unless we have to. Let's get this over with."

***

Vikar summoned the Arrezkan ambassador, Johannes Bondt.

"Their majesties are open to the offer of marriage between the Princess Saskia and Prince Oreyn. Naturally the prince wishes to know more of the young woman before he agrees to share his life with her. And there would be the matter of the dowry."

"Of course, of course." The old man offered an avuncular smile intended to disarm. "We are prepared to discuss the matter."

"Are you empowered to engage in preliminary talks?"

"I am. Though not to make any promises."

"Then just between us, why does Wouder want this alliance?"

"I don't suppose there is any single pressing reason, Vikar. Rather, there are several tactical ones that might be satisfied if our kingdoms were allied."

Tactical. That wasn't something he'd expected, but he supposed he ought to have done. "Lostri and Eresumma?"

"I've not said so, but I've not dismissed the notion either," Bondt replied, proving why he'd been such a successful negotiator for so many years. He was good at saying much while saying nothing. "I happen to know that Feracia has made an offer."

"I couldn't say."

"I said I know this, Vikar. I've known for a while."

"Of course you have. Foolish of me to imagine otherwise."

"And how does the Pellires family view that offer?"

Vikar made a vague gesture. "We are weighing our options."

"What options do you suppose you have?"

"Princess Darcha of Albhain is—"

"Twelve years old."

"We can wait," Vikar said. "We are in no hurry."

"Albhain wants no part of the Pellires family as it stands now, allied by marriage to Feracia, and represented—please forgive my blunt speaking—by a lazy cretin who beats animals and servants."

Vikar was silent.

"I hope I have not given offense."

"Not to me. Johannes, I know Oreyn is no prize. I honestly don't understand why Wouder would sell one of his daughters in marriage to him for any tactical advantage. I don't know why Queen Annemeike would allow it."

"I am not at liberty to disclose my king's plans. Or the queen's. All I can say is that the match is advantageous enough that they are willing to take the chance."

"All right, I will advance the suit on this end. Will you do the same on yours?"

"I will."

"When can we look forward to meeting the princess?"

"Let me contact King Wouder. I'm sure he's anxious to resolve this."

And then, with no time to lose, Vikar approached the Feracian ambassador to tell him that they would consider the Feracian offer of marriage.

Messengers went out to the ambassadors of King Rugenius of Vartaris, and Connla of Albhain suggesting that Corraçao would be open to an alliance between its royal family and theirs. If he was going to negotiate, he was going to do it from a position of strength with multiple offers to dangle in front of the representatives from Arrezko.

He was going to get a good price for Oreyn before he left this place.

***

He felt the tug of the cards a few nights after his return from Albhain. Jeskil. It wouldn't do to ignore him; his cousin was relentless.

"Hallo, Cousin, what can I do for you?" he asked the small figure that leaped up as he laid out his deck upon a table worn into silky smoothness by generations of use.

"I wanted to see how your plans are progressing."

"Quite well."

"Have you resigned yet?"

"Not yet, no. We're in the midst of some delicate marriage negotiations."

The little flickering figure put its fists on its hips and regarded Vikar with a sardonic expression. How on earth did Jeskil put so much personality into these insubstantial messengers?

"You mean," he said, "that you're back to being Counselor Revin of Corraçao."

"Only until my business is completed," Vikar protested. "I told you."

"Your business will never be completed."

"It will, I sw—"

"No, Cousin, never swear to something we both know is untrue."

"What do you want me to say?" Vikar asked, suddenly tired of defending himself. This was his life, his choice.

"That you are finished beating your head against the wall of state. It's not your country."

Vikar felt sad, suddenly, as if he had lost something precious. "You and I have no country anymore. We have to make the best of what we have left."

"The circus is my country, Cousin. It could be yours as well."

The silence stretched out between them, as if there was nothing more either of them could say to convince the other. Finally, Jeskil said, "You know I'm behind you no matter what you do, don't you? We're family. Family first, Vikar."

"Family first," Vikar echoed. It was one of the last things Caelea had said to him. "And honor?"

The little figure laughed. "Have it your way. You always do."

12.

Rain Moon, CR 549

Replies to Vikar's official overtures came in quickly. It seemed that even Oreyn was worth some consideration in the royal marriage market despite his unfortunate reputation. Albhain graciously pointed out that the Princess Darcha was far too young to form any such alliance, but it was not outside the realm of possibility that, at some time in the future, Prince Roran might make an offer for one of Oreyn's sisters. It was a polite refusal, better than Vikar had expected from the greatest power on the continent, one that had no investment in sugarcoating its disdain.

Vartaris was interested but not willing to commit to anything beyond a negotiation. Providing the auguries were positive, they said, they would be open to further talks. Vikar didn't expect much, but it was enough to give his position a bit more weight.

Feracia was thrilled that Corraçao was prepared to accept their offer, and Vikar was forced to reply that they had accepted nothing but the possibility of a negotiation. Hartan was Wismar's agent in this, and he was aggressive in pushing the suit. His reply was petulant, implying that Corraçao was reneging on a promise. Vikar, who was mightily tired of the Talians, replied that under the circumstances, if the Duchess was offended, Feracia could shop her out to someone else.

A reception was arranged for the representatives of each royal house. Pelle and Roxanna would, of course, attend, and Oreyn if he could be reined in. Offers would be discussed, nothing would be decided, but it would show them all that Vikar, and therefore Corraçao, were not without options. Even the Albhanian ambassador was willing to attend in spite of his government's rejection of the Corraçao suit. It was a generous gesture.

On the night in question, the ambassadors, representatives, their aides, guests, husbands, and wives all milled around the reception room, eating and drinking, making what passed for small talk at that level of government. Ambassador Johary from Vartaris told a long, involved story about pirates from the Aryvian Sultanate attempting to raid some of Vartaris's outlying islands but being pushed back by the Peorans, who subsequently ate their captives. "They sent the skulls to King Rugenius who, fearing to offend, has put them on display in the throne room." Several of the ladies gasped, and Johary chuckled. "Personally I think he likes the effect."

Just then the arrival of the royal family was announced, and Pelle entered, followed by Roxanna and the children. Pelle's mouth was drawn down at the corners, making his thinness even more alarming. Oreyn looked sullen, the girls cowed and unhappy, but Roxanna was queenly. Vikar was not unaware of the irony that this interloper who had gained the throne by guile was the most regal member of the family. They took their places, and Roxanna began to speak for them.

"We are so pleased to welcome all of you to this gathering. Our son, the heir to the throne of the great country of Corraçao, is of an age to be married, and therefore we have decided to give due consideration to all the offers before us."

"Can we get on with this?" Oreyn asked. "I want to meet the girls."

Roxanna colored, and Pelle tried to cuff his son, but Oreyn ducked away.

"We are prepared to hear your offers," Roxanna said. "Counselor Revin, will you present each representative to us in order of arrival?"

The first, predictably, was Hartan, who had arrived two days before anyone else. He had the duchess in tow, a small, weedy girl with white-blonde hair, a snub nose, and far too much jewelry for a girl her age. She was smiling in an unfocused way, as if she wasn't sure who she should be smiling at.

"Your majesties, I have the honor to introduce the Duchess Wilhelmina Haase fonFulkenheim, heiress to the Fulkenheim lands and titles."

The girl curtsied, and Oreyn laughed. "Uncle Hartan, you've brought me a pet monkey! How thoughtful."

Hartan snarled at his nephew, but Vikar noted that the smile never left the duchess's face, as if she didn't understand that she'd just been basely insulted. Or possibly she'd not been educated to speak the common tongue of Eiliron.

This time Pelle's blow connected, knocking Oreyn backward. "You will keep your mouth shut or leave this hall," he hissed. And Roxanna leaned forward and said, "Oreyn, behave like a prince or leave here now."

She turned to Hartan. "Brother, we apologize. This is not an easy situation for our son, who has many concerns about marriage and his kingdom."

"We will speak of this again," Hartan promised.

"I don't doubt it," she replied.

Oreyn was glaring at his parents, murder in his eyes.

Ambassador Bondt came forward and presented Pelle and Roxanna with a miniature portrait of the Princess Saskia. "Their serene majesties, King Wouder and Queen Annemeike, send their highest regards to Corraçao and its ruling family, and an offer of marriage between Prince Oreyn and Princess Saskia."

"She didn't come herself?" Oreyn asked. "I'm not marrying a picture."

"Oreyn, be quiet!" Roxanna snapped.

"Are you empowered to negotiate terms?" Vikar asked, trying to move the audience out of the muck of Oreyn's bad manners.

"I am."

"Then we look forward to discussing this with you, and perhaps meeting the princess in the not-too-distant future?" Roxanna told him. "She looks like a lovely girl."

"Thank you, Majesty."

Oreyn jumped up and grabbed the portrait from his mother. "Well that's an improvement at least," he said.

"That's enough. Nori-Gant!" Roxanna barked. "Take him away now."

The nurse came forward out of the shadows and caught hold of Oreyn's arm. He dropped the miniature and seemed to relax. "We're leaving now, my little one," she told him, and he followed her out without a word. Her witchery over the boy was worrisome, but for that moment, Vikar was grateful for it.

"Our apologies," Pelle said.

"No need, Majesty. It's a difficult time for the boy, as we have heard." Bondt's expression was one of practiced sympathy. "I look forward to our discussions." He bowed and stepped back.

Ambassador Johary was next. He bowed, greeted the king and queen, and then said that Vartaris was not prepared to make an offer at this time. Behind him, in the crowd of Vartarian nobles, stood the Princess Catenia, Hartan's wife, with their two eldest children. Vikar had put a watch on her as soon as she had entered the palace, but he had to step carefully to avoid insulting both the Feracians and the Vartarians. "The auguries, you know," Johary explained. "They were confusing."

Catenia nodded to Hartan, who raised his eyebrows and returned a sly smile. They'd certainly had a hand in keeping Vartaris out of these negotiations.

Finally, the Albhanian ambassador came forward and greeted the royal couple warmly, and with assurances of the great affection King Connla had for his royal cousin Pelle. "His Majesty is unhappy that his daughter, the Princess Darcha, is too young for such a marriage, but assures their majesties that Prince Roran will be of an age to marry as your daughters become old enough to make a match. He wishes me to say that we might revisit a union between our countries at that time, if you should choose to negotiate one."

"Thank you, my lord," Roxanna replied, though without warmth. She understood that Albhain wanted no part of her son, nor did they need Corraçao's goodwill.

There were no other offers to consider, so Roxanna thanked everyone and took herself off. Only Pelle remained, and all he wanted was food. He was always hungry, but the more he ate, the thinner he grew.

Roxanna went directly to Oreyn's apartments. She was angry at him for his behavior, but also outraged on his behalf for the slights of Vartaris and Albhain. She found her son with Nori-Gant. "Leave us," she told the woman.

"I don't think you want that." There was a warning in the nurse's voice.

"Oh very well, I don't care. Oreyn, your behavior was—" But before she could finish, he leaped up and struck her hard in the face with his open hand, knocking her down. He began to kick her, and Nori-Gant stopped him, telling him to sit down and keep his mouth shut. Then she extended a hand to Roxanna and muttered, "Told you."

"I'm your mother, Oreyn! How dare you?" Roxanna sputtered as she got up off the floor, wiping the blood from her lip. Oreyn wasn't cowed.

"And I am going to be king soon. If you ever speak to me without respect again, if you ever correct me or shame me in public again, I will have you put away, you venomous reptile. When I'm king, I will find a dungeon so deep that everyone will forget you ever existed." His fists were clenched so tight the skin had gone white.

She shot a look at Nori-Gant, who shrugged as if to say, "I can't do anything with him," which was an obvious lie. Roxanna suspected that she approved of what Oreyn had done; it was just another wall she was building between mother and son.

Roxanna removed herself from the room with as much dignity as she could muster, though she heard Oreyn hissing "snake" under his breath.

But she knew she'd made a choice and was paying for it now, letting the old woman nurse her child, letting her love him, raise him, become a mother to him by slow, almost imperceptible degrees, usurping Roxanna's place not only in his life but in his heart.

But in spite of all the abuse, all the vile behavior, Oreyn was part of her, and she loved him in a way she hadn't thought possible. Every other affection she had ever felt, even her passion for Pelle in those early years, paled by comparison to the love she felt for her children, particularly her firstborn. He was a monster, but he was her monster.

She would have had more children had Pelle not become incapable. She would have populated a small country with her children and grandchildren if she could have done. She loved them fiercely and forgave them for everything. And that, she knew to her sorrow, was one reason why they had become who they were.

And the way he looked at his sisters. It made her uneasy.

At Roxanna's request, Nori-Gant had piled magicks upon magicks to make Oreyn stronger, fairer, more a prince, more like his father. But magic couldn't make him kind or decent, or even stable. She had begun to understand why magic was a capital crime in Feracia.

With a bruise darkening on her cheek, Roxanna went to Revin, who was the only man she felt she could trust. The irony of that was not lost on her. "I need advice," she said, limping past him into his office.

"I would have said medical attention," he told her, pulling up a chair and making her sit. "Who did this? Was it Oreyn?"

She had forgotten how much this man saw. "I'm worried for the kingdom," she confessed.

"You should be. Your son has become a liability."

With a sigh, she nodded and said, "His behavior... I fear he has ruined his chances of a good marriage, and perhaps that of his sisters as well." She covered her eyes with a hand and was horrified to realize it was shaking.

"No, Arrezko is still willing, as is, of course, Feracia. That they're here at all proves that." Then Vikar's voice softened. "May I give you something for the pain?" he asked. She nodded.

He fixed her a draught of a mild painkiller. "Drink it all; it will help." Then he sat down opposite her. "We have been uneasy allies at best, and I have had occasion to wonder if I did the right thing in protecting you, but here we are, and we have to make the best of things."

Over the years she had learned to appreciate Revin's honesty and intelligence, as well as his devotion to Corraçao. She was willing to listen to anything he had to say. "What do you suggest?"

"First, I think we need to arrange marriages for the girls, and send them away to be fostered."

It was like a blow to her. "You want to take my girls from me?" He would leave her with nothing to love and care for.

Vikar's voice was firm but kind. "You know how he looks at them. You know it's only a matter of time before he harms them in some way. I want to send them to Albhain and Vartaris. Connla and Rugenius are willing to entertain the possibility of betrothals and fostering."

She sighed. "Because this court is unwholesome."

"Because we would insist on it. The princesses must be safe."

"It would be a kindness," she murmured. "I see that, of course. But my husband hates me, my son hates me, and with my girls gone, there is nothing for me but a slow decline." She felt old for the first time in her life, but understood the wisdom of Vikar's plans. "I will do whatever you think is best, Counselor. I want my girls to be safe. That's more important than anything else."

"And I want the kingdom to be safe. Local marriages will strengthen our alliances as well as protect the princesses."

"Thank you."

"Now, I'm sorry, but I must ask about the king's ill health. He has been failing for years now, we both have seen it. But in the month I was gone, he has become a wraith. Tell me, please, what kind of magic has been worked on him?"

"Magic? Not by my hand or my will, Revin, I swear it to you. I love the man. Though in his illness he has lost so much of his sweetness. Do you mean that you think someone is harming him with magic?" She was shocked, though she supposed she ought not to be. "Nori-Gant," she breathed. "You believe it's Nori-Gant, don't you?"

"The old woman works the magic for her own ends?" he muttered. "I don't know. What would she gain by it?"

"She'd put her darling boy on the throne."

"True. I've also wondered if she does it at your brother and sister-in-law's bidding."

Roxanna's jaw set in anger, and she slammed her fist down on the wooden table. "If we find proof she has been harming Pelle, I will have her quartered and throw the pieces to the pigs. I will put her head on a spike." She was surprised to see Revin smile a little.

"Please don't destroy my table," he said with gentle humor. "We have to find out what she's done to him—if it is her doing—and if she is working for someone."

"Torture her."

"While I appreciate the directness of your plan, we would do better to step carefully. I don't know what she's capable of, and her magicks are so alien to me that I can't find the threads."

"Find someone," she begged. "Find someone who can stop her."

"I will do whatever I can. In the meantime, do I have your leave to negotiate for betrothals and fostering for the princesses?"

"Yes. Yes. Do what you must to keep them safe."

"And I will present the offers of marriage for Oreyn from Arrezko and Feracia as soon as I have them in hand."

"Arrezko," she said. There was no question of an alliance with Feracia.

"What?"

"We will accept the offer from Arrezko. We will not ally with Feracia."

"Um, are you certain? Have you spoken with Pelle about this?"

"I don't need to, Counselor. I want nothing more to do with my brother's plans, and Pelle cares nothing for what happens to his children."

Vikar bit his lip and looked as if he was about to suggest a little more consideration of the matter, but she stood and looked down at him. "I appreciate your help and your counsel, I respect your opinions even if I do not always agree, so please respect my wishes in this. I will not tie my son or my kingdom to Feracia or be in any way beholden to Hartan and his wife."

"Understood," Vikar said. She would not be moved in her decision, and he was wise enough to accept it.

"Counselor, my husband doesn't care," she told him. "About anything. He is waiting to die now." She felt tears rise, and she turned away. "My brother will be displeased, I expect."

"An unlooked-for perk," Vikar said, and in spite of the flood of misery she had been feeling, she laughed.

"I am always glad to have some common ground with you," she said. And she left him to his work.

Not ten minutes after Roxanna left, a knock sounded at the door, and Vikar opened it to find Bondt standing before him, a broad smile on his face.

"Shall we get these children married off?" he asked, and Vikar said, "We can discuss it." Even if Roxanna wanted this marriage, it couldn't hurt to negotiate for good terms. That's why he was there, after all.

Bondt sat down in a chair in front of the fire, stretching out his long legs with a sigh of relief. "Foul weather we're having. But at least there's a good, roaring fire and, perhaps, something warm to drink? Is that mountainberry brew I smell?"

"There's always a jug of it on my hearth," Vikar told him and poured two cups. "Now let's talk terms."

Bondt presented his king's offer, which was generous enough that Vikar wondered what Arrezko hoped to get out of the relationship. Then, since all the cards seemed to be in his hands, he asked Bondt outright what King Wouder stood to gain.

"You're old enough to recall the fall of Eresumma and the partition of Lostri. Do you also recall that Feracia invaded Arrezko that same year?"

Vikar nodded. He was sharply aware of every incursion made by Feracia in those wars. "That was when Albhain stepped in."

"Yes. Too late for Eresumma and Lostri, alas, but Albhain's aid helped us beat back the Feracian forces, though we were unable to regain the territory we lost."

"So this is about Feracia and the disputed territories?"

"To some degree, yes. We recognize the ties between Feracia and Corraçao and are, to be quite blunt, not anxious to see those ties strengthened with another marriage. Arrezko and Lostri's government in exile both have much to lose if Corraçao becomes an ally of Feracia, and perhaps much to gain if Feracia is surrounded by allied countries. More leverage, I think we could say."

Vikar had suspected something of the sort. To be allied with Arrezko would be nearly as good as an alliance with Albhain. "Bondt, I appreciate your candor, and I understand your concerns. I cannot give you a final answer at this time, but I will take this to their majesties for consideration."

"Then have them consider this, Revin; if the prince weds Saskia, in addition to her dowry, Arrezko cancels all debts it holds against Corraçao."

It was an enormously generous offer; too generous. Vikar couldn't help but wonder if there wasn't some other reason why the Arrezkans were so set on this marriage.

As if Bondt could read Vikar's thoughts, he nodded and said, "Arrezko has a long memory, my friend."

"And you are allied with the government of Lostri in exile."

"We are. And their interests are similar to our own."

"And the Princess Saskia is content to play pawn in this game of yours?"

Bondt sat back and laced his fingers over his ample belly. "The princess is a remarkable young woman. She is committed to this marriage because she understands that it will strengthen both kingdoms. You might better ask if your prince is willing to do his duty to his country."

Vikar wondered if Saskia had any idea of what her future husband was really like. Even a remarkable young woman might find herself questioning her commitment to a marriage with someone like Oreyn. But it wasn't Vikar's place to warn either Bondt or the Arrezkan monarchs.

"He will do what he's told," Vikar promised.

"Are you sure?"

"I am."

"Well then, I will send a message to King Wouder." He grinned. "Because I'm guessing you'd rather eat ground glass than have a Pellires married off to that little Feracian wraith."

"Poor girl."

"She seemed addled," Bondt observed. "Not much of an offer, was it?"

"It did have its advantages." Chiefly that Vikar didn't imagine the girl would make any trouble no matter how miserable Oreyn made her. There was something to be said for a slow, tractable girl who would do what she was told and produce a pack of princes.

At that, Bondt stretched and stood up. "I do think we understand each other, Revin. Yes?"

"I believe we do." They shook hands.

"I will suggest to the king and queen that Saskia might want to meet her future husband before the wedding."

Vikar agreed. He walked Bondt out and took the opportunity to stroll down to the garden, which was silent and empty in the gathering dusk. The rain had stopped, and the cooler air cleared Vikar's head as he paced the cobbled paths. He glanced up at the sky, dappled with stars, and smiled, remembering how very like Azur, Oreyn was. How nearly like a twin. Jeskil would fight him, of course, and Reyna, but based on what he'd observed, and what members of the troupe had told him about the boy, Azur might have just enough ambition to step into the role, if it was offered.

With luck, this marriage would work out, Oreyn would grow up and become a decent king, so Vikar could resign his position without guilt. Without luck? There was one more way that a strong, capable Pellires heir could inherit the throne of Corraçao. And then Vikar would have to stay, at least until Azur found his footing. But the boy was smart and decent, and he would make a good king.

And the world would be better without Oreyn, Vikar supposed.

13.

Heat Moon, CR 549

It was unsurprising that the level of tension at court was high the week that the princess's party from Arrezko was due to arrive. Oreyn had been balky about the marriage but had recently become almost enthusiastic on the subject. Vikar guessed that Nori-Gant had something to do with it, whether by magic or by the tangle of emotions by which she bound the boy.

The heat was terrible that year, and Pelle was often absent from court, leaving Roxanna to tend to all the functions. She was a surprisingly capable monarch, serious but fair, a welcome change from Pelle's expansive frivolity that had cost the kingdom so dearly over the years of his reign. At least now, assuming the marriage would take place, Corraçao's considerable debts to Arrezko would be erased. Vikar felt that the marriage ceremony would be like a break in the heat; he would finally be able to breathe more freely once both were over.

Since the disastrous day when Feracia and Arrezko had both made offers of marriage, Roxanna and Vikar had worked together to secure agreements with Albhain and Vartaris for the princesses. Once Oreyn's wedding celebration was over, Maerys would be sent to Vartaris to be fostered with an eye to a betrothal to the Vartarian heir, Fortunatis—a coup if it came off. Rhaenne would be returning to Albhain with their deputation to be fostered until such time as she was old enough to marry Roran, who was only a second son and unlikely ever to inherit the throne. But it was a good match. And it was good to get the girls away from their brother. He hated them and they him. Roxanna had done well for her girls, and in spite of all his past reservations about her, Vikar had come to appreciate her intelligence and her diplomatic abilities. Had she ever showed that face to the Corraçaoan people, they would probably have come to love her rather than seeing her as the outsider who took Caelea's place. He should have counseled her to put aside all her natural reserve and show her abilities. He'd made foolish mistakes by focusing too much on Pelle and the children.

***

The Arrezkan party arrived in Trennin on a blisteringly hot afternoon and immediately withdrew to the quarters that had been prepared for them, much to Oreyn's annoyance.

"I want to see her!" he insisted. "I won't marry a fright."

"What difference does it make?" Roxanna asked him. "Close your eyes and do your duty."

He glared. "I want to see her now," he said, his fists clenched.

And as she often did, Nori-Gant stepped in and soothed him with a touch. "Time enough, little one. Come along."

Vikar found it unnerving how blank the boy went at those moments. Clearly Roxanna did as well because she sighed and shook her head. "I don't know what's right for him," she admitted to Vikar. "I never have known. And I have made such mistakes..." She let the thought trail off.

Vikar wasn't sure there was any right when it came to Oreyn, but he didn't say as much. "We will get through this," he promised her.

She reached out and touched his shoulder. "I wish we had been friends at the start," she told him just before she went off to tend to Pelle, whose mood had turned poisonous with the heat.

The meeting between the bride and groom occurred the next morning. Pelle was sullen and withdrawn, taking out his bad mood on Roxanna and the children. Oreyn was agitated, and the girls found places to hide from all the drama. But if Roxanna was anything but collected, she didn't show it. She was gracious to the Arrezkans, welcoming to the Princess Saskia, greeting her with the warmth of a mother greeting a daughter, and her steely demeanor cowed even Oreyn, who in his turn greeted the princess with civility, though without warmth.

The boy had to be pleased, Vikar thought. Saskia was a statuesque golden beauty with a peach blush to her cheeks and bright blue eyes that hinted at both a strong will and a sense of humor. She was a girl whose future was guaranteed, who had the weight and influence of the wealthiest country in Eiliron behind her. Vikar thought that she was what Roxanna could have been, had Roxanna been loved and supported by family and kingdom.

Oreyn was uneasy and sullen, though he didn't subject the gathering to one of his fits of temper. Instead, like his father, he withdrew emotionally. Saskia pretended not to notice, though she did try, from time to time, to bring him back into the conversation about the wedding.

In the end, Oreyn gave his assent to the marriage with a stiff nod, and Saskia, when asked, replied, "With pleasure, Your Majesties." It was agreed that the wedding would take place during the harvest festival, and Vikar allowed himself to hope that this union would work out after all.

At the close of the eventful day, he shared a cup of mountainberry brew with Roxanna, who told him, "Oreyn says she's too beautiful," leaving Vikar momentarily at a loss for words.

"Too beautiful?" he asked, trying to fathom what that might mean.

"Prettier than he is, I'm guessing. No, don't say it. I know he's a disaster."

In spite of himself, Vikar laughed. "If they will just give Corraçao an heir and a spare, disaster is averted," he reminded her. "And they can go off to live at separate ends of the kingdom if they like."

"That's what I told him. They'll make beautiful babies."

"That they will. To beautiful heirs," he said and tapped his cup against hers. "It's what we work for, isn't it?" They drank to the promise of a new generation.

"I don't know if I should stay in Corraçao after the wedding. Both Rhaenne and Maerys have asked me to come live with them in their new homes, but I don't know if that would be wise. And I do not want to go back to Feracia. Well, there's nothing for me there, in any event. What do you counsel, Counselor?" she asked with a smile.

"I think there's a place for you here, Your Majesty. You are the queen."

"Revin, I think you know as well as I do that Pelle is dying. When he does, I will be nothing again. Dowager queen, a woman with no husband, no children left to raise, no power or influence."

"Influence you would have," he countered. "As much as you choose to have, that I will promise you."

"Perhaps." She sipped the hot brew. "I will have to think on it. But not tonight."

"Perhaps not for a long time," Vikar countered.

She gave him a quizzical look. "We shall hope that is true," she told him.

***

The date of the wedding gave guests from all over Eiliron time to travel to Corraçao. Wouder and Annemeike of Arrezko arrived first with their unmarried children in tow, bursting with excitement over Saskia's betrothal.

It was a handsome, high-spirited family, all of whom seemed to bring fresh air into every room they entered. Roxanna envied them and their obvious affection for each other, and hoped that they would be good for Oreyn, and more, that Saskia would be good for him.

The betrothed couple had spent little time in each other's company since the date was settled, and Oreyn was uncharacteristically reserved around Saskia. They were always chaperoned, of course, and Roxanna told herself that once they could be alone together, once they could come to know each other, they would also come to care for each other.

She wished she could have married her girls into that family. They'd be well cared for. And loved. She wanted them to be loved the way she had once hoped to be loved.

When the Drurins of Albhain arrived with Roran, Roxanna wasted no time in introducing him to Rhaenne. That they seemed to like each other immediately made her happy. That King Connla and Queen Maeri seemed to like Rhaenne was a relief. It would be a good match, Roxanna decided. A safe one.

But she wasn't as sanguine about the meeting of Maerys and Fortunatis of Vartaris. They were clearly unimpressed with each other, though polite. Fortunatis seemed like a dullard, quite unlike his younger brother, Prince Rugenius, who enchanted

Maerys with his exquisite manners and all the attentions that Fortunatis should have paid her.

And then, when Hartan and Catenia arrived, Roxanna's mood soured.

"I've been avoiding them," she confessed to Vikar over their now-traditional evening mountainberry cup. "I honestly hate the sight of them."

Vikar nodded. "At least Wismar stayed away. His presence would have made things awkward when the representatives of Lostri's government in exile arrived."

"Perhaps that's why he stayed away. Remind me why we invited any of them?"

Vikar shrugged and sipped the hot brew. "It was political."

"Oh, politics. Of course. I wish I could see all of this as a simple political situation."

"I know it's more than that to you, but—"

"It wasn't criticism, Counselor. I do wish I didn't have such a personal investment in the outcome of the wedding and the two fostering agreements."

"They're your children; how could it not be personal?"

She nodded, appreciating that Revin understood what it was she was feeling, or at least why. She'd come to enjoy their evening discussions of state business, discussions that occasionally veered into the personal. Revin was a thinker, something Roxanna valued. "Counselor, promise me that you'll stay on in this capacity for my son and his wife. When the time comes," she added.

"I will give it due consideration," he promised. "The welfare of the kingdom is important to me. Speaking of which, I have not seen the king in days. Is he ill?"

"I don't know. Since the guests began to arrive, he's been in hiding. He's not happy about any of this and accused me of trying to replace him with Oreyn. I fear I was unkind in my response." She frowned into her cup. "I barely remember loving him. I know I did once, but when I search my feelings…" She let her thoughts trail off, then she looked up and blinked. "I'm sorry, Revin, I don't mean to make you uncomfortable."

"I'm not," he said, though she thought it was probably a lie of kindness. And in truth Roxanna felt guilty complaining about her life since, on the surface, it had been all she'd wanted. She had a secure position and was beholden to no one. And if the one man she'd ever truly cared for had changed so much that she barely knew him, well there were worse things to live through, she supposed. She would see her children safe and retire to live quietly.

Though sometimes it was difficult to envision that hermetic life, she felt even more so when one of the wedding guests, Sultan Orhan of Aryvia, who had always been attentive and even flirtatious, openly courted her over dinner a few nights before the wedding.

"With your son married and your daughters betrothed, your most important work here is finished," he pointed out.

"Thank you, my lord, for pointing out my redundancy," she replied, making him smile.

"That wasn't my intention. Far from it", he told her. "I only observe that you…that you will have more freedom after they are all settled." He leaned closer, and Roxanna could smell a warm, woodsy scent rising off his perfectly curled black hair and his tawny skin. There was no denying that he was a handsome man, as darkly attractive as Pelle had been brilliant and golden, the moon to Pelle's sun. "Thou art fair as a star in the night sky," he whispered. And for a moment, her breath quickened, though she tried to hide it.

"Sultan Orhan, please, I am a married woman."

"And I am a married man, several times over. In Aryvia we believe that marriage is a blessing to be shared."

She knew that under the laws of the Sultanate, men could have as many wives and concubines as they chose.

"I would not fare well as one of many, I fear."

Orhan took a sugared hawnut from his plate and placed it on hers. "If there is not enough to share, we do not offer."

"I do not speak of wealth, sir."

"Nor do I, my lady," he countered, and her breath caught as she took in the many possible meanings of his words. A shiver ran through her.

She clamped down on it. She couldn't do anything that might jeopardize the standing of her children in Eiliron. "You will say no more about this matter to me, my lord."

"If that is what you wish, then I shall withdraw the offer and speak no more of it."

"It is."

"But we will remain friends?" he asked.

Friends? Was that what they were? "Of course," she told him.

"Then I am satisfied." He turned smoothly and engaged the guest to his right in a conversation about trade.

14.

Harvest Moon, CR 549

The weeks passed quickly with all the preparations for the wedding. With Pelle unwilling to cooperate, all the work fell to Roxanna. And though she had the help of Revin and his staff, it left her with little time to attend to anything else. She left the children to Nori-Gant and was pleased to find that the old woman had convinced Maerys that her betrothal to Fortunatis was a good thing.

"Say what you like about the woman," Hartan observed as they dined together a few nights before the wedding, "but she does have her uses."

"Nevertheless I'll be glad to see the back of her," Roxanna admitted. She assumed that with Oreyn married and the girls gone, she could send Nori-Gant back to Vartaris with a nice pension and never have to think about her eating habits again.

"Yes, I expect it's time to cut the cord. Oreyn needs to be an adult now."

Easy for him to say, she thought. And later, when she found her son cowering in his room, weeping with anxiety over the wedding, she wondered if perhaps she would ever stop needing Nori-Gant. She wondered if she'd ever be free of her son, and then was filled with shame at the thought that she did not like

Oreyn. She loved him, she would do anything to help him, but like him? No, not in the least.

***

The day of the wedding was clear and bright, and the guests gathered in the great hall to watch the uniting of the two kingdoms. Wouder and Annemeike stood with Saskia, Pelle and Roxanna with Oreyn. Pelle, who looked fragile and uncomfortable, made no responses to the ceremonial questions, so Roxanna was forced to speak for him. Oreyn's responses were so quiet, the prelate was forced to ask him twice if he was prepared to do his duty to his wife and their children.

And when it was finished, Oreyn turned away from the expected kiss, and Pelle muttered, "Finally, we can eat." Roxanna was nearly weak with relief to have it done.

To her surprise, the wedding dinner was a light-hearted affair. With the pressure off, Oreyn loosened up enough to kiss Saskia's cheek when Wouder made a toast to the couple.

They looked beautiful together, Roxanna thought. Two fair and perfect children uniting two great kingdoms. She had done well. Now it was their turn to serve their people.

But as the night wore on and the newlyweds were gently urged toward the bridal chamber by both families, Oreyn grew sullen and withdrawn. In the end, Saskia retired, and he disappeared for the rest of the night.

"Jitters," Wouder said. "I had a bad case of them on my wedding night. He'll come around." He was a hearty, good-natured man, as easygoing as his wife, a man who would make a great ally for the future.

But on the second and third nights, Oreyn again avoided the marriage bed, and Roxanna began to worry. She went to Nori-Gant.

"Can you convince him to do what must be done?"

"I've tried," the old woman told her. She looked as if she'd aged a decade in the last few months. "The boy is afraid."

"Of what?"

Nori-Gant shrugged. "It's one of the few things he will not tell me."

"Can you do more?"

"Magic, you mean? No. I fear it would drive him to madness."

"Then teach him his duty. You're the only one who can. I have no hold on him," Roxanna admitted, understanding that she was giving up any claim to her son for the sake of the kingdom. Her role in his life was over; Nori-Gant had won.

Two more nights passed without the necessary end to the wedding ceremony. The Arrezkan guests made uneasy preparations for leaving Corraçao. While Queen Annemeike was delicate in her concern, her husband, whose patience was finally fraying, was blunter.

"What ails the boy?" he demanded over a family dinner which Oreyn did not attend. "Anyone would think he had no stomach for his duty. And with a wife so beautiful too!" Saskia stared down at her plate and said nothing.

Roxanna noticed that Pelle was flushed with embarrassment. "I will settle this," Pelle promised Wouder. He gestured to Revin, and Roxanna heard him whisper, "Find the brat, and take him to my study. Keep him there."

Later, when Revin returned and nodded to Pelle, the king rose unsteadily but with a set to his jaw that Roxanna recognized as a single-minded determination to have his will done without question or excuse. She grabbed her husband's arm.

"Let me go to him."

"It's my place." He didn't look at her. "Let me be his father for a change."

"You will not hurt him," she said, and he shook her off.

"See to our guests," he hissed at her and left the hall.

She shot an agonized glance at Revin, who came immediately to her side. "The prince is docile," he assured her. "There won't be a fight."

"Please," she said, and he understood what she wanted.

"Of course." He bowed and left the hall. She watched him go, turning back to her guests only when she heard Annemeike asking about one of the dishes.

"I'm sorry, I didn't hear—"

"This cake, I've never had anything like it. Where does it come from?"

With a sigh, Roxanna turned her full attention to the conversation. "A specialty of my home province in Feracia. We eat it only on special occasions."

"Most delicious," Annemeike replied. "Don't you think, my dear?" she asked her husband.

"It's a cake," he said, and silence fell on the company, finally broken when Saskia stood up and said, "If you will excuse me. I'm quite tired." It was going to be a long night, Roxanna thought.

Not long after both families had retired for the night, a commotion began in the tower that housed the family quarters. First there was shouting that came from the bridal chamber, then screaming. Roxanna, who was up reading, was the first to arrive in the hall outside the chamber where Oreyn and Saskia stood, howling at each other. Saskia was clutching a dressing gown around herself; there was blood on her lower lip, and a bruise darkening the left side of her face. Oreyn, half clad—and half mad from the look of his eyes, had claw marks down the left side of his face. His language was more suited to a waterfront brothel than a royal bedchamber. Where he had heard such things, Roxanna didn't like to think.

She tried shouting them down but couldn't make herself heard above their rage. Saskia was screaming, "Don't you touch me. Don't you ever touch me again, you monster!" and Oreyn was insisting that it was his right to do as he wished to her. *Dear saints, what had he done to the girl?*

And then Oreyn lunged at his new wife, fists clenched and ready to strike, and without thinking, Roxanna put herself between them. She got a fist in the face that knocked her backward into Saskia's arms, and both women fell back onto the stone floor of the corridor. Oreyn picked up a carved statue of Saint Grillo that was resting in a wall niche and advanced on them with murder in his eyes.

But as he lifted the heavy wooden statue, Pelle's voice rang out in the corridor as strong and commanding as it had ever been. "Oreyn, put that down now!" He shouted as he advanced, followed by a brace of guards, and Oreyn, who had never heard his father's voice sound with such authority, faltered just long enough for Revin to snatch the statue from him before Pelle's fist connected with Oreyn's face. The prince tumbled sideways, falling hard on his mother. Saskia scooted out from under Roxanna and back into her chamber. The sound of the door being locked echoed in the silent hallway just before Oreyn began to howl for Pelle's blood. He tried to scramble to his feet, but Revin muttered a few words, and the prince slumped, silent again, dazed-looking. Then his eyes closed and he fell back onto Roxanna, profoundly asleep.

"What did you do?" Roxanna asked as Revin and Pelle pulled Oreyn off her.

"He's asleep, nothing more," Revin assured her. Then Pelle sagged down onto the stones and began to cough violently.

"It's impossible," he wheezed between coughing spells. "The child isn't fit for a throne or a family."

He was right. She knew he was right.

Revin helped her up, then went to Pelle's side. "Calm, be calm," he said, and before long the wheezing and coughing eased, replaced by Pelle's short, gasping breaths.

"What can we do?" she asked the two men.

"One of the girls will be named heir," Pelle told her. "Which one has a brain?"

"They're too young," she said, and the look he gave her chilled her.

"I'm not dead yet," he said. "Have the courtesy to not treat me as if I was." He coughed again. There was an ominous rattle in his chest.

"No, my dear, I never intended—" she began.

"Revin, give me a hand up," Pelle said, and Revin helped him to his feet.

"Pelle..." But what was there to say, really? She had seen his end for a long time and feared it was closer than any of them wished. "You will be king for many more years," she said, trying to sound as if she believed it.

He turned away from her. "Revin, we need a solution. And we need Oreyn somewhere he can't hurt anyone until we can sort this out." He limped off to his chambers, supported by Revin.

Roxanna stood alone, looking down at her son, who looked angry even in his sleep. She gestured for the guards to take Oreyn back to his rooms. "Lock him in," she told them. "Set a guard on his chambers."

She was placing the statue of Grillo back in its niche when Saskia's door opened and the girl strode out. She was dressed for travel, not at all surprising. "My dear—"

"I am returning to Arrezko," Saskia said. "Please don't try to stop me, and please don't ask me to explain."

"I am so very sorry," Roxanna whispered. There was, after all, nothing more to say than that. "You must do what seems best to you." She wanted to say more, to explain, to tell her that Oreyn had often been a joy to her as well as a trial, that he had been a sweet child at first, and that she had had so many hopes for his future. But then Saskia's ladies arrived to help her pack, and Roxanna simply nodded and turned away. She didn't want any of them to see the tears that had begun to spill onto her cheeks.

The next morning, the Arrezkans left at first light. Pelle did not come to see them off, but both Roxanna and Revin came to the courtyard where their entourage was assembled. Revin spoke quietly to Wouder, whose normally cheerful face had turned stormy. Roxanna apologized again to Saskia, and the girl nodded, eyes fixed on some point in the distance.

The lively family was subdued now, as they took Saskia, and all of Roxanna's best hopes, back home with them. The weather had turned raw and cold overnight, but Roxanna had not asked them to stay on; there was no point. So she stood in the courtyard, wrapped in a plain woolen cloak, and watched as they left the castle, mute with misery and shame.

She'd tried to overlook Oreyn's behavior for too long, the rages and the irrational fears. She'd tried to make him into a golden prince who would be loved by the people the way his father had been. And this is where they were now.

"Your majesty?"

She turned to face Revin.

"We must talk," he told her, and she nodded and followed him back into the castle.

Once they were in her sitting room and she had dismissed her women, she said, "Before you say anything, I need to know if you can fix him."

"Oreyn?"

"Yes. You have magic. You keep it secret, but I saw it last night, and I need to know if you can fix him."

"No."

"Why not?" She was so cold. She couldn't recall ever feeling this cold. She was shaking with it.

"Because I don't begin to know what's wrong with him. Magic without knowledge is dangerous, criminal. We need a real-world solution, Your Majesty. And I have several in mind."

She sat opposite him in front of the fire, and she leaned toward it, drinking up its heat. "Very well. What can we do?"

"The first option is the king's choice, and the obvious solution. We bring back one of the girls and designate her the heir. Maerys would be my first choice as the elder, and arguably the more intelligent of the two girls, though Rhaenne might prove more tractable. With luck, the king will live until Maerys reaches her majority, and if not, you would become her regent."

"And my son?"

"The best thing for him would be to live a quiet life with a magical order in Albhain where they can restrain the worst of his behaviors and perhaps bring him some peace."

"Perhaps fix him?"

Vikar hesitated, then said, "It is not outside the realm of possibility, but we cannot count on it."

"What else?"

"There are Pellires cousins among the ruling houses and the nobility. I would have to consult the lineage, but one of them may prove acceptable."

"So there is no option in which my son will sit on the throne?" she asked, and hated the look of pity that crossed Revin's face.

"Arrezko will annul the marriage sooner rather than later, and even if the reasons for it never come to light, which is unlikely, the chances of a second marriage are dim. You would almost certainly be forced to accept a Feracian alliance, and if Oreyn proves unable to rule, which I believe we both know to be the case, the Feracians will control the throne. I would bet we'd see your brother made regent with the power of the Feracian throne behind him."

Roxanna nodded. "Let me think on these solutions. Is Oreyn awake?"

"I don't believe so, and that might be to the good. Sleep heals."

"Nothing will heal my son, I fear," Roxanna told him.

As Revin rose from his chair, there was a pounding on the door and the sound of shouting in the hall. He pulled the door open to see a wild-eyed guard with a raised fist. "What's wrong?"

"It's the king, sir. He's dead."

***

Although Roxanna had been prepared for the loss of her husband for a long while, she had not expected it to be accompanied by a gnawing emptiness, as if grief was devouring her from the inside. She followed Revin and the guard to Pelle's chamber where the king lay abed, his sunken flesh blue-white and waxen. Revin began to study the scene.

"What are you doing?" she demanded, feeling close to screaming at him. Her nerves were shot and she wanted to scream at someone.

"Looking for magical traces. This was no natural death," Revin told her, touching the bleached flesh. "His color suggests he died of suffocation." When he turned and saw the expression on her face, he said, "Your Majesty, please sit." And then as if in apology, he added, "I have to wonder. It's part of my job." He told the guard to bring some water for the queen and went back to his examination.

She found she couldn't speak for a time, but finally, after watching Revin inspect everything, she observed, "Even in death he doesn't seem peaceful, does he? My poor Pelle. You will see to the arrangements?"

"Of course," he promised, and she was content.

From Pelle's chamber to her own felt like a journey of miles instead of steps, but she held fast to her composure until she was inside her rooms, alone, door closed against prying eyes. And then she sank down onto the floor and wept.

She wept because she had loved Pelle, and because she had known for years that he did not love her. She wept because her children had lost their father. And she wept because she feared what would happen now. There should have been more time. Why was there never enough time?

Later, when she had cried herself out against the unyielding stone floor, she washed her face, changed her gown, and went to Oreyn's room. To her surprise he was up, looking bright and beautiful, like a smaller version of his father, and her heart lifted.

"I wondered when you would come to pay your respects to your new king," he said. He looked triumphant, and the love she was feeling for him curdled.

"I was paying my respects to your father." She wanted to ask him why he was not doing the same.

"He was a broken-down wreck. It was time for him to go," Oreyn said as he studied the map that lay in front of him, tracing the route of the west branch of the Janesse river down to the Strait of Restmark. "It seems to me that once I'm rid of the Arrezkan girl, I'll need to take another wife. I want a Peoran one."

"We—Peorans are not—they're a tribe of savages," she blurted.

Then he did look up. "Speak respectfully of my mother's people."

It was like a physical blow, this rejection by her own child coming on top of being widowed so suddenly. "She is not your mother!"

"Nori-Gant was always more of a mother to me than you were. She took care of me, nursed me, loved me."

"I loved you!" Roxanna insisted, angry now. "You are my son, and I love you."

"I never felt it," he said and looked back at his map.

"Oreyn, please. Your father is dead, and you and your sisters are all I have in the world. Can we not be a family?"

He grimaced but said nothing.

No use in pressing him on this, she realized. There would be time enough. She would put it right. "I must see to bringing your sisters back for the funeral."

"Oh don't bother. I've already given orders to burn the body and scatter the ashes on the rose garden."

Anger flared. "You don't dare show such disrespect to a king!" she shouted at him.

And Oreyn shouted back, "He is not a king. He's a piece of dead meat!" Then more calmly he added, "This is my kingdom now, and I'll do as I like. I am the anointed now, or will be as soon as we find a priest to do the job." He straightened and approached her, a bland smile on his face that was more frightening than his rages. "You are either with me or you're not," he told her. The threat was almost palpable, and in spite of herself, she shrank back from him.

"I'm your mother," she whispered. "And he was your father."

The expression on his face changed briefly to one of confusion before the bland expression returned, and he laughed.

"Not anymore." He went back to studying his map. "You're dismissed."

***

"Counselor, the queen is here to see you."

Revin looked up and nodded. He had been expecting her, but he had not expected her to be in such a state. She was shaking with anger.

"Have you heard about his orders to burn the king's body? How do we stop him?" she asked. "How do we control him before he destroys everything?"

"Yes, the captain of the guard informed me, and I countermanded the order. There will be a state funeral," Vikar promised as he led her to a chair. "You have my word on it."

"I don't know what to do. I'm afraid of my own child." She sank down and shuddered.

Vikar took her hand, a breach of royal etiquette, but he knew it was the right thing to do. "I am not afraid of him, nor are the palace guards, who prefer things to run smoothly. We will all work to make this right. I swear it."

"What of the army?" They both understood the power the military could hold for good or ill.

"They've been ordered to barracks. I will be speaking to the generals this evening. I believe we can count on their loyalty to the throne, if not the new king."

"Are they different?" she asked.

"Very."

She sighed and squeezed his hand before withdrawing it. "He wants to divorce Saskia and take a Peoran wife."

While Vikar had expected the divorce, he had not expected that Oreyn would want to remarry. He had certainly not expected that he would choose a Peoran wife, though he supposed he ought to have guessed. "Peoran? It's the witch's doing, I'll be bound. We'll find a way around this."

"He said something else that disturbs me." Roxanna repeated as much of the conversation as she recalled. "Then he said that it was time for Pelle to go." She seemed to be grasping for a way to speak of the unspeakable. But Vikar understood what she was saying.

"Only if someone else did the deed," Vikar told her. "Oreyn is not subtle; he would have left obvious indications of his involvement. But... the nurse?"

"After all these years, when she might have done the same or worse? Why now? Why, when the future of the royal family has been thrown into question by what happened between Oreyn and Saskia. Whatever it was," she added, and shook her head. "Neither of them have spoken of it."

Passing over the events of the wedding night, Vikar mused, "Indeed, why leave the country in turmoil?"

"Magic gone awry?" she asked.

"I found no sign of magic on him. Not even a breath."

Roxanna closed her eyes. "I'm no longer sure if I find that reassuring."

"I don't," Vikar admitted. "But I may be overthinking this. I've asked Doctor Tomeran to look for any signs of foul play when the body is prepared for burial."

"Poison, you mean?"

Vikar nodded. "Let's not assume anything. The king was not a well man. The stresses of the last year may have affected his heart." He noticed that Roxanna's face was twisted into a grimace of anger and grief. "Majesty?"

"Whoever hurt him, I will strip the skin from their bodies with my own hands. And then I will roll them in salt." She looked up. "You're shocked?"

"More surprised than shocked. I've long understood how dangerous a woman's rage can be. But it's another thing entirely to hear it spoken."

"To remain apart from this is beyond me, Revin. Not only do I have much to reproach myself for in the things I did to win him and keep him, but I promise you I came to love him truly even before our marriage, and had hoped—" The words caught and she covered her face with her hands. "How does one endure this sort of pain?"

"Living a day at a time is the only remedy," he told her. "Just live. It will get better. Now, do you feel able to help me plan the funeral and compose the letters that must go out?"

She wiped away the tears and nodded. "Of course. Where shall we begin?"

"A date," he said. "We'll chose a date to send Pelle to his final rest and work from there."

Once the date was chosen and the arrangements made, the messengers went out to the nobles of Corraçao and all the kingdoms of Eiliron with news of Pelle's death. Oreyn pretended not to notice that his orders regarding his father's body hadn't been carried out. Vikar wondered if he even remembered giving them. The boy's mental state concerned him, but there were other things to worry about just then.

Tomeran had reported certain oddities about Pelle's body. "A darkening of the heart," he told Revin. "As if it had been badly bruised. And there were also small perforations in the arteries. I have never seen anything like it before."

The symptoms seemed familiar to Vikar. "Anything else?"

"Of course I was not able to examine any other organs, only the heart when it was taken for preservation in the Hall of Kings. But I did see the chest cavity, and it looked similarly bruised." He paused. "This was no natural death," he whispered, despite being alone with Vikar.

"You will say nothing of this."

Tomeran nodded. "Understood."

After the doctor left, Vikar went to his library and pulled down a volume on poisons. He needed to be certain of his suspicions. It took him some time to track down the symptoms Tomeran had shared, plus what he had found in the king's chamber, the sheets wet and stained blue-black, and a chamber pot filled with black liquid. But finally he matched all those indications to chirdal, a fermented poison made from a plant root native to the mountains that ran along the border between Lostri and Feracia. He had expected a Peoran poison because he believed that Nori-Gant had killed Pelle to ensure Oreyn's ascension to the throne. But the location of this root was very specific: cold climate, high altitude. Of course the old woman could have bought the chirdal somewhere; it was rare, but not impossible to find if you knew who to turn to.

There was a knock at the door. It was the messenger he'd sent to Wismar of Feracia reporting the death of Pelle. "I did not deliver the message," the young woman confessed. "I think they already know. Feracian troops are massed on our border, Counselor."

Vikar was rattled. He had not expected open aggression from Feracia. "You will keep that news to yourself," he ordered her.

"Yes, sir."

"And send General Pascion to me."

She left, and he put his book back on the shelf. With Feracia still being held to the terms of the treaty with the other nations of Eiliron, this move was almost more dangerous to Wismar than to Oreyn, especially if there was any chance that Wismar had ordered or been in any way complicit in Pelle's death.

Pascion arrived, and Vikar filled him in on recent events. "I will, of course, be contacting Arrezko and Albhain for support, but until then I need troops at the ready."

Pascion sighed. "I think not, Counselor. I'm sorry."

Careful to keep his voice emotionless, Vikar said, "Explain yourself, General."

"You know as well as I do that the young king is not fit to rule."

"So you betray your country to the Feracians?"

"No sir!" Pascion protested. "This is the help we need to ensure a smooth transition of power if Prince Oreyn is judged incapable. The Feracians—the queen's own people, I remind you—will help us put the right ruler on the throne of Corraçao. If not Oreyn, then one of the princesses, with a Feracian regent until she comes of age."

"You're willing to trust that the people who almost certainly had King Pelle poisoned will give up power in Corraçao if it's freely given?"

He expected shock, surprise at least, but Pascion just shook his head. "No, Counselor, it was the nurse, Nori-Gant, who killed the king. The Feracians had nothing to do with it."

"What am I missing? What makes you think—"

"The boy has confessed that he asked her to kill his father."

"What? Why was I not told?" Vikar felt as if his head might explode. "What gave you the right to question him?"

"You would have protected him, would you not?"

"I would have found a way to the truth. We could have dealt with this together. I thought I had your support."

"You were meant to. I'm sorry," he said again, "but you know the army must and will act in the best interest of the country."

"As do I!"

"That remains to be seen. We will discuss it again when Hartan of Feracia arrives in Trennin."

Hartan. Of course. It began to make sense.

"Until then, sir, I regret to inform you that you, Prince Oreyn, and the queen are all under house arrest. You have free access to the living quarters, of course, but on no account will any of you be allowed in the public areas of the castle, nor will you be allowed to leave or have any contact with anyone but your guards. Should you have any requests, please speak to one of the guards who will be stationed outside your chambers."

"And may I communicate with my fellow prisoners, or is that forbidden as well?"

Pascion had the grace to look embarrassed. "The king is under close guard, so no, there can be no communication with him. With the dowager, yes, I will see to it."

"Why is the king under close guard?" Vikar asked.

"We believe he is a danger to himself or others." Pascion's brow furrowed. "Counselor, those rages of his, they're growing worse."

Rather than respond, Vikar asked, "Pascion, what did the nurse say when you confronted her?"

"She laughed."

"Is she under close guard?"

The general looked embarrassed. "She has disappeared. I hope we've seen the last of her."

"As do I, but I doubt it. Do I have leave to investigate her chambers?"

"No sir, I'm sorry. Not at this time."

"All right. Thank you for the information."

"I really am sorry about this, Counselor Revin. I hope we can clear up this misunderstanding quickly."

"Misunderstanding. Interesting word," Vikar murmured as Pascion left his chamber.

15.

Moon of First Frost, CR 550

"He must have been planning this even at the wedding," Roxanna said. She and Vikar were sitting together in her receiving room, sharing a meal. "But why? What does Wismar gain?"

"I don't know," Vikar admitted, though privately he thought he'd have been tempted to remove Oreyn from the throne too if he'd had the means.

"Has your famous intelligence network failed you?"

"Archness doesn't become you. But in fact, yes, this is a failure of intelligence. We've never had a strong presence in Feracia, but we should have suspected that something like this might happen in spite of the treaty."

"Hartan will be here by evening," Roxanna said. "I'm sure he'll tell us exactly what will happen then. My brother loves to talk, especially about himself."

But despite Roxanna's predictions, Hartan arrived in Trennin and immediately retired to Pelle's rooms to "eat and rest after a long journey." It was the following morning before he called them all together to discuss what was happening. Vikar was not shocked to see Nori-Gant standing beside Hartan's chair. The situation was becoming clear.

"I'm sad that Feracia needs to take a hand in this situation, but it was unavoidable. It seems that the death of King Pelle has left the kingdom in less-than-capable hands."

Oreyn was bound and gagged, held by two guards; he must have been impossible to manage any other way. He was glaring death at Hartan.

"With the support of Corraçao's army," Hartan said with a nod to Pascion and the other generals, "we propose to step into the gap left by Pelle's untimely death, and serve as regent to the new king, our nephew, until such time as he is deemed capable of reigning wisely and without our help." Apparently he felt emboldened enough to use the royal "we."

Oreyn made an animal noise and tried to shake off his guards. Vikar noted that Roxanna's face was carefully neutral. The cool, collected exterior was back in place. "Brother," she said, "we welcome your help and advice, of course, but your approach has not been a friendly one. If you withdraw your troops from our lands, we will gladly discuss on what terms we will be prepared to accept your advice and aid."

"I can't do that, sister," he replied. "It is my insurance against your compliance. I should also inform you that the Princess Rhaenne will be returned to Corraçao soon. There is a better marriage planned for her in Feracia."

"No!"

"You have no say in the matter," Hartan snapped. "King Wismar has been generous enough to arrange this marriage. As for Oreyn, Wismar has a niece who will suit him."

This time the objection came from Nori-Gant. "No!" she shouted. "That is not what you promised me."

Hartan flushed. "Be quiet, old woman!"

But there was no suppressing Nori-Gant. "I will not. I have tended to this child since before his birth. I have made him what he is today," she insisted.

Hartan sneered. "Look at him! He is no credit to you. Now be silent."

"I have done your bidding since before his birth, Hartan Talian, and nursed him at my own breast. I took his love and loyalty away from his parents, I ensured there would be no other women producing bastard heirs, I saw to the ruin of his wedding night, and to the weakening and ultimate end of his father as you asked. You promised me that I would have sway over the boy's future, and now you think to cheat me?" Her rage filled the room. "You will regret ever crossing me. I have done magic for you, Hartan Talian, against all the laws of your kingdom, and you will repay me as promised or I will carry this story to your king and curse your name for generations!"

Hartan lifted a hand. Nori-Gant spun around, saw the soldier looming behind her, and shouted, "I do curse you and all your line!" just before the soldiers grasped her by her beringed arms and dragged her out of the room, screaming curses the whole way.

No one moved until the sound of her shrieking died away. Hartan turned to Roxanna. "You should be grateful to me, sister," he said. "I've removed her malign influence from your family. For her crimes, for the murder of your beloved husband, I will have her burned. I know you'll enjoy that."

Oreyn began to scream into the gag that covered his mouth, sagging between his guards who dropped him on the floor. There he lay thrashing as if he was having a fit and beating his head against the stones.

"Get him up! Get him out of here!" Pascion shouted, and the guards hauled Oreyn to his feet and dragged him out of the room.

Roxanna stood. Her voice was low, but steady. "I curse you too, brother. For the death of my husband, for the evil magicks worked on my son—"

"By your request!" Hartan shouted as he approached her with rage in his eyes. Vikar caught hold of her arm and dragged her back.

"Never! I wished him only well!" she shouted back at her brother. "I wished him safe and strong, and as much like his father as he could be. I never wished for that madness she cast on him, or to have her steal his love from me! I curse you for the blight on my life, the theft of my future, the lies you told, and the plots you carried out against those whom you should have cared for."

Vikar stepped in between them then, because he could see by the expression on Hartan's face that Roxanna was in grave danger.

"Prince Hartan!" He injected just enough magic into his words to put up a wall around Hartan's rage. "Emotions are running high. May I suggest that we all retire to think about what will be best for the future of Corraçao?"

Hartan huffed like an angry bull, but the wall kept him in his place.

"We can meet again tomorrow. At noon." And again, Vikar injected just a touch of word magic into the exchange and saw that Hartan relaxed slightly.

"You both had best be willing to meet my demands," the prince said before he turned and left the room.

The queen turned her anger on Vikar. "How dare you?" Roxanna growled.

"Save your life?"

"Intrude."

"We can discuss this in private," he told her, and he felt all the tension in her release as she sagged in his grasp. "Let me help you, Your Majesty. You have had a difficult month." Again, a touch of word magic. Just a touch. Because the Talians could be their own worst enemies.

The magic fell away from Roxanna as Vikar pulled her along the corridor, and she stopped short, tugging her arm from his grasp, then smashed her fist into the side of his face. "How dare you lay hands on me? How dare you use magic on me?"

In spite of himself, Vikar was impressed; the woman could throw a punch. He rubbed his jaw. "You and your brother were about to do or say something that would make this situation much worse. I did what I could to stop it so we have time to think."

"About what?"

"Saving Oreyn and the throne. Come with me now," he told her and strode off, hoping that she would do as he asked.

"Talk to me," she said in a low voice as they reached Vikar's chambers.

"If we can get away from Trennin, I can get us into Albhain where we'll find sanctuary and aid. I hope," he added, ushering her inside.

"How do we get away?"

"With Oreyn it won't be easy."

"I won't leave without him."

"I don't expect you to, but you must give me leave to do whatever I think is necessary."

"Magic, you mean? Of course. Why not? It's done nothing but harm him all along. Why not let it save his life?" She sank into a chair and buried her face in her hands. "I should have sent Nori-Gant away before any of this started. I wanted so much to be everything Pelle needed, so I used her," she confessed. "And my family paid for it." She paused, closed her eyes, and took a calming breath. "I need to speak with her."

"There's no point." Vikar knelt in front of her and took hold of her wrists, pulling her hands from her face. "You did what you thought you had to. We have all done what we thought we had to do. Perhaps all this is our fault, but it's done, and we have to find a way to fix what we can."

"How is it your fault?"

"Peoran magicks are unfamiliar to me, and they're said to be primitive and ineffective. I believed that and underestimated the damage Nori-Gant could do."

"And here I thought you knew what you were doing," she said, and it took him a moment to realize that there was a spark of humor in her eyes and in her words.

"I thought so as well," he said ruefully. "My queen, we will come through this."

"I fear my son will not," she told him as the spark faded from her eyes. And though he didn't say as much, he thought the same thing. "Nevertheless, I need to speak with her. Can you see to it?"

He wanted to say he couldn't, that it was too dangerous, that they had no time. But somehow he understood that this wasn't a queen wanting to interview a traitor, but a mother wanting some sort of resolution to her worries, her questions and concerns. "I'll talk to Pascion," he told her.

And in the end, Pascion was not immune to the same argument that a mother's love had been betrayed. He sighed and nodded. "Go now. Hartan will burn the witch at dusk, and good riddance. I'll tell the guards to let you through."

Vikar led Roxanna down to the cells. "Don't let her touch you," he said. "I believe that Peorans may have a powerful touch magic that I do not begin to understand." Then he shaped a protective shield around the queen. "The protection won't last long, and we don't have a lot of time anyway, so keep it short."

She nodded and stepped through the door into a corridor lined with cells. They were all empty save for the one that held Nori-Gant. The woman was sitting on a cot, back straight, hands folded. She looked tired "Come to ask me one last favor?"

"No. You took him from me; I deserve to understand why."

"Payment then. Yes, of course, I owe you that much. The why is simple. Your brother promised me that he would make a marriage for the boy with one of my own people."

"A Peoran?"

"Why not? Hartan married one. A relative of mine." She sighed. "I would have thought Catenia would speak for me, but apparently she has not. So much for family, eh?" Then she seemed to soften. "But I did come to love the child. I do love him." When their eyes met, for just a moment, it was two mothers sharing a bond. "But I can do nothing for him now. I'll be dead"—she looked up through the barred window—"quite soon, I expect. And that will be the end of our sweet boy."

Roxanna went cold. "What do you mean?"

"I've held him together by magic for years. It was for his sake that I took all of Pelle's energies to give power to my magicks. Your husband failed because he wasn't needed."

"Did you kill him too?"

"Oreyn wanted him gone, and I never could deny him anything. Silly child was impatient. I scolded him for that. Do you know what he said?"

Roxanna shook her head.

"He said, 'Take what energies you need from my mother and sisters. I don't need them.' What a clever boy," she said with something like pride.

Roxanna pushed the thought away. "But what did you mean that it's over for him?"

"When I die, my magicks die with me. They will unravel quickly, I fear, in weeks." She sighed. "Or perhaps days. It would be a kindness to kill the boy now before it happens. He's quite mad, you know."

Roxanna felt sick. "Did we make him that way?" she asked, though she feared the answer.

Nori-Gant shook her head. "I could never have hurt him like that, nor could you. He was born wrong. I don't know why. I loved him so fiercely I kept the worst of it at bay, but it's stronger than I am."

Roxanna grasped the bars of the cell so tightly her hands grew white. "What is going to happen to him?"

"I have no idea."

"What?"

"I don't. I can't. The madness runs deep, and I've never found the wellspring."

Roxanna stared at the nurse, felt the wetness of tears on her cheeks. And though it cost her dearly she managed to choke out, "thank you for trying to save him."

"I took him from you."

"Nevertheless it was always for him, wasn't it?"

Nori-Gant looked up, nodded. "Yes." She sighed again and seemed to deflate. "I have not done right by you, Roxanna. I have believed their lies and my own. I see now that you truly loved your son, and so I lift my curse on you and your daughters. You will not suffer any longer for my mistakes."

"And my brother?"

"Will suffer and die, and soon be forgotten."

"Is there anything I can do for you?" the queen asked the nurse.

"Don't let my boy see me burn."

Just then Pascion appeared with half a dozen guards. "It's time," he said, and Nori-Gant laughed.

Roxanna stepped away from the cell and wrapped her arms around herself. "Can we not stop this?" she begged Pascion. "For the sake of the young king?"

"No, Your Majesty." Just that. No excuses, no explanations. It was a done thing as far as Pascion was concerned.

"Then as your queen I am commanding you to keep my son from seeing this barbarity. Send guards. Ensure that he knows nothing of what is happening."

"As you command." Pascion sent four of his men to the king's quarters with orders to keep Oreyn from knowing what was occurring. Then his men took Nori-Gant from her cell and marched her out into the courtyard where Hartan waited. Pascion offered his arm to Roxanna, but she shook her head, preferring to walk with Vikar, who waited just outside the cell block.

"Did you learn what you needed to know?" he asked as they followed the old woman's final walk.

"Only that nothing really makes sense anymore," she told him. "And that all this," she waved her hand, "will cost my brother dearly."

In the courtyard two stakes had been erected, and between them, a pile of wood. The old woman was tied between the stakes, arms tightly bound above her head as if she was asking favor of the heavens. She stared at Hartan with a curious mixture of amusement and loathing.

"You will burn, Hartan Talian. Like me, you will burn. And your flesh will be consumed, and your children will curse your name. You will be called traitor and fool by generations to come. This I promise you."

Hartan's jaw tightened and he gave a signal, then one of the soldiers stepped forward and set a torch to the pile of wood. It caught with an audible whooshing noise, fed by some kind of alchemical accelerant, and the flames shot upward, enveloping the old woman.

She never made a sound. Hartan looked disappointed.

Roxanna sagged against Vikar. She whispered, "I hope she didn't suffer too much."

And Vikar patted her hand. "I saw to it."

"So end all traitors and witches in this kingdom," Hartan announced. He stared directly at Vikar. "All magickers."

"A wise policy," Vikar said smoothly. "And now I must see to the queen."

"Dowager queen," Hartan corrected.

"Of course," Vikar said as he led Roxanna out of the courtyard. "Whatever you say."

***

Vikar was not idle that day. Between his influence and the prevailing dislike of Hartan and Feracia, he had no trouble finding confederates. Sheep carcasses from the kitchens were magicked into simulacra of Oreyn and Roxanna, and put in their beds. Oreyn himself was heavily drugged and put into the back of a peddler's cart. A glamour disguised both Roxanna and Vikar, and Vikar's loyalists saw to it that they were safely out of the castle and on the road before midnight.

Roxanna was very quiet as they fled the city, and though she relaxed visibly once they were outside the gates, she remained silent and withdrawn.

"Is there something you need to say?" Vikar asked her as they trundled along the road toward Lakan, which lay on the border of Albhain.

"I did not expect anyone to be willing to help us."

It was not what he expected to hear. "Why?"

"I have never been liked at court, and Oreyn"—she sighed—"he has been cruel and vindictive, and I wasn't able to curb him. Perhaps I wasn't willing to put myself at risk. I don't know."

"They're good people, the Corraçaoans," Vikar said.

"Yes. I see that now. So many mistakes," she said. "So many lost opportunities to be a good person too. I'm ashamed."

"You need to stop." His tone was sharper than he'd intended, but he didn't try to soften what he'd said.

"What?"

"If you're going to indulge in self-pity for the entire trip, you can walk."

She stared at him, eyes wide. "What?" she said again.

"I don't think I can stand days of breast-beating and self-recrimination. It's so boring to listen to."

There was a long moment of silence, and then Roxanna began to laugh. She laughed until tears ran down her face. "You're a horrible man," she said, wiping her eyes. "Thank you."

"Do you know why I like you?" he asked her.

"Because you're paid to?"

"Because you have such a lively sense of the absurd. I never realized it before we began to talk."

"I found it helped when I was growing up."

"Particularly with a brother like Hartan?"

"How did you guess?" she asked him, but he could see that she was smiling in the light from the full moon.

When they stopped to rest, Vikar checked on Oreyn, who was still unconscious. Once they'd eaten, Vikar pulled out his deck of cards and attempted to contact Jeskil, but there was no response. Jeskil knew they were coming; Vikar had contacted him before they left Trennin. But he wanted to keep his cousin informed about their progress.

They were on the road again when Oreyn finally woke with a shout of terror. Roxanna, who was sitting with him at the time, tried to calm him, but he was having none of it.

"She's dead! She's dead! She's dead!" he wailed.

"Oreyn, please."

"Take your hands away, don't touch me!"

At the sound of flesh striking flesh, Vikar halted the cart and climbed in back to find Oreyn about to strike his mother a second time. "That's enough!" he shouted, grabbing the boy's arm.

"Don't you touch me," Oreyn said, trying to wrench free. "You don't dare touch your king like that. I'll have you killed, I'll have you cut into pieces and burned, I'll—"

Vikar stopped the tirade with a slap to Oreyn's face. He hadn't meant to do it, but the boy had shattered his last nerve.

"You hit me!"

"It's not pleasant, is it?" Vikar asked him tartly as he helped Roxanna to sit up. "And I promise you I will do worse if you don't calm down and leave your mother alone."

"I'm your king. And she's not my mother."

"You're nobody's king right now, boy, and she's the only mother you'll ever have. Stop acting like a fool and listen. We're trying to save your life. You know your uncle would not hesitate to kill you if you get in his way, don't you?"

Oreyn glared at him. "He wants to make me king."

"He wants power," Roxanna told him. "He wants the throne of Corraçao for himself, I'm sure of it."

"We are in the middle of nowhere," Vikar told him, "so if you believe you'd be better off with Hartan, you're welcome to get out and walk. See if you can find someone to help you before you're murdered on the road. But if you continue with us, you will behave in a seemly manner or I swear to you I will tie you up back here and stuff a dirty rag into your mouth. Do you understand?"

Oreyn scowled but asked, "Where are we going?"

"To Albhain, to ask for help from King Connla. If Feracia has broken the terms of the truce, the other countries of Eiliron must stand behind you."

Vikar thought that there was something not quite right about the way Oreyn looked, flushed and feverish, as if he was sickening for something. "Come ride with me in front," he said to Roxanna, giving her a hand up. "Let the king consider his diplomatic options."

When they were seated and on their way again, Vikar asked her, "Are you all right? Did he hurt you?"

"I'm fine. It was nothing. Revin, the nurse told me that Oreyn was born wrong, that she was never able to find the wellspring of his madness, only to curb it. Do you think--." She broke off, seemingly unable to voice her concerns.

"Majesty," he began, and then, more quietly, he said, "Roxanna, tell me what she said. Everything. It would help me understand who he is, I think."

He listened as she described her interview with Nori-Gant. Vikar remained silent for a long time. Finally he said, "So it was not so much magic that harmed him as helped him. I'm not sure if we can work with that or not."

Roxanna went pale. "Before she died, Nori-Gant tried to tell me that her magicks would die with her. I thought she was lying to get me to save her life. What can we do?"

"Let's get safely to Albhain first, and then we'll worry about it."

Just then there was a sound of riders coming their way, and Vikar said, "Go in back and keep him quiet."

Roxanna climbed into the back of the cart and pulled the canvas flap closed behind her.

Vikar drove along at a leisurely pace, letting a mild glamour swirl around him, just enough to make him seem like a thoroughly harmless old peddler.

The riders came into sight, and he strained to see their colors. It was a mixed group of Corraçaoan and Albhanian soldiers. And at the head of the party...

"Cousin!" he shouted as relief made him giddy. He halted the cart and waited until Jeskil rode up with the soldiers at his back. "I didn't expect this."

"I can't trust you to do anything by yourself," Jeskil said. "And Connla was worried. He had a message about returning Rhaenne to Corraçao. It wasn't hard to convince him to send an escort. And when I explained to the captain of the Lakan garrison that a usurper had invaded the capital, he insisted on bringing his own escort. Captain Phrin, Counselor Revin."

The captain rode up and gave a soldierly nod. "May I ask where the king is?"

Vikar moved the canvas and told Roxanna and Oreyn to show themselves. "As you see, he and his mother are both safe."

"Captain, your concern for our safety is much appreciated," Roxanna said. Oreyn looked dazed and said nothing.

"Majesty, it will be an honor to escort you to safety in Albhain, and serve as your personal guard there."

"Thank you," she said. "I am much relieved." She came out and sat down beside Vikar, looking every inch the queen.

And then she saw Jeskil. "You!"

"Majesty, I believe we have much to discuss. But for now, I think we must make haste."

***

Vikar knew the boys were watching as their entourage arrived at the winter camp, knew they saw Oreyn and would mark his singular resemblance to Azur. He'd have to talk to them sooner rather than later, but for the moment all he wanted was a bed.

"You'll be fine here," Jeskil was assuring Roxanna and her son. "No better place to hide than a circus. For now, we have a spare vardo which I think you'll find quite comfortable, but I promise you a proper suite of rooms as soon as we can prepare one."

Phrin and his men took Roxanna and Oreyn to the circus wagon Jeskil had set aside for their use and stood guard around it.

"So much for blending in," Jeskil observed. "You look like you're on your last legs."

Vikar nodded. "Just about."

"Food?"

"No, just a bed. Oh, and the boys were watching."

"I know. So was Reyna. I'll talk to them."

"Thank you, Cousin. Now give me a place to lay my head and leave me to my rest."

Jeskil went to the kitchen of their apartments where Reyna and the boys all pretended to be surprised to see him. "Back so soon?" she asked.

"Mama, you knew he was home," Donnr insisted. "We saw him!"

Reyna bit her lip. "Well," she said, and the older boys both laughed.

"We did see you," Azur told him.

"And we have questions," Vari added.

"I know, and yes we will talk. But I want my supper."

While the family ate, they caught him up on what had been happening at the camp during his absence. After dinner, Mera took the little ones off to bed, and Jeskil sat back with a hot mug of mountainberry brew, finally able to relax after a tense trip.

"All right now, husband, our sons and I want some answers."

"Who was that woman with Uncle Vikar?" Vari asked.

"And who was that boy who looks like a pitiful copy of me?" Azur held Jeskil's gaze, and Jeskil sighed.

"Family, we are giving sanctuary to the king of Corraçao and his mother, the dowager queen."

"That woman," Reyna sniffed.

"That's a king?" Azur and Vari laughed.

"His father just died, he's been deposed by his uncle, and he's quite ill," Jeskil said quietly, and their laughter faded.

"Sorry," Vari said. Azur just looked annoyed at having his fun spoiled.

"Why does he look like me?" Azur asked.

Jeskil looked to Reyna for help. He had hoped this day would never come, so he had never prepared a speech.

Reyna reached out and took Azur's hand. "You look alike because you have the same father." Then she took Vari's hand. "You three boys all do."

"Wait... what?" Azur said, just as Vari said, "But different mothers, yes?"

"Yes."

She told her story. Jeskil told Caelea's story. The boys listened, Azur's face vivid with emotion, Vari almost unreadable.

In the uncomfortable silence that filled the room after they finished, Vari said, "Azur will be impossible to live with from now on. Your Majesty this, Your Majesty that, off with their heads."

Everyone at the table burst into laughter as the tension broke.

"Oh no," Azur insisted, wiping his eyes. "That's not the job for me."

"You'd love it!" Vari accused.

"Would not. Well, maybe a little."

Jeskil could tell that the boys were trying a little too hard to downplay the news, partly out of love for Reyna and himself, and partly because they both needed time to assimilate what they'd just learned. It hadn't been an easy thing to reveal to them, and it couldn't have been easy for them to hear.

"If you boys want to talk about this," he began.

"We're good," Azur said, much too quickly. And the look in Vari's eyes told Jeskil that there would be questions. Eventually.

***

Roxanna was lying in the bed at the front of the circus wagon. She was bone weary but wakeful in this new place. She heard movement, and then suddenly Oreyn was standing above her.

"Mother, I can't sleep," he whispered. It was something he'd sometimes done when he was a child, before Nori-Gant's influence over him became complete, and Roxanna knew what he wanted. She lifted the covers and he climbed in beside her, turning onto his side so she could hold him while he slept. She could have forgiven him of anything at that moment, just to hold him again the way she had when he was a child.

"All will be well." She stroked his hair and wrapped her arms around him. "All will be well," she said again as he tugged her arms more tightly around his chest.

"Mama," he whispered, and soon enough his breathing became deeper and slower.

She held him, and slow tears ran down her face because she could feel his body heat like an uncontrolled fever. Like burning. Her child was burning from the inside.

***

When Vikar finally awoke, Jeskil told him that Roxanna wanted to see him. "She's been plaguing me for hours, Cousin. Please talk to her."

"Do you know what she wants?"

"No."

He wasn't ready for another problem so soon, but he dressed and went to meet Roxanna where she sat in the empty circus hall, staring up at the stage. "I hear you're anxious to talk to me," he said.

"He's dying, I think."

"What?"

"My son. He's burning up, Revin, as if he was tied to the stakes beside Nori-Gant."

Vikar sat down hard on the bench beside her. "Are you sure?"

"I held him while he slept last night. I know what I felt. I know he realizes something is terribly wrong with him, but I don't think he understands what or why. She's going to take him from me, isn't she? She's dead and she's still holding on to him. Revin, I am resigned to the idea that my son will never sit on the throne of Corraçao, but I need to make his future safe. Comfortable if we can. Whole if that is possible. Can we not save his life?"

Vikar didn't suppose it was, but didn't say as much. "I will do all I can," he promised. "I'll contact the magisters and see if there is anyone who might understand what's happening."

"Thank you." Then she looked him in the eye. "What is it you want to do?" she asked. "About Corraçao, I mean. I know you have a plan."

"I do. One that preserves the appearance of stability, if not the fact of it, and will give the people a figure around which to rally."

A tiny frown line appeared between her brows. "How will you do that? Not one of my girls, they're too young, and my brother and Wismar will find a way to take advantage. I want them out of danger. I will not destroy what's left of my family for the sake of a throne."

"No, not the girls. Come with me." He stood and held out his hand. With a sigh, Roxanna took it and followed him to where the puppet theater was rehearsing. Merrypike was on the stage, and as Roxanna and Vikar drew closer, the puppet cried, "All hail the Queen of Diamonds."

Roxanna looked shocked, then she laughed. "Queen no more, my lord Merrypike," she said.

The puppet seemed to study her for a moment, then he asked, "Then have you come to join the circus?"

"What would I do?" she asked him. "I have no talent for entertaining."

"You have walked a fine wire for years, my lady," Merrypike said.

Roxanna's laughter faded. "Show yourself, sir. I don't spar with those I can't see."

Merrypike slumped, and Jeskil came around the side of the theater to join them. "Your pardon, lady," he said. "I'm often caught up in my own wit."

She hesitated for a long moment, then asked, "But sir, how can that be when it's so small?"

Jeskil roared with laughter. "Cousin, you must convince her to join us."

"I brought her here to meet the boys," Vikar said.

"You're sure?"

Vikar nodded.

"Azur, Vari, come on out here. There's someone you need to meet."

Roxanna's face froze when she saw them. Jeskil stepped forward.

"Queen Roxanna, may I present my sons, my adoptive sons," he added after a moment's hesitation, "Azur and Vari."

She was silent for a time, her face pale. "I see their parents in them," she whispered. Then she turned to Vikar. "Did you know? Why was Corius taken from Corraçao?"

Jeskil turned to the boys. "Go on off and help rig the wire." Once they were gone, he turned to Roxanna. "You and I had a long conversation about that just after his birth." The expression on her face made him chuckle. "No, I didn't think you'd remember it because I was convinced even then that it wasn't you.

"We think it may have been your sister-in-law glamoured to look like you," Vikar told her.

"Did you know about all this?" she asked.

Vikar gave his cousin a sardonic look. "Not until fairly recently, no. But given the circumstances I think Jeskil did the right thing for the child."

"The woman I spoke to wanted me to murder the prince."

"A child? A babe in arms? What sort of monster--." She looked from Jeskil to Vikar. "So this is why you came to me and asked those questions." And then she turned back to Jeskil. "And you stole the child rather than killing him."

"I don't kill children."

"And the dancer? I presume Azur is her son and not stillborn?"

"You have a good memory as well as sharp eyes," Vikar told her.

"Reyna would never have given up her son to the throne," Jeskil added. "Again. We did what was best for the child."

"Reyna?"

"Paradis. That's her name. She's my wife," Jeskil said. "And she believes you wanted Vari dead in spite of everything. Don't worry, I'll talk to her before you meet."

But as the promise left his lips, Reyna approached, crimson with fury. She planted herself in front of Roxanna and slapped the queen hard across the face. "You stay away from me and my children!" she warned. "Or you will regret it."

"Oh wife, no!" Jeskil said, snatching her back. "No, peace! I'll explain."

"Madam Gild, I wished no harm to you or your children. Please believe me," Roxanna insisted, hand pressed to her cheek.

"I'll believe you when the moon turns to dust!" Reyna shouted as Jeskil tried to pull her toward their apartments.

"What shall I swear by?" Roxanna asked her as the mark of Reyna's hand grew livid on her pale face.

"The lives of your children."

Roxanna's face froze, and for a moment Vikar feared what might happen. But then her expression grew solemn, even sorrowful. "Madame Gild, I would do it in a moment, but I fear my son is already dying, and I will never see my daughters again. May I swear to you on my own life? On my name? On the memory of my husband who we both loved?"

Reyna stared at her. She shook off Jeskil's hand. "I don't know what to believe," she admitted and turned away.

"What a tangle," Roxanna breathed as she watched Reyna retreat with Jeskil following. "That poor woman."

"We can unknot it with the truth. But the point of my bringing you here was to introduce you to Azur. He is like enough to your son as Oreyn was, that with a glamour or two, no one would guess that he was not the king."

"What is he like?"

"A good man. He has a noble nature and has been reared by good people. He's not as clever as Vari, but then few people are."

"Vari is the true king, though, isn't he?"

"The people would never believe it. Attempting to put him on the throne would send the kingdom into chaos."

"A tangle," she said again.

"You must consent if we are to make the switch."

"If you will ensure that Oreyn will have the care he needs, I will consent," Roxanna told him. "Corraçao needs a good king now, and my family needs peace."

Roxanna made her way back across the field to the wagon where Oreyn waited. She noted that the shutters on the windows had been closed, as had the upper half of the door. No light, no air, no prying eyes, she supposed. Oreyn was in hiding. Accordingly, she tapped lightly before she opened the door.

"Go awa—oh, it's you." Oreyn sat hunched on his bed, lost in deep shadow.

"Have you eaten?" she asked. First things first.

"Not hungry."

"You must eat." She reached out to touch him, and he flinched away from her as if he feared a blow.

"Don't touch me. I'm on fire. Don't touch me. He burned her, didn't he? I feel it inside my bones. I can feel the fire."

Roxanna sat down on the bed. "I've asked Revin to get help for you. I'm sure--."

He snarled at her. "I'm burning up from the inside. What help is there for me? No, stay away!" he shouted slapping at her hands as she attempted to embrace him. "I will burn you to cinders, too. Why did you let her take me from you?" he demanded.

It was a terrible question, and the answer, she thought, was worse. And yet he deserved to understand.

"When I married your father," Roxanna began, "I wanted to give him a son, a strong, beautiful, smart boy who could follow him to the throne, a prince who would be loved by his people and who would be a better king than his father had ever been."

She told him the story, editing nothing about her own part in it. She told him that Nori-Gant had been gifted to her by Hartan and Catenia. That the nurse was said to have virtues beyond that of the normal wet-nurse. "They said she would help me make a perfect heir. And you were perfect, Oreyn. The most beautiful child I'd ever seen. Your father and I were so proud, so overjoyed that the kingdom had an heir. But I come from a country where magic is outlawed and so I knew nothing about how it works. I didn't realize that spells came with a price."

"I don't understand."

"The price was your love," she told him.

He was silent for a long time and then he said, "It wasn't only that, was it? I was born wrong. I've been on fire my whole life, and it's your fault. Yours and hers. My mothers," he spat. "As if either of you ever truly loved me."

Roxanna was about to protest when he said, "Well I'm still glad she's dead. You should be dead too for what you did to me. I wish we were all dead. The world would be better off without us."

"I swear to you I will do whatever can be done to help. I love you." No matter who he'd become, no matter how horrible he'd been or what he'd done, she did love him. He was part of her. And it tore her apart to see him suffering like this.

But he stared at her as if she were a stranger, and a chill ran up her spine.

***

A few days after their arrival, an ambassador from King Connla came to the circus camp with news. Roxanna and Vikar met with him in private, hoping for Connla's support. Vikar wondered what it might cost but didn't express those concerns. They'd know soon enough.

"King Connla is prepared to stand with Corraçao's government in exile." Ambassador Gethin paused and looked around. "May I ask why the young king is not with us?"

There was a heavy silence, and then Roxanna spoke. "My son has been through a great deal in the last weeks and is recovering from a severe irritation of the throat, which he caught during our journey from Trennin. He still has difficulty speaking and tires quickly."

It was the agreed-upon story, but Vikar could see that it wasn't good enough, so he turned to Roxanna. "Your Majesty, in light of the importance of this meeting, may I suggest that I bring King Oreyn to this meeting with the understanding that he will not have to speak and may leave if he feels fatigued?"

"I am content," she replied. "Ambassador, will that be sufficient?"

"Yes, madam, it will."

"Very well, Counselor. Please bring my son," she said. "If he feels able."

Vikar left the meeting, but instead of going to Oreyn, who could no longer pass for anything like a king, he went to Azur, who was busy repairing some of the puppets. "Clean yourself up," he told his nephew. "Wrap your throat in a scarf, and put on warm clothes. You're going to be a king for an hour or two. Oh, and do try not to look so oppressively healthy. You're recovering from an illness, and you have an irritated throat. Can you do it?"

Azur gave him a look. "Keep my mouth shut and look like a sick boy king? I think I can manage it."

"Can I come and watch, Uncle?" Vari asked with a cheeky smile.

"You may not. This is going to be hard enough as it is."

On the way to the meeting, Vikar explained the situation to Azur. "And this is why you find it difficult to speak. You may nod occasionally, nothing more."

Azur nodded and touched his throat with a helpless gesture, and Vikar nodded his approval.

When Vikar returned to the meeting with Azur, the mood was tense, but at the sight of Azur the ambassador stood and bowed. "Your Majesty, it is an honor."

Again, Azur touched his throat with that helpless and now slightly apologetic gesture. Then he extended a hand to the ambassador and smiled.

The boy was good, Vikar thought. Azur sat between Vikar and Roxanna, who did not look at him.

"As I said, King Connla is prepared to stand with Corraçao's government in exile and, further, to negotiate on behalf of the house of Pellires with Lostrian and Eresumman representatives here in Albhain."

"And Arrezko?" Vikar asked.

"We believe Vartaris will support Feracia," the ambassador said, sidestepping the question. "It has much to gain from the alliance and very little to lose."

There was a silence. Then Roxanna spoke. "I take it that King Connla has heard certain rumors about my son's marriage."

"Madame, it is not my place—"

"Nevertheless, if it affects anything about our negotiations, we must discuss it."

Azur looked at Vikar and raised an eyebrow. Vikar shook his head almost imperceptibly.

"Very well," Gethin said. "King Connla has expressed his unwillingness to negotiate with Arrezko on your behalf because of the delicate situation between King Oreyn and his wife. He says it's a family matter and should be dealt with by the families."

"The situation is unfortunate. The children had no real chance to come to know each other," Roxanna said. "My son was under malign magical influences by my brother's hand, and it goes without saying that neither he, nor Saskia had much experience of the world. They were hesitant, uncertain; my husband forced the issue. Now, of course, we know that it was because Pelle was quite ill and wanted to assure the safety of the succession before his death. But it did the children no good at all. I firmly believe that we can work through the problems if given time. I'm sure you understand me, Ambassador Gethin."

Gethin flushed. "Why yes, I believe I do. Children are so often unprepared for the responsibilities of marriage."

"Just so."

Azur bowed his head, presumably to hide the expression of stunned disbelief on his face.

"How if we undertake to negotiate directly with Arrezko?" Vikar asked.

Gethin looked relieved. "It is what we hoped for."

"Once their support is gained, what more can we expect?"

"Once they have joined the alliance, we will obstruct Feracia's routes to the sea on the north, east, and west of Eiliron."

"It's not enough," Azur rasped. Then he feigned a coughing fit. "The south," he gasped. And he was correct. The south was the weak point in any attempt to isolate Feracia, now that Hartan held Corraçao.

"No, alas it is not, but we have no way of besetting the Janesse from within Corraçao," Gethin replied. "And I am not certain that we have the ships and men to extend the barricade that far."

There was another uncomfortable silence. Azur coughed delicately into his handkerchief and slumped in his chair.

"Ambassador, it may be that I can provide an ally who has the ability to ensure the closure of the Janesse at the Strait of Restmark to secure the coast of Corraçao," Roxanna said.

Both Vikar and Azur turned to stare at her in surprise.

"That would be perfect. It would cut off Feracia comprehensively. But..." Gethin let his thought trail away as if they would all understand why he didn't believe such an ally could exist.

"The Sultan of Aryvia has proved to be a good friend to Corraçao in the past, though never in an obvious way. It may be that if I contact him and explain the situation, he would send his ships to aid in our mission."

Vikar was gaping at her; he couldn't help himself. Sultan Orhan a friend to Corraçao? In what reality was that true? Orhan was a friend to Orhan.

"Madame, you have taken a great load off my mind. I will tell the king all that we have discussed here, and once Arrezko and Aryvia have joined the alliance, we will have the power to isolate Feracia from the outside world and force capitulation."

"I hope it will be that simple," Roxanna said, rising and taking Gethin's hand. "Thank you, Ambassador Gethin, for being so candid with us."

Gethin took his leave, bowing to Azur and shaking Vikar's hand. Once he was gone, Vikar turned to his nephew. "The south?"

"It was obvious," Azur told him, unwinding the scarf. "Saints, I'm so hot." He shrugged out of the heavy jacket.

"What do you know about it?" Roxanna asked him.

"I can read a map. Eiliron has a long southern coast, and no one was offering to protect it."

She stared at him for a long while, then nodded. "Thank you."

"I am glad to help Corraçao," he replied and left the room.

Roxanna looked over at Vikar. "You chose well," she told him, her voice wistful. "He'll be a good king."

***

"Where have you been?" Oreyn's voice, once so pleasant and low, came shrilly out of the gloom of their apartment. "You've been gone for hours. No! Don't open that curtain." They lived in perpetual darkness.

"The room is stuffy, you need air." It was more an odor of decay than stuffiness. Decay and cooked meat.

"No."

"Oreyn—"

"No!" It was more a scream than a shout, and it set Roxanna's teeth on edge. His voice was changing again. Everything was changing, growing worse.

She knew why he kept the curtains drawn. He was covered in blisters and raw flesh now, the physical changes utterly out of control. He was in constant pain and spoke only about death and dying.

"Darling, won't you see a magister? There may be something they can do for you."

"No! I'll see no one."

"Is there anything I can do for you?"

"You can expire."

Roxanna turned away.

"I didn't mean it. Mother?"

"It's all right, I understand."

"I want to die."

She sat beside him and put her arms around him, but he was stiff in her embrace as if he couldn't bear her touch. Or perhaps it was just that he couldn't bear a human touch now that he no longer felt human.

"Where were you?" he asked, pressing his ravaged face against her arm. "I was afraid."

"I met with Connla's ambassador. We spoke about Corraçao, about how to force your uncle to withdraw."

"Why bother? I'll never sit on the throne again. I want to die, and I want you with me."

Her heart began to ache. "I will always be with you, but I hope you'll stop and think about this. There may be a way."

"I have thought about it, Mother, and this is the way, this is the right way for me, for you. The world will be better without us."

For a moment she couldn't think clearly. What was it he'd just said to her? "Oreyn, I—"

"You said you would be with me." He pulled away from her, then grasped her face in his hands and forced her to look at him, at the ruined face of the boy who had once been the most beautiful child she had ever seen. "You did this to me. If I were still king, I'd have you put to death for this and enjoy watching you perish."

She felt wetness on her face; his flesh wept now. She tried not to shiver.

"This can't be the only way."

"Coward!" he spat and shoved her off the bed.

She left his chamber and went to her own to wash and collect herself. She was shaking.

She was sitting alone when Vikar came to her door. "Am I disturbing you?" he asked.

"Not at all. I'm glad of the company." It was in her mind to tell him what had passed between Oreyn and herself, but before she could approach the subject, he said, "What you said earlier, about Sultan Orhan helping our cause..." He let the thought trail off, and she didn't bother trying to follow it. She was so tired.

"What about it?"

"You don't have to sell yourself to get his help. We can manage."

"Sell myself?" What was it he was saying?

"Orhan does nothing out of kindness," Vikar said. "He is guided wholly by self-interest."

She could hardly believe he was saying this to her. Why would he care how she obtained Orhan's help? It made her angry, and anger felt better than the gnawing despair that had settled on her after speaking with Oreyn. "What makes you think I'd be selling myself?" she asked. She could see that it hurt him, and she didn't care.

"I'm sorry," he mumbled. "I shouldn't have—my mistake."

"Yes, it absolutely is. You forget yourself." She put all the ice of a Feracian winter into her voice.

The color drained from his face. "Your Majesty, I humbly beg your pardon." He bowed and fled the room.

***

It was late when Roxanna made her way to the Gild apartments. She tapped, then tapped again, and the door opened on a sleepy-eyed Reyna, clutching a robe around herself.

"What do you need, madam?" There was no warmth in Reyna's greeting but neither was there hostility.

"I'm sorry, but I must speak to your husband. It's"—she began to tremble—"my son," she said, and a sob choked her.

Reyna hesitated a moment before she opened the door to Roxanna. "Come in, please. Come sit."

"I'll be fine," Roxanna said. "I just..." She slumped into a chair and bowed her head. Reyna reached out and took Roxanna's hand.

"Your son... I'm so sorry he's ill. Is there anything I can do?"

Roxanna shook her head. "He's dying, and he welcomes it. I've lost him."

"Oh no. It's that bad?"

Roxanna looked up as Jeskil sat down beside Reyna. "Yes."

"Perhaps the magister—"

"Oreyn refuses to see anyone. I've tried to convince him, but he won't have it. He wants to die. He wants me to die with him." It was a relief to say it out loud, to share it even if Reyna gasped in shock.

"I can't fail him again," Roxanna whispered. "I need your help, Master Gild."

"I understand. I can help."

Horrified, Reyna pulled out of Roxanna's grasp. "You will not!"

"Peace, wife."

"How can you even think of killing your own child?" Reyna glared at them both. "Perhaps I was not wrong about you," she said to Roxanna who reached out and caught hold of Reyna's arm.

"He is burning from the inside as if someone had filled his body with hot coals. His flesh is blistering and sloughing off. He touched my face and his skin came away on mine. How can I not help him do the one thing he asks of me? Could you deny your child that mercy? Could you?" There were tears, but she barely felt them coursing down her cheeks.

Reyna's face went from pink to white as she understood what Roxanna was saying. She pulled away. "I didn't…" Then she fled the room.

Roxanna sighed. "I fear I've brought discord to your home." She wiped her face on her sleeve.

"She's volatile. She also believes deeply in the bonds of family."

"I would save him if I could, but I don't think it can be done."

"You want to comfort him as he passes."

"Yes."

"But not join him."

Another, deeper sigh. "No. I do not want to die. Is that wrong of me?"

"If you could save him by dying," he began, "it would be one thing. But this pointless death? No, it's not your responsibility to give up on your life and your other children just to join him in death. But that's not why you're here, is it? I can help, but I ask one thing. I want to see him and speak to him before I involve myself in his death."

"He won't see you."

"I will make it clear that it's his only option," he told her. "You won't have to do a thing."

"What you'll see," she began, "I can't describe it."

"I've seen magic gone very wrong."

She wondered if he could have seen anything worse than what was happening to her son in the darkness of his room.

***

Though Jeskil needed Roxanna to introduce him to Oreyn, he would not allow her to stay with them as they talked. "This is a private choice for him," he told her. "You can't be part of it."

She had expected Oreyn to be almost hysterical at the sight of another human being, but he seemed subdued, as if he had no energy left for anger or fear. "Go away," was all he said.

"No, Your Majesty, you and I have business." To Roxanna, Jeskil said, "Leave us now. I will come to you when we're finished here."

She waited outside despite the cold, wrapping herself in a plain woolen cloak, emptied of every emotion. She stared blindly into the darkness and didn't see Reyna approaching until the woman was close. She looked up, not knowing what to expect, but Reyna's face was sorrowful. She sat down beside Roxanna, took her hand, and the two women sat together in silence. Not a queen and a dancer, but two mothers confronting grief.

It was nearly an hour before Jeskil emerged. He showed no surprise to find Reyna with the queen, holding her hand. He looked terribly sad. "I couldn't dissuade him," he told Roxanna, sitting beside her on the bench. "And I confess I didn't want to once we'd spoken. He knows he's dying but doesn't wish to suffer any longer than he has to. And yes, he's still determined that you must die with him."

Roxanna felt Reyna's grip on her hand tighten. "I cannot fail him," she said.

"You won't. We will give him the illusion that you are both taking your lives. I told him I would return tonight with a painless solution. Come to me at dusk and we'll prepare you for your ordeal. And it will be," he told her. "You must understand that."

***

At dusk, Roxanna returned to the Gild apartments. Jeskil invited her in and sat down with her. He handed her a vial. "Drink this now."

"What is it?"

"An antidote for what you will drink later."

Chilled at the thought, she hesitated, but finally she drank the contents of the vial. "And then?"

"And then you'll go to Oreyn and give him this bottle. Tell him there is enough for both of you. He will drink, you will drink, he will grow drowsy. I suggest you pretend to do the same. Say your goodbyes. It won't take long."

"I can't bear this," she whispered.

"We can stop now, but I believe he will find a way to kill himself and you as well if we don't cooperate with him. I'll come with you and give him the poison." He stood up. "It's time to give him peace and stop his suffering."

As they entered Oreyn's chamber, he said, "So it's time now?"

"Yes, Your Majesty, it is. I've brought the tonic you asked for. Enough for two."

"Make her drink first; I don't trust her."

Jeskil handed the vial to Roxanna, who downed a bit less than half of the bitter liquid. Then she passed it to Oreyn.

"I keep thinking there should be some kind of ceremony. I suppose we're beyond that." He drank, gagging a bit, but finishing what was left. "So that's done."

"Unless you wish me to stay, I will wait outside and see that no one disturbs you," Jeskil said. When there was no objection, he left the room.

"Will you let me hold you?" Roxanna asked Oreyn. It seemed important to her to touch him. "I'll try not to hurt you."

"As if that ever stopped you," he replied. He was shaking.

Roxanna sat down on the bed and pulled her son into her arms. There was nothing left of him. His hair had fallen out, and he was so covered in sores and grotesquely blistered flesh that he barely seemed human. There was a smell of burnt meat about him; he was little more than cooked flesh on rackety bones. "If I'd known—" she whispered.

"It's too late for that." Then he asked, "Are you sleepy? I'm getting sleepy."

"Yes," she lied. "Yes, I feel quite tired."

He relaxed in her arms. "This is good. This is what I wanted. We monsters belong together."

She held him as his breathing slowed, and finally with one last exhale, she felt him simply stop. He was gone. It was the only peaceful thing he'd ever done in his short life, and it was terrible. And then he fell to ashes in her arms. It was too much for her and she howled in horror and pain, and grief.

Jeskil came in response to her cries, and saw the pile of ashes. "Dear saints," he muttered. "Are you all right?" he asked her.

After a long pause she replied, "I don't think I will ever be all right again."

"Go wash and change your clothes. I'll take care of... this."

She couldn't quite assimilate what had just happened, nor could she feel anything. The world had gone cold and empty.

When she rejoined Jeskil, Revin was there with him, and Oreyn's ashes were gone.

"What have you done with him?"

"He will have a decent funeral," Jeskil promised her. "But now, as far as the world knows, the young king is here recovering from an illness and mustering support for his campaign to win back his throne. You must focus on that."

In spite of herself, her breath caught on a sob.

"Are you all right?" Revin asked her. She clenched her fists, nails digging into her palms, to keep herself from breaking down entirely.

"I'm still here. That's all there is now. What is the plan?" She didn't want anyone's sympathy.

"I'm sending Phrin and his men to Lakan to secure the fortress there. The east remains loyal to the Pellires, and Phrin will ready them for our return."

"And you both believe that the people will accept Azur in Oreyn's place?"

The two men nodded.

"Then my work is done."

"No, not yet. It's essential that you're seen beside him. Mother and son fighting to reclaim their kingdom," Revin told her.

Jeskil added, "And you have to tutor Azur in how to be a king, and how to be Oreyn. He needs to know who he's becoming."

"Revin can do that."

"Not all of it. He needs to learn how to behave."

"Not like my son. Anything but that. And what of Arrezko?"

"We are negotiating. I've told a few half-truths that may bring them around," Revin told her. "Evil plan hatched by usurper to ruin the marriage with magic, and so forth. Guaranteed to produce sympathy, particularly as I've told them that Oreyn became quite ill just before you fled Trennin."

"Hanging on between life and death is always good for provoking sympathy," Jeskil agreed.

Her child was dead and this man was joking. "I would like to be alone now," she said, cutting off any further discussion.

"Of course. We'll take care of everything," Revin promised. He shooed Jeskil out but paused at the door. "Is there anything—?"

"Nothing," she snapped.

The door closed softly, and she was alone with her memories.

Roxanna understood that both Jeskil and Vikar had important work to do. Jeskil was arranging for a provisional capital based in Lakan with support from Connla. Vikar was on his way to Arrezko to negotiate for Saskia's return to Corraçao, and Roxanna certainly didn't envy him that task, but it left her alone in a strange place, weighed down by grief and guilt and forced to teach a stranger how to be her son and a king.

It was painful to look at Azur and remember a time when her own son was as bright and beautiful, to realize that Azur was a better man and would be a better king than Oreyn could ever have been. When Azur asked her what sort of person Oreyn had been, she didn't know what to say. Horrible? Mad? Petty and cruel? He was all those things.

"He was not a good man," she told him. "He was wrong, inside himself."

"I'm sorry," Azur said. "That must have been hard for you both."

"Just be yourself, and you'll do well," she told him. "We are explaining that there was a magical influence on him which has been lifted now."

"Was there?"

She sighed. "Yes, no. I don't know. I've never known what ailed my son. But that's not important right now. The important thing is that the world must believe that you are Oreyn. I can teach you something of how he spoke and moved, and you are a near double for him physically. The only people who might know otherwise would be his sisters. Your sisters," she corrected.

"Tell me about them."

She told him that Oreyn's relationship with his sisters was troubled. "He hated them, and they feared him. He was often violent." She explained that Maerys, who was the stronger and more stubborn of the two girls, was being fostered in Vartaris as future wife to Fortunatis, and how her sweet Rhaenne was betrothed to Roran of Albhain.

"She's here? In Albhain?"

"Don't worry, she doesn't know that we are. And she's a good child and will accept what I tell her about you."

"And your daughter-in-law, Saskia of Arrezko?"

Roxanna bit her lip. "She's a clever young woman, and a strong one. I expect she'll require more than a bit of wooing."

He flashed a smile and said, "I'm good at that."

It didn't surprise her at all. "Let me show you some of the gestures he used. They will not go unnoticed by those who want to believe you are Oreyn."

***

Jeskil sent Phrin and his men off to Lakan with the promise that King Oreyn would join them there once he had recovered from the malign magic that had made him so ill. "He understands that there is a great deal to be done, and is counting on his loyal subjects to help him bring peace and stability back to Corraçao. He regrets his current infirmity."

"My men and I stand ready to do whatever we must for him."

"Then secure Lakan for him. When he arrives, it will be the seat of his government until we retake Trennin."

He knew it would be done. Phrin and his men were ferociously loyal to the throne, and would secure as much of the east as they could. But Jeskil also had another, less obvious weapon in this war. Though he hated to send his people out on the road in the winter, it was necessary to spread the word of how the young king had been evilly used by his uncle and the Peoran witch who did Hartan's bidding. He even sent troupe members into Vartaris to sow discord there. If the Vartarians could be divided, Hartan's support among them might suffer.

Once they were all on their way, he just had to be patient. Travelers were good at spreading news throughout the seven kingdoms, and the troupe members were familiar to the people who loved the circus. They would be believed. They would raise feeling against Hartan, and that feeling could easily be turned to forcing Wismar to intervene. Played correctly, this could prove to be a nearly bloodless countercoup.

Aware of the need for speed in arranging the closures of Corraçao's waterways, Jeskil helped Roxanna contact Aryvia via the cards.

"There are magickers in Aryvia?" she asked, clearly uncomfortable.

"There are magic users everywhere. But there are many different sorts of magic. Fortunately, the cards are useful enough that they're in wide use even outside Eiliron. Come and sit with me, and concentrate on this card." He handed her the Fire King card. "Think of Orhan as you do."

"No." She dropped the card. "I'll do no magic."

He supposed she had reason. "I will be doing the magic, but I need you to provide my focus."

She closed her eyes, took a deep breath, and nodded, picking up the card again and staring hard at it. "Very well, I am thinking of—oh!" The figure of Orhan stood before her on the table. Even in miniature he seemed bigger than life.

"I am delighted to hear from you. I have been worried."

Once she recovered from her surprise, she said, "Your Majesty, I have a great favor to ask you." Then she turned to Jeskil and whispered, "Must you be here?"

"Yes, I must."

"I am at your service," Orhan said, drawing her attention.

"My son has been deposed and cruelly used by his uncle. He is recovering from the illness laid on him, and once he is well again, he and I will be attempting to win back his throne."

"What may I do to help?"

"Orhan, I need your ships. We can attempt closure of all the waterways to the north, east, and west but cannot obstruct the southern coast of Corraçao."

"The intent is to cut off Feracia's access to the outer world?"

"Yes."

Orhan nodded. "This is a big undertaking for my Sultanate," he told her.

"I have nothing to offer in return save the gratitude of the king. And the deepest thanks and affection of his mother." There was a tone to her voice that Jeskil recognized as a promise and an invitation, and he wondered if any man had ever successfully resisted her. Certainly his cousin had not, though he suspected Vikar was willfully oblivious to his feelings for Roxanna.

"Lady, your affections are all I ever desired. My ships will leave at first light to take up critical positions along the southern coast." Then he said, "Master Jeskil, I see you there in the shadows. I believe you will owe me a favor as well, if this plan should succeed."

"I will happily discuss the matter with you once we have the young king back on his throne."

"Fair enough," Orhan said, and bowed again. Then the little figure disappeared.

"You know him?" Roxanna asked as she laid the card back on top of the deck.

"I have worked for him in the past."

"Tell me, then, why the Fire King card?"

He gathered the cards and put them back in their bag. "Aryvia is a kingdom not just of humans but of spirits of fire and air. Orhan's power keeps them bound to his kingdom."

"Orhan's power?" She stood and smoothed her gown. "How little I know of the world," she said before she left the room.

Jeskil wondered if she knew anything of her own power to bewitch.

***

While Jeskil and Roxanna dealt with the allies of the Pellires family, Vikar had a more difficult and delicate job to do. He journeyed to Arrezko to confer with Wouder and Annemeike on behalf of the young king, and when it was plain that he had come to convince them that their daughter belonged in Corraçao with her husband, the atmosphere became chilly.

"Our daughter considers the matter closed, as do we," Annemeike said. "You have made a long trip for nothing."

"Would it make a difference to hear something of why the young king behaved badly?"

"There's something that can excuse his behavior?" Wouder asked. "Mind you, none of us know the whole story. Saskia has never spoken of the events of that night. But we saw clearly the damage he did to her. Great saints, man, my daughter wept for days!"

"If I may explain... and perhaps your daughter might wish to hear this as well?"

"I don't know," Wouder grumbled, but Annemeike looked thoughtful.

"Perhaps," she said. "But you'll explain to us first. I won't have her made miserable over nonsense."

Vikar nodded. "As you wish."

"Then please sit down with us, take some refreshment, and speak your piece. We will decide whether Saskia needs to hear what you have to say or not."

The tale was simple, worked out ahead of time and so close to the truth that any possible discrepancies could be overlooked. He explained that Hartan's coup had been planned years in advance, and to that end, he had secured a nurse from Vartaris to care for the queen, and later Prince Oreyn. Roxanna, being raised in a kingdom where magic was proscribed, never suspected that there was anything wrong with the nurse.

"You know that Hartan married the Princess Catenia of Vartaris." Both monarchs nodded. "What is often forgotten is that Catenia's mother was Peoran. She supplied the nurse to Hartan, a witch attached to her mother's family."

Yes, that struck home, he saw. Wouder and his wife looked shocked.

"I see that you understand my meaning. Hartan and his wife-to-be planned some mischief before Oreyn was born. And while I'm not at liberty to disclose everything that was done to the boy and his mother"—here he hesitated, injecting a bit more drama into his narrative—"and his father, whose death was not natural, I can assure you that Oreyn's behavior, his seeming madness, was absolutely a product of years of magical abuse by his nurse. I was in the room when she confronted Hartan, demanding her due for the years she'd spent poisoning the house of Pellires on his orders."

"Why did no one stop her?" Annemeike asked. She'd gone pale.

"It was a slow, patient process, difficult to detect for anyone not trained in the very specific Peoran magicks she used to drive Oreyn to madness. Even now, as he recovers in Albhain, he is tormented by the memories of what was done to him and what he did to others. But," he added quickly, "I know the young man well, and know his strength. With time and the help of those who love him, he will recover, and he will be a good king. And I believe he will be a good husband if given the chance. He entreated me to go down on my knees to your daughter and beg her to accept both his apologies and assurances that he is not the man she fears she married. He promises to do the same when next they meet."

"And the goal was to capture Corraçao?" Wouder asked. Annemeike dabbed at her eyes with a handkerchief.

"The original goal was to make Oreyn unmarriageable to anyone not under the control of Feracia. Wismar presented a young woman who was rejected by King Pelle, and not long after, Pelle died."

"And you are sure the death was not natural? Pelle had been ill for a long time."

"I made a cursory examination of the body myself and was convinced of foul play. Then one of the court doctors confirmed my suspicions."

"This is insupportable!" Wouder shouted. His face was pink with outrage. "How dare they?" He was understandably sensitive to the notion of regicide.

"It's Feracia," Annemeike murmured. "They dare all, as you well know, my dear. Arrezko briefly lost territory to them decades ago. Only the aid of Albhain drove back the invasion." She leaned forward. "So the plan was to put the boy on the throne and marry him to a Feracian woman?"

"Precisely, Your Majesty. But the magicks used on him had made him intractable and highly erratic. It led to a falling out between Hartan and his witch when the plot was exposed. Hartan had her killed, and the dowager queen and her son fled the country. Without the malign influence that had been on him his whole life, Oreyn has reverted to being who he should have been all along. Mercifully, Peoran magicks wear off if not refreshed."

"And you want us to support Corraçao in this effort to cut off Feracia's trade routes?"

"Yes, Your Majesty."

"And to deliver our daughter to King Oreyn when he retakes the throne."

"Before would be better," he said. "But essentially, yes, that's what we hope for."

"And if she will not go?" asked a high, clear voice behind him. Vikar rose, turned, and went down on his knees to Saskia.

"Majesty—"

"Oh get up, you look like a fool. I've heard all you had to say but have heard no guarantees."

"What guarantee would you need?"

"Not one you can give, I'm afraid." Saskia sighed. A livid scar on her lip was the only flaw in her beauty. "I will consent to meet with my husband, nothing more."

"It's enough for now," Vikar assured her.

"You're sure, darling?" Annemeike asked her.

"I'd go if only to slap his nasty face again," her daughter replied.

16.

Bright Moon CR 550

Jeskil brushed a speck of lint from his jacket. He wore the deep green livery of an ambassador of Albhain, representing the alliance of Eiliron in negotiation with Wismar of Feracia, though "negotiation" was probably too generous a word under the circumstances. The closure of all of Feracia's routes to the sea, which had lasted through the winter, coupled with the fighting in the east of Corraçao and a strong resistance to Hartan's governance throughout Corraçao, had made itself felt in the mountain kingdom.

"Gild!" Wismar glared at him from under his unruly mop of white curls. "What are you doing here?"

"As you see," Jeskil said with a gesture to his badge of office.

"You're not representing Connla, are you?"

"And the Alliance, Majesty." He made a pro forma bow. "I bring terms."

"Alliance? Terms?" Wismar's already sour expression darkened. "What terms?"

"Your Majesty, we both know your trade routes have been obstructed by an alliance of countries that take a dim view of the overthrow and murder of kings. Your economy is suffering, and what benefits have you seen from the governance of Hartan Talian? The people of Corraçao resent Hartan the Usurper, as they call him, and you know that eventually he will be driven out of the kingdom."

"All unprovoked acts of aggression," Wismar retorted. "Though I have nothing to do with Hartan's ambitions."

"You have supported Hartan's capture of the throne of Corraçao."

Wismar scratched his beard and studied Jeskil. "That's a lie. I have not. I'm as shocked as anyone by the events in Corraçao." The lie came easily enough that anyone who didn't know his reputation might believe Wismar's denial.

"Hartan and his wife say that your aid placed them on the throne of Corraçao, that it was your plan all along."

Jeskil hit a nerve, and Wismar's fists clenched. "Also a lie," he said, but he was clearly rattled.

"Then deny it. Denounce them publicly. Deny their implication that you were involved in Pelle's death and the overthrow of the legitimate heir."

"Gladly," Wismar said, recovering his aplomb. "It's nothing to do with Feracia, Gild. I shall issue a statement today denying all knowledge of and complicity in Talian's actions, not just by the throne of Feracia, but by its people as well. We are a well-intentioned race as you know."

"I know Feracia well, Majesty. My people were Eresumman and Lostrian."

At that, Wismar dropped all pretense. "Tell your master to leave us in peace. Tell all your masters that their siege is an act of aggression that won't go unanswered."

Jeskil tilted his head like a cat considering its prey. "You suggest that Feracia is prepared to go to war against the alliance?" He tilted his head. "With Albhain, Arrezko, Corraçao, and Aryvia? Even Vartaris, though it is not part of the alliance, is distancing itself from the events in Corraçao. King Rugenius has called his daughter home to answer questions about her part in them."

Wismar scowled. "What is it you want?"

"King Oreyn wants his throne back. He holds Lakan and much of the east, but he does not want to wage a war against the usurper because his subjects will suffer and die. He wants Hartan removed, peacefully if possible, something you can do easily. Once it's accomplished, the siege will end."

"And if I say I can do nothing?"

Jeskil held out an envelope with the seal of Arrezko, but Wismar only stared at it. "Shall I tell you what it says?" Jeskil asked.

"You read it?"

"I was told. As an emissary I had to know what information I was delivering."

Wismar snatched the envelope and ripped it open, reading over the letter within. "You all think you're so clever," he said. "How did you win over Arrezko? What did you promise to do about the unconsummated marriage?" he sneered.

"Whatever was decided between Arrezko and Corraçao is not at issue. What is at issue is whether Feracia can repay the significant amount of money it owes Arrezko." He gave a little shrug. "Soldiers need to be paid." And then Jeskil tired of Wismar's dodging. "Your Majesty, you have very little in the way of options. Either you can do nothing and remain besieged while the Pellires fight to regain the throne of Corraçao, or you can remove the single obstacle to the throne, a man who is still your subject. You have no other choices."

The old man rubbed his forehead. "The barricade will be lifted once Hartan is removed?"

"Yes."

"And the repayment of the loans?"

"Something you'll have to discuss with Wouder, though I expect he'll be receptive. Particularly as his daughter has agreed to meet with the king to settle their differences."

"All right then. Hartan will be removed." His smile was brittle. "I won't endanger my kingdom for the sake of one of my servants. Satisfied?"

Jeskil bowed and replied, "We await word of Hartan's return to Feracia."

17.

Rain Moon CR 550

An easterly storm was battering Lakan when the news arrived from Trennin. Hartan, who had briefly styled himself Hartan I of Corraçao, had fled with his family to Vartaris after a visit from the Feracian ambassador. Jeskil got the message in the cards and conveyed it to Vikar and Roxanna.

Roxanna was unaccountably unnerved by the news. "Is Azur ready?" she asked. "Doesn't he need more—?"

"I think he'll do very well," Vikar told her.

"Any shortcomings can be easily explained away. My troupe has been on the road for months, spreading the story," Jeskil told them. "Feeling is running high in sympathy for the young king so badly used by his uncle."

"It helps that Hartan was a terrible ruler," Vikar said with a wry smile. "Had he held the capital much longer, I think Corraçao would have accepted an ape as king if it meant being rid of him."

"Thank you so much, Uncle." Azur had come in behind Jeskil and was looking amused. "Good to know I'm a step above ape at this point." He looked every inch a king now after months of grooming and lessons. He held himself proudly, moved with grace, and behaved with the sort of good-natured benevolence that won hearts just as his father once had done. Roxanna hoped he'd be loved by the people of Corraçao. She knew that with the help of his family, he'd be a good king. "When will we leave for Trennin?"

"We'll send troops ahead to make sure we have the sort of welcome we want. There are a few generals who need to be relieved of their commands before I'm satisfied that the return will be safe."

"And Captain Phrin?" she asked. "His loyalty and service deserve recognition."

"You know my mind. We will promote him to general and send him to clear the way for the triumphant return of King Oreyn."

Everyone in the room looked at Azur. "About that," Azur began.

"You're not having second thoughts?" Jeskil asked.

"No, not at all. I can do this. But the name bothers me, and I have it in mind to make a change. I want to use my own name. Azur. Azur I of Corraçao."

Everyone stared.

"I have a plan," he said. "I thought we could make the name change a ceremony of rededication to the kingdom. The old name is attached to the evil that was done, and so on, so let's shake all that off and start fresh with a new name to"—he waved his hands as if trying to catch the whole of the idea—"to underscore our determination to rededicate ourselves to the welfare of the kingdom." In the silence that followed, he said, "You don't like it?"

"I think it's brilliant," Roxanna told him. "It's exactly what's needed." Her fears for him vanished with that moment of comprehension. He was ready.

18.

Moon of First Leaf CR 550

The king's return to Trennin came as the first flowers blossomed, lining his way into the city with a glow of white and pink, accompanied by the sweet scent of hawflowers and early-blooming mountainberry. Azur, clad in blue and gold, rode at the head of the party, Roxanna behind him, beside Vikar. *Let the boy have the attention, let him be a king*, she thought.

And the people screamed their approval and their welcome.

General Phrin met them at the eastern gate and escorted them to the royal residence. People scattered flowers on the streets, children thrust bouquets into Azur's hands, and a few even found their way to Roxanna, much to her surprise.

Just before they were to enter the castle gate, Azur stopped his horse and held up one hand for silence.

"What's he doing?" Vikar hissed at Roxanna.

"I don't know."

The cheering died away, and Azur spoke. "My people, I am both honored and humbled by your welcome."

The cheering began anew. Azur again held up his hand. "I return to you a different man, one determined to give service to his kingdom. Together we will make this Corraçao's golden age!"

There were screams of approval from the crowd, and Roxanna muttered, "He *is* a king."

"I thank you," Azur said to the cheering masses, "and I am here for you, my people. *We* are Corraçao!" He shouted, and the citizens went wild.

Vari, who had ridden up to where Vikar and Roxanna waited, chuckled quietly and said, "What a showman. And he means it too. He wants this." When both of them turned to look, he said, "He told me so. He said he felt it was his destiny to be a good monarch to his father's people."

"And what will you be?" Roxanna asked him as the company began to move through the castle gate.

Vari shrugged. "Perhaps a counselor? Or perhaps I'll go back to Albhain and become a magister. Or stay with the circus. Anything can happen, can't it?"

Roxanna felt a little thrill run through her. Anything could happen. The future was there for the taking. She had only needed these two remarkable brothers to help her see that.

***

Once inside and away from the crowds, Roxanna relaxed. It had gone well, she thought. Between the light glamour Vikar had placed on Azur to make him resemble Oreyn more closely, and Azur's easy way with the people, they had passed a critical test. If the people believed in him, everyone else would fall in line.

"The family chambers have been cleaned and aired," General Phrin told her as he took them up to the royal quarters. He didn't have to do it; as a general he could have delegated the job to a subordinate, but he was seeing his duty through. He was a good ally, she thought.

"The queen is already in residence," he told them. Everyone stopped and stared.

"What?"

"Queen Saskia, Your Majesty. She arrived a few days ago."

Azur shot a glance at Roxanna, who said, "We look forward to meeting with her as soon as we have settled. Please ask her to join us tonight for dinner."

"Of course."

"General Phrin, we thank you for your efforts on our behalf," Azur said. "You have been a true friend to Corraçao and the Pellires."

Phrin's face glowed with the praise. "Thank you, sire. That means a great deal to me."

Once he had left them at the royal apartments with Vikar, Roxanna said, "So... Saskia. Are we ready for her?"

"I will crawl to her if I have to," Azur assured her.

"Not too abject," she replied, but she saw a look in his eyes that reminded her of Pelle. This young man had a way with women, she decided. If anyone could win Saskia back, it would be Azur. "But I leave it to you. And now I'm going to rest." She had suddenly lost her last reserve of energy and was close to sleeping on her feet. "I will see you at dinner."

Once in her chamber, she sank down on the bed and closed her eyes, but sleep wouldn't come. Tired as she was, her mind wouldn't stop racing around all the questions she still had. Would they be a success? Would the people accept Azur? Would he be a good king? And most immediately, would he win Saskia's heart, or at least her loyalty?

With a sigh, she sat up, stretched, and wondered if Doctor Tomeran was still in residence. Her aching muscles could do with a powder or ointment. Or perhaps she simply needed a long soak in a hot bath. But rather than summoning a servant for any of those things, she went to her desk where she found a stack of papers waiting for her, mostly requests for aid, some quite old, come in just after she'd fled with Oreyn.

It felt like years she'd been gone from Trennin.

At the top of the stack was an envelope addressed in a fine hand, and she knew without opening it that it came from Orhan. A debt waiting to be paid, she supposed.

The day is won without a single casualty, my queen, and I am taking my fleet home, though they remain at your service, as do I. Once you have settled your business, send for me, and I will come to you in Trennin to take you back with me to Aryvia, as agreed.

She didn't recall agreeing to leave Corraçao, but it hardly mattered. There was no place for her here.

I long to show you the beauties of my kingdom almost as much as I long to hold you in my arms. Ever your servant, Orhan.

There was a kind of relief in knowing that her future was, at least for a time, settled on the shoulders of someone else. She was tired in her very soul.

This time, when she lay down on her bed, she slept.

The maidservant woke Roxanna at dusk to ask if she wanted to dine with the others or have her meal brought to her. "I'll go down to the hall. Fetch me some water."

She stripped down to her under-gown and ruffled her hair, in which she was already seeing the odd strand of silver among the gold. She wasn't an old woman yet, she told herself, and she wasn't going to disappear from the world.

She washed and dressed herself in a dark blue gown. The maid brushed her hair and put it up into a chignon. She searched for her jewels, which she hadn't thought to take when she fled Trennin, but they were gone as she suspected. Not that it mattered to her. She would have given most of them to Saskia in any event. But she regretted the loss of the simple golden band Pelle had given her before their marriage. Inside was an engraving: *My heart is yours forever.* She hated the idea that Catenia might be wearing it.

On her way down to the dining hall, she met Saskia in the hallway. They greeted each other, though without much warmth on Saskia's side. Still, Roxanna needed to thank her for giving the king a second chance. "You have given the country a second chance as well," she told her. "And I appreciate it."

"It remains to be seen, madam, whether I will be staying." Saskia swept on ahead of Roxanna into the dining hall where Azur waited with Revin. They were conferring so intensely that, at first, they didn't notice the two women enter the hall. Once they did, both stood. Azur looked embarrassed. Vikar whispered something to him, and Azur shook his head. "I will always stand in the presence of my mother and my wife," he told the counselor.

Then he made a move toward Saskia, hand extended, and she moved away. "If you don't mind, I'm rather hungry. I'd prefer to discuss our situation later."

"Of course." He moved past her to Roxanna and kissed her cheek. "Mother, thank you for coming down. Revin and I have been discussing the rededication plans." He held her chair for her before doing the same for Saskia, whose expression suggested confusion and annoyance. Perhaps she didn't really want to be here, Roxanna thought. Perhaps her parents had forced her to come back to Corraçao.

"I think his Majesty has some excellent plans," Vikar said. "In the Pellires tradition there will be a country-wide celebration."

"Can we afford it?"

"No, but we can't afford not to, can we?" Azur asked. "I don't propose anything outrageous, but we want the people to feel part of the rededication."

"We'll work something out," Vikar promised. "We've discussed the name change, and I believe it makes sense."

"Name change?" Saskia asked.

"The name Oreyn Pellires is associated with grievous wrongs," Azur explained. "No matter the reason for them, it's up to me to show my people that those times are over. I propose to take the name Azur I as a symbol of my own rededication to the kingdom. A new beginning."

"You think you can wipe out a bad reputation by renaming yourself?" she asked.

He tilted his head and considered her for a moment before he said, "No, but I can show that those days are past. I am myself again."

"I see." She sounded unconvinced. "My, this looks good," she added as the server put her plate in front of her.

Saskia was silent for much of the meal, but it was clear that she was listening with interest to the conversation between Azur, Revin, and Roxanna. Her expression gave away little, though sometimes she frowned as she stared at Azur. Then, as the meal ended, she said, "I would appreciate being allowed to speak to my husband in private."

Roxanna looked to Vikar, who gave an almost imperceptible nod. "Very well," she said. "I have much to do. You will excuse me," she said as she rose. Azur and Vikar rose as well, and Vikar moved to her side.

"I'll see you to your apartments," he said, and she took his arm. It took every ounce of her strength not to look back at the two young people who were about to have a conversation that might affect the future of the kingdom.

"I owe you apologies," Azur said after the others had left. "I can only say that my behavior—"

"How could you have spoken to me like that?" Saskia demanded. "Those things you said to me, the things you told me you wanted to do to me." She shuddered, and Azur wondered again what sort of misery Oreyn had inflicted on her.

"I know, and I am so very sorry."

"When you said you wanted to chop off my fingers and eat them—"

"I... what?" he blurted, then caught himself. "I was wholly under the influence of the Peoran witch. You know they're cannibals."

"And the things you said to me, vile things about my body and what you wanted to do to it. You must remember. Surely you recall what you said about the donkey?"

"Donkey?" Azur was starting to panic. What kind of monster was he impersonating? "I can only say I'm sorry, and it wasn't—"

Saskia sat back in her chair. "Who are you?"

It took him a moment to understand. "Um, what?"

"You're not my husband or you'd know that what I just said to you were lies. Who are you?"

"Well, I'm much changed because the influences—" He was trying hard not to stammer.

"Oh, stop. You're no more Oreyn than I am. So who are you?"

"I am a Pellires," he told her. "That is the truth."

She nodded. "Yes, I see it clearly. All right then. We have a lot to discuss if we're going to carry this off."

How she had seen right through him he didn't know, but he rose, went to her side, and knelt. "I told Vikar to tell you that I would kneel before you and beg your forgiveness," he said, looking up into her beautiful blue eyes. "And I do ask you to forgive me for attempting to deceive you." And then he reached up and gently touched the new scar on her lip. "Did he do this to you?"

She pulled away. "Oh for heaven's sake, get up. Don't be ridiculous. There will be conditions, of course, one of which is that there will be no marital relations."

That was a blow to the ego, but he nodded. "So you will help?"

"Who wouldn't want to be queen of a country like Corraçao?" she asked, and he thought he saw a smile quirk her lips. "Yes, we can carry this off, I think."

He gave her one of his most beautiful, innocent smiles, one that always melted women, and she just laughed at him. "Don't ruin our agreement by trying to charm me."

"I wouldn't dream of it," he said, standing and bowing to her. *This might just work*, he decided.

***

The days and weeks didn't seem long enough for everything that needed to be done for the rededication. For days they'd argued about how best to involve the people in the process, what to give them, until Vari said, "Why not give them hope and purpose?"

"We mean material things, lack-brain," Azur said with a fond smile.

"I know you do, and I think that's a mistake, empty-skull," Vari shot back, and the brothers elbowed each other roughly until Jeskil rapped on the table.

"Sorry," they chorused.

"Vari, what do you mean by hope and purpose?" Vikar asked.

"The country has been through a difficult time by all accounts." He looked to Roxanna, who nodded. "Why not give the people the opportunity to add their efforts to the positive changes? Ask them for their service. Not in huge things but in small things that can build bridges. Help your neighbor, work for the local school or church. Pull together to bring Corraçao back to its glory."

"And what would that glory be?" Azur asked.

"Solvent, beholden to no one, a country where the monarchs are the servants of the people, not the other way around."

"How on earth do we accomplish that?"

Vari shrugged. "I'm working on it," he admitted. And everyone laughed except for Saskia.

"I think I can help here," she said. "In my country there's a tradition that twice a year, the monarchs labor alongside ordinary workers for a day. My father has cleaned stables, and my mother has milked cows. They come away from each new experience with a greater appreciation for their people, and the people see that their monarchs are just like them in many ways."

Azur was staring at her with undisguised admiration. "That's brilliant! We can do that. Can't we?" he asked Vikar.

"Um, I don't see any reason why not. We make it a part of the rededication that it will be a new tradition as it is in Arrezko."

"And begin with a journey around the kingdom," Jeskil said. "No, hear me out," he insisted as a chorus of voices expressed skepticism. "A progress through the kingdom to show the people that Azur I is sane and whole, and a good, hardworking man. It would reassure everyone."

"I could sit with the people, learn about them, their lives, their jobs, their families—"

"We could," Saskia corrected. "We both have to participate."

"She'll be a wonderful ambassador," Vari told them.

"The new Queen of Hearts?" Jeskil asked.

Saskia shook her head. "No, not that. But a queen for all the people, not just the rich and powerful."

And for a moment, Roxanna was ashamed of the way she'd begun her life as queen, wanting only Pelle, and the comfort and security of being queen. She had never thought to serve the people, though as Pelle drifted out of public life, she had been forced into it. And by all accounts she'd done a good job. Still, it wasn't what she would have chosen.

And now these children were showing them all how it should be done. Azur might not have been her child, but she was proud of him. She was proud of all of them.

From there the process became more solid, more focused on the logistics and scheduling. Roxanna listened but had nothing to contribute. For all the work she'd done in Pelle's stead, she really didn't know the kingdom at all, or its people. And now it was too late to change that. Just another regret to add to the long list.

She did think about the messages she'd had from Orhan asking her when he could come to claim her, as if she were some sort of prize. It rankled. Attractive as he was, it did rankle.

***

The date for the start of the celebration was set. Emissaries were sent out to towns and villages all over Corraçao, explaining what this rededication meant and what would happen as the royal couple progressed through the kingdom to celebrate with their people. As expected, the plan wasn't popular with the nobles, but Azur and Saskia didn't seem to care. Roxanna envied their self-assurance.

She would not be going along. It wasn't her place. She represented a past that was better forgotten, while the children were the future. And she had had another message from Orhan. *I will arrive in Trennin within the month.* Nothing more, not that she needed him to explain.

On the night before the beginning of the rededication, she went to Vikar.

"To what do I owe this honor?" he asked. They'd been formal around each other for many months now. Perhaps it would make things easier, she thought.

"You know I won't be accompanying the children on their travels. But I am also not remaining in Trennin. I'm leaving the country with Sultan Orhan."

She wished she could see his face more clearly in the light from his fire, but the movement of the light disguised his thoughts.

"I understand," he told her, his voice flat.

"I—" She sighed. "Vikar, can we part as friends?"

"How?"

"Shake my hand and wish me well," she told him. "Please. I don't want to part feeling estranged."

He stood and lifted her out of her chair, pulled her close, and kissed her in a way that communicated so many emotions that she couldn't find her way out of the tangle. "Wait, no," she gasped and pulled away. "It's not possible." She thought her heart would break as she said it.

"I know. But it wasn't possible to let you go unless you knew how I felt."

And then her heart did seem to break into a thousand little pieces, and she felt tears rise in her eyes. She fled without another word.

19.

Flower and Berry Moon, CR 550

Roxanna stayed to see the first of the celebrations, the day when Azur was crowned and named Azur I, and Saskia crowned as his queen. It was the first time he would address his people as their true king, and while he was nervous, everyone else had perfect faith in him. He was that sort of man, who inspired trust and love.

He would be a greater king than his father, greater by far.

She saw them off a few days later, watching them ride slowly through the adoring crowds who were chanting, "Azur! Saskia!" Vikar, Jeskil, and Vari went with them, and Roxanna was left alone to wait for her Sultan.

He arrived a few days later, sailing up the Janesse to the harbor at Trennin, and arriving at the castle with a trio of personal guards, huge men with skin that glowed like fire. Were these the legendary djinn of Aryvia?

"Did you think you'd have to fight for me?" she asked him with a wry smile.

By way of reply, he pulled her into his arms and whispered, "I want you. You are promised to me."

But she disengaged herself and patted his arm. "Not here. Not where I lived with my husband. And not before we are wed."

He stepped back and studied her. "You are a woman of tact and delicacy. I like that," he told her. "When you are packed, we will sail back to my kingdom."

"I'm not bringing much," she told him. "This life is over."

In the end, she packed two bags of clothing and a few keepsakes. They were loaded on the ship, and Orhan himself escorted her to the harbor. When he showed her to her quarters onboard his magnificent ship, she realized that they were also his. He intended to share with her.

"The captain stands ready to marry us," he told her.

"Then I am ready too," she said and took his hand. Her old life was over, and she had determined to make her way into a new one. Orhan was a gift she was giving to herself, a little respite after so much sorrow. Or at the very least a way of forgetting for a time. But she would not endanger the reputation of her children by being less than the legal consort of a king.

It was quickly done, and when he came to her that night, she welcomed him with pleasure if not joy, and let him quiet her too-busy mind for a time. He was skilled, and she was parched for touch. But Vikar's kiss remained as a bittersweet memory even while she and Orhan lay together, listening to the lap of the water on the ship's hull.

"I don't love you, you know," she told him.

"Nor I you. But it doesn't matter," he replied, and she was satisfied that they understood one another.

They sailed with the sun for seven days. On the eighth, as she stood on the deck, looking out over the vast ocean, she caught sight of what looked like a mountain. Turning, she sought out Orhan and pointed to the horizon. "Is that part of Aryvia?"

He came to her side and wrapped her in his arms. "That is Saharawad, home of the fire spirits of my country, and the people who serve them." He pointed to the left where she could see great cliffs rising from the sea. "And that is Dhiwar, our largest island. It's where we are headed."

She watched the horizon as they approached the islands and the sun sank down behind them. And then, unexpectedly, Saharawad belched a plume of flame into the sky. Roxanna gasped, and she heard soft laughter from the crew behind her. Again, Orhan came to her side.

"They're used to it. It's Saharawad welcoming us home."

"The spirits know?"

"Of course. I am lord of fire and air. Why would they not greet my return?"

"There's so much to learn," she whispered.

"Nothing you need now. Your beauty is enough for anyone."

She stiffened in his embrace recalling that for all that they were husband and wife now, she remained a kind of prize.

When they finally arrived at Orhan's palace, dawn was approaching, and she was tired and travel weary. She wanted a bed, her own bed, and an uninterrupted night's sleep.

"I will have you shown to the women's quarters," Orhan told her.

"The women's quarters?"

"The zarai. Where you all live."

"Who?"

"My wives, my consorts, my odalisques." He looked baffled that she wouldn't know this. "But of course your people keep themselves to one mate. I should have explained. We will talk later." And with a kiss, he left her standing in the hall with her things.

A lovely, dark-haired woman came to greet her and lead her to her new chamber. "I am Maryam."

"Are you one of Orhan's wives?"

"Oh no, just a woman of the zarai. I think you will like it here."

And it was beautiful, like nothing Roxanna had ever seen. But so hot! She fanned herself, and Maryam said, "Your clothes are too heavy. I'll see that you have lighter ones."

Like her own brightly colored silks, Roxanna supposed. They were beautiful too. Everything was beautiful and strange, and she had so many questions.

Maryam showed her to a bedchamber. "This is yours. The bath is down the hall, and we dine in the room just beyond. I'll come to get you for the first few meals so you learn our schedule. Everyone is excited to meet you."

"And where is Orhan's chamber?"

"In the main palace."

"How do I get there?" she asked.

Maryam looked confused. "You will be taken to him."

"But what if I want to go now?" Roxanna could see that she'd shocked the girl.

"You do not just go to his Majesty. He will send for you when he wishes your company." She set Roxanna's bag on the floor. "You should rest now."

"Wait, will you show me around the palace later?"

Maryam looked scandalized at the request. "We do not leave the women's quarters unless we are sent for." She turned and left quickly before Roxanna could ask any more awkward questions.

But what did the girl mean? Surely she had the freedom of the palace. Surely she was not a prisoner. She set her other bag down and walked purposefully back the way she'd come. As she reached the entrance to the women's quarters, there was a flash of light, and one of the huge flame-skinned men sprang up out of nowhere to block her passage.

"Get out of my way," she ordered.

"Go back."

"I will not!" she replied. "Get out of my way."

There were a few moments of silence when she thought she might have won the skirmish, but then he said, "Do not make me hurt you."

"How dare you?"

"I guard these quarters," he told her, his voice a low rumble. "It is my life. You will not pass me. Go back."

There was something in his voice that told her that she couldn't win the argument, so she returned to her chamber. It opened onto a balcony with a view of the sea, and the sun met the horizon low in the sky.

Why had she come? This was not what she had expected or wanted. She realized that she was a prisoner to a man who valued only her beauty. Even being away from Eiliron wasn't worth this. It had been a bad bargain.

And then she remembered that she'd made many such bargains in her life and had lived through the consequences. One more would hardly kill her. If anything, she decided, she would learn more about the world outside of Eiliron.

And she wouldn't be a prisoner forever. She would see to that.